In TONGUES of the DEAD

In
TONGUES
of the DEAD

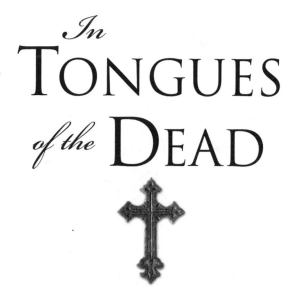

BRAD KELLN

ECW Press

Published by ECW Press
2120 Queen Street East, Suite 200
Toronto, Ontario, Canada M4E 1E2
416.694.3348 / info@ecwpress.com

LIBRARY AND ARCHIVES CANADA CATALOGUING IN PUBLICATION

Kelln, Brad
In tongues of the dead / Brad Kelln.
ISBN-13: 978-1-55022-830-4

1. Title.
PS8571.E586416 2008   C813'.6   C2008-902387-0

Cover and Text Design: Tania Craan
Cover Image: iStock
Part Title and Endpaper Images: Voynich manuscript, courtesy of
the Beinecke Rare Book and Manuscript Library, Yale University
Image of Cross: © Gary Woodard
Typesetting: Mary Bowness
Production: Rachel Brooks
Printing: Thomson-Shore

This book is set in Goudy and printed on paper that contains
30% post consumer recycled content.

The publication of In Tongues of the Dead has been generously supported by the Canada Council for the Arts which last year invested $20.1 million in writing and publishing throughout Canada, by the Ontario Arts Council, by the Government of Ontario through Ontario Book Publishing Tax Credit, by the OMDC Book Fund, an initiative of the Ontario Media Development Corporation, and by the Government of Canada through the Book Publishing Industry Development Program (BPIDP).

 Canada Council Conseil des Arts
for the Arts du Canada
 Canadä
ONTARIO ARTS COUNCIL
CONSEIL DES ARTS DE L'ONTARIO

PRINTED AND BOUND IN THE UNITED STATES

ECW PRESS
ecwpress.com

for Ben & Jake

ACKNOWLEDGEMENTS

Books are not written without tremendous support and encouragement. This one is no exception and I am sure I will never be able to thank everyone. I must first thank my wife, Glenna, and my sons, Ben and Jake, for their support — directly when they give encouragement — and indirectly when they leave me alone to write.

I also want to thank all those who contributed to the creative process either by listening to ideas and giving their own, reading advance copies, or answering technical questions. This includes but isn't restricted to Barry Banks, Ken Bowes, Tony Bremner, Trevor Briggs, Linda DeBaie, Anne Godley, Lindsay Hernden, Kelly Rowlett, and of course, Glenna Kelln.

Jack David and ECW Press deserve a big helping of gratitude for taking a chance on this book. Edna Barker is a wonderful editor and a joy to work with.

Finally, I need always thank my number one fans — my parents Robert and Janette.

Although the book you are about to read is a work of fiction, many of the mysteries discussed are real. The Voynich manuscript exists, and all references to its contents and history are accurate. In addition, all references to the Bible and the biblical mystery of the Nephilim are true.

. . . to another the ability to distinguish between spirits, to another the ability to speak in different kinds of tongues, and to still another the interpretation of tongues. All these are the work of one and the same Spirit, and He gives them to each one, just as He determines.

— I Corinthians 12:8–11

PART I

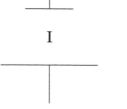

I

THIRTEEN YEARS AGO

Benicio Valori took a deep breath and looked at the small crowd gathered in the auditorium at Columbia's Department of Psychology. He recognized twenty or so graduate students and faculty members, and also noticed quite a few strangers. As he spoke, he searched for his girlfriend, Jenna Dodgson. She was easy to find: her raven hair reflected the auditorium's lights, a smile on her face. God, how he loved those dimples. She was in the back row next to Benicio's best friend, Jake Tunnel, another psychology student. Jake and Jenna had listened to Benicio practice his speech many times. Yet here they were, showing their support. He could do this. He cleared his throat and began to explain his dissertation. His voice carried a vague hint of his native Italian.

Benicio knew his words would hit the room like a bomb — especially with the Jewish and Christian people in the audience. "Nowhere has mythology influenced the practices of organized groups as much as in religious domains," he said slowly. "Ancient lore and mythology were often the basis on which social policy was secured. As an example, in the Old Testament, in Genesis, the Bible describes a time when angels came to the Earth and had children with women. The resulting offspring were known as the Nephilim."

Benicio heard expressions of disbelief. Then a bearded man said, "I've been a Lutheran all my life. I taught Sunday school for fifteen years. I've never heard such a ridiculous thing."

"It's true," Benicio insisted. "Genesis six, verse four: 'The Nephilim were in the earth in those days, and also after that, when the sons of God came unto the daughters of men, and they bore children to them.'"

"Ridiculous," the bearded man repeated.

Benicio nodded. "I agree with you. The story is a metaphor — the Bible is full of them. These stories weren't meant to be taken literally. They were meant to be discussed, debated, and explored. Unfortunately, organized religions have often taken myths and allegories to be literal truths. For example, some religions still desperately cling to the notion the Earth was constructed in six days — literally."

He paused, waiting for more comments or questions. There were none, so he continued. "I should give you some background to the story. The angels were a special order known as the Grigori, which means the silent ones. God sent them to Earth to watch over the earliest of Earth's people. But the Grigori broke two major rules. One, they started teaching secrets from the kingdom of heaven. They taught man about herbology, astrology, sorcery, and divination. God never meant for man to know these secrets. The Grigori had angered Him. And then they began to lust after women. They eventually gave in to their desire, and the half-angel, half-human offspring, the Nephilim, were born.

"Verses in the Bible tell us that God viewed this union between angel and woman as an abomination. He looked upon the offspring as mistakes, monsters, and He banished the Grigori from ever returning to heaven. He turned His back on the Nephilim, cursed them, and abandoned them. They became soulless husks, left to slowly die out. God eliminated the fallen angels by banishing them, their offspring by letting them die, and all trace of the Grigori's teachings by making men mortal. The secrets of the kingdom of heaven were hidden once more."

Benicio smiled, then continued, "The Bible is full of fantastic stories. Myths that were never meant to be taken literally. But churches have used these myths to justify some of their cruelest decisions. In the Middle Ages the Catholic church decided leprosy was a sign of a person's direct descent from the Nephilim. It was the church's way to justify its complete disdain for lepers. After all, God had cursed the Nephilim. Even the word *nephilim* has sometimes been translated as *the dead ones*.

"As a result, anyone suspected of having leprosy in the Middle Ages was routinely subjected to the Mass of Separation — a religious ceremony in which the leper was cast away from society. The belief that Nephilim were dead to begin with led some religious authorities to insist that the leper stand in an open grave as the Mass of Separation was performed. Once the leper was pronounced dead, the church frequently took all his worldly possessions. A fairly self-serving practice." Benicio paused and caught Jenna's eye. She smiled. He was going to marry her one of these days.

"We know now that leprosy is an infectious disease — not an indication that someone is descended from Nephilim. The Nephilim and the myth that angels once had children with women were just stories. The church used the myth to promote its own agenda — to account for leprosy and obtain people's money. The psychological effect of taking mythology literally is enormous. Indeed, our world is full of myths we have taken as reality, and such interpretation shapes our understanding of self in ways we could not have imagined."

As Benicio provided specific details of his research on mythology and self-perception, Cardinal Sebastián Herrero y Espinosa sat near the back of the room, feeling unnatural in his civilian clothes. He decided he'd heard enough, and slipped out the side door. He would contact the young scholar soon. There was no way around it: Benicio Valori would join the Holy Church.

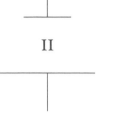

II

Father Ronald McCallum drew in a deep breath as he entered the library on Thursday morning. *His* library — that's how he'd thought of it for the twenty-two years he'd been in New Haven.

He filled his lungs with the musky smell of paper — a curious combination of dust and age. The odor had been a constant companion here at the Beinecke, which housed Yale's rare book collection.

The Beinecke Library, built by architect Gordon Bunshaft in 1963, was a magnificent edifice constructed to hold more than 160,000 rare books and manuscripts on six levels. A unique feature of the library was a massive glass enclosure that ran through the center of the building. Each floor of the facility wrapped around this central shaft, and thus natural light filled each level. The first floor housed many rare collections that rotated through climate-controlled display showrooms open to the public. The other five floors housed collections of literature, theology, history, and the natural sciences.

Father McCallum knew he could spend every day examining the priceless manuscripts — some of the finest books ever crafted — and still not have scratched the surface of each text. He was honored that the Holy Church had posted him here.

"Hey, Mr. McCallum!"

Father McCallum looked over and smiled warmly at the young security guard. No one knew to call him Father — he never wore his priest's habit. There were always new faces at the security posts, and he couldn't remember all the names — though he shouldn't be surprised; after all, he was almost sixty. His memory for names was starting to wane. These days he opted for a polite nod.

He kept moving, on a direct path to his private office, a path he followed every morning. Even after so many years, he still felt like a spy when he walked into the library. No one knew he was on a mission directed by the Vatican, under orders straight from the sacred office of the Holy See.

He gazed at the twenty-foot-high shelves lining the main holding area but kept walking rapidly toward the back corner, keeping his loving glances at the books to a minimum lest he get distracted and spend the entire day perusing one single shelf. He turned a corner and approached a door.

Father McCallum punched a combination into the door's handle and stepped into a stairwell, then made his way down to the labyrinth of small offices in the basement. He rated an office because of his title: Curator of Ancient Books and Manuscripts. But he'd had to wait fifteen years to get it because there were more curators than offices. Only the senior curators were given a place to hang their jackets.

He opened his office door slowly, careful not to let it bang against his bookcase. He slid into the tiny room, guiding his ample belly past the pile of paper on the edge of the desk. Once inside, he pushed the door shut and hung his coat on the hook on the back. Father McCallum couldn't turn without brushing against the bookcase or the desk. He leaned over the desk — it was too much trouble to get to the chair — and looked at the phone. The message light was not blinking. *Nobody loves me*, he thought, smiling. He frowned when he saw the two-way radio surrounded by triple-A batteries. In the three years he'd had the radio he'd worn it only once. It had started beeping and he couldn't figure out how to answer it. It had been sitting on his desk ever since. He left the office, careful to lock the door behind him, and began his *real* work.

His secret mission at the library was simple: watch the Voynich manuscript. The 500-year-old book had been discovered in 1912, and since then no one had been able to translate a single word of its more than 230 pages. Experts had analyzed the language and revealed that it had a structure, proving the book was written in an unknown language or at least concealed in a code so elaborate even the most sophisticated computers could not decipher it. The Vatican had long believed it was a book of singular religious importance, and kept an agent close at all times. The exact nature of the Vatican's concern was never revealed to Father McCallum, nor did he ask. He understood his role, and that was all a servant of the Lord needed. But he was curious, so he'd paid attention to the book's history. He knew it had been given to Yale in 1969 by H.P. Kraus, an antiquarian book dealer from New York, and that mainly it just sat in the library in a sealed display case. Occasionally cryptologists and historians delicately examined it, but they rarely handled the manuscript itself: they used the microfilm and Internet versions that had been made of each and every page of the Voynich, which were available to anyone. Father McCallum often wondered about the logic of guarding the manuscript when the contents were public. He'd gathered his courage on one occasion and asked the Cardinal Prefect about it. "A day will come when eyes will look directly upon the manuscript — and read," the cardinal had said. Father McCallum accepted that. It wasn't his place to question his role.

He headed upstairs to the main floor to check on the Voynich room. This was always his first stop after he dropped off his coat. He needed to make sure the book was undisturbed, and he always checked the tour schedules and visitor times to see who was coming. After that, he usually toured the library to see what jobs were on the agenda. Some days he restocked collections or compiled research lists for academic staff from Yale and other universities. Occasionally a professor gave him a subject to research. Father McCallum loved combing through indexes to find the most relevant texts. He felt like a detective, searching through ancient volumes for clues to questions about "historical influences on Darwin's theory of evolution" or references to "a fossil bat, Icaronycteris, from the Eocene period." Some of the subjects seemed like scientific mumbo jumbo, but as soon as he started reading, he would become interested.

He approached the separate alcove that housed the older collections and noticed a group of children. There were often class trips at the library, designed to give children a sense of history and to create a curiosity about books. Father McCallum supported the school visits wholeheartedly. He knew the younger kids thought he looked like Santa Claus, so he took advantage: he espoused the rewards of a career in academia or the library sciences. He wished he could add a recommendation for a life devoted to the Holy Father but couldn't risk blowing his secular cover.

This particular group of kids was leaving the room where the Voynich was kept. He would check the manuscript, then catch up with the children. He pushed open the door, listening for the slight hiss of pressured air — the room was sealed to preserve the manuscript — then saw a young boy in front of the glass case. Obviously a straggler from the class. He watched the boy for a moment, then approached.

The boy was staring into the glass case that protected the Voynich manuscript with an intensity that struck Father McCallum. He thought: *This isn't a boy, but a small mannequin.*

He stepped toward the boy, then crouched, knowing that a towering man could be intimidating. The boy seemed not to notice him. The priest wasn't good at judging a child's age, even after the countless school groups he'd talked to, but guessed the child was probably six or seven. He could see the boy's lips moving ever so slightly as he studied the manuscript.

"That book is over five hundred years old," he said softly, not wanting to startle the child. He smiled warmly.

The boy didn't react. His lips continued to move, and Father McCallum thought he could hear the boy murmuring, as though he were reading. He strained to hear but couldn't make out the boy's words.

"It is a very important and very mysterious book. We still

don't know how to read it," Father McCallum continued.

The boy didn't acknowledge him.

Father McCallum gave the boy another moment and then asked, "What do you see when you look at those pages?"

Slowly, the boy said, "It is the language of the forsaken. The tongue of the dead."

Father McCallum's heart leapt into his throat. "What do you mean? Who are the forsaken?"

"Half man, half angel," the boy said, still without looking at Father McCallum. "God's secrets."

"What secrets? How do you know this?"

The boy finally turned to the priest, his face completely vacant. "I can read it."

"What can you read?" Father McCallum asked, trying to quell his panic and disbelief.

The boy turned back to the book, ignoring the priest's question.

"Read it to me," he whispered. His voice shook. "What do you see?"

The boy remained silent. Father McCallum waited a few moments, then felt the air stir. He turned his head and saw a very young woman standing behind him. He hadn't noticed the hiss of the door opening.

"I hope he's not bothering you," the young woman said, smiling.

Father McCallum braced his hands on his knees and pushed himself to his feet. He felt unsteady. "No, not at all. Not at all."

"Little Matthew is sometimes in a world to himself. He wasn't doing anything bad, was he?"

"Of course not. We were just having a chat about this rare book here." He waved at the Voynich.

The young woman laughed. "Must have been a fairly one-sided chat," she said. "I'm Matthew's aide. He's autistic and hasn't ever spoken." She turned to the child. "Come on, Matthew." She reached for him, but the boy walked past without looking at her.

"Um," Father McCallum said, realizing they were getting away, "I'm a curator here. I wonder if I might join your tour."

She shrugged. "Sure."

He started toward her, regaining his composure. "I love seeing the children discover the magic of this book collection. What school did you say you're with?"

"Sacred Heart Elementary."

He made a mental note. *Sacred Heart Elementary. How fitting!*

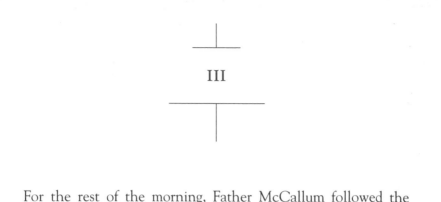

III

For the rest of the morning, Father McCallum followed the first-grade class as they toured the library, led by his colleague, Rhonda. He added the occasional comment but mainly focused on young Matthew, who remained silent and disengaged. The priest watched him and gathered information: the aide's name was Samantha, and she stayed close to Matthew. After the tour, Father McCallum watched the class go out the main doors, then rushed to his office for his jacket. He would be taking lunch early today.

***

The security guard watched Father McCallum hurry toward the west staircase. He stood, moved from behind his desk and laced his fingers behind his back, smiling at the old man's obvious urgency.

The bulky flashlight on his belt banged against his thigh, and he looked at it casually. He wasn't used to the guard uniform, but it suited his purpose: keeping watch over the Voynich manuscript.

He made his way to the front door and stepped outside, took a deep breath of the cool fall air, and murmured a quick prayer to God, thanking him for the day. It felt great to be alive.

He watched the children as they walked through the courtyard, making their way to the yellow school bus. One of the children was walking more slowly than the others. The boy suddenly stopped and turned back to the library. He seemed to stare straight at the guard.

The guard matched the boy's gaze without reaction.

The school aide seemed to realize the boy was lagging behind and stopped, urging him to rejoin the group. A few minutes later the children were all on the bus.

The guard stared at the slowly moving bus. "Soon," he whispered, "you will be dead and it will all be done. You are the last."

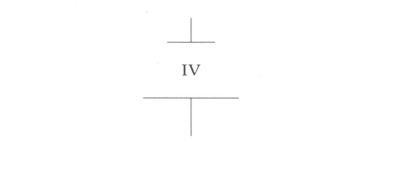

IV

"There are two ways to be dead — the loss of life and the loss of the spirit." MacKenzie Oak spoke as if he were beginning a lecture.

Dr. Jake Tunnel nodded, pushed back in his leather chair and occasionally made a motion with his pen, as though he were taking notes. He wasn't. If he wrote down everything his patient said, he'd run out of paper.

"I'd much rather lose my life than my spirit," MacKenzie continued. "I want to live out the rest of my life on this world and go to the next. I refuse to be the walking dead."

Jake stopped himself from saying something about zombies; MacKenzie didn't need encouragement. Jake knew his patient's lecture was a strategy to avoid talking about the real reason he was sitting in a psychologist's office. Big, burly MacKenzie Oak was an alcoholic and addicted to gambling — or at least to using video lottery terminals. The man had worked for Canadian Pacific Railways for forty-two years, and now he was wasting his life savings and gambling away his pension. His wife had confronted him about their dwindling bank account, and MacKenzie turned to his former employer for help. The CPR's Employee Assistance Program referred him to Jake, who specialized in addictions. And an EAP meant Jake didn't have to worry about payment. He felt callous when he listened to a patient pour his or her heart out for fifty minutes, then had to ask, "How will you be paying for all this help?"

"You can teach your patients about being alive again," MacKenzie Oak continued. "You can introduce them to a higher power of faith. You can help them find reasons to live — not just be alive."

Jake casually checked the small clock he kept hidden from the patient couch: only ten minutes left in the session. Time to get to the real therapy. He hated cutting a patient off, but sometimes he had to be firm.

"Yes, but we're here to talk about you, Mac. We need to get back to the reason you came to my office."

MacKenzie instantly looked contrite.

"I know it's difficult," Jake said in a soft, nonthreatening manner. "Why don't you give me an update on how you've managed with the gambling over the last week?"

MacKenzie hung his head. Jake waited patiently, and finally the bearded man began to talk. He had told Jake he was full of guilt, because his church taught him gambling was sinful. And he felt guilty about how he was treating his wife, to whom he was devoted. "I've betrayed her," he told Jake.

"It's been a rough week then," Jake said gently.

MacKenzie nodded.

"How much?" Jake asked.

"Too much."

Jake waited.

"Five hundred," MacKenzie finally said.

"And the drinking?"

His patient looked up. "Nothing," he said almost proudly. "I did like you taught me. I used one of the *drastic measures*. I was at the machine and ordered a beer without thinking. I was about to take a drink but I stopped myself and right then and there I dumped that beer on the floor."

Jake laughed, "Right on the floor, eh?" MacKenzie finally smiled.

"Yep, the whole damn thing right there on the floor, and I told myself I'm not going down that slippery slope. I remember you saying it's that damn first step and then the next steps are so easy. You just slip and slide your way right into an all-out relapse. Well I wasn't gonna do that. No sir. And even though I got a stare or two, like I was crazy, I made like it was an accident, and the people around me sank right back into themselves."

"I'm proud of you, Mac. You've taken some pretty big steps. I think it's been almost a month since your last drink."

MacKenzie nodded, but his face was sad. "But I still didn't get away from the machine after the beer thing. I still wasted all that money."

"Hey, you beat the booze — you can beat the machine. Just don't knock yourself down — you know what that does."

"Puts me back in the cycle."

"Yep. The cycle of guilt and remorse that drives you right into the addictive behavior."

"You've been real good to me, Dr. Tunnel. I just wanted to say —"

"No, no, Mac. It's my job, and you're doing all the work. I just wish all my patients were as thoughtful and motivated."

"I know, but —"

"No buts," Jake insisted. "You keep on working hard like you are, and we'll put all this stuff behind us. Now get out of here. I'll see you next week."

As soon as MacKenzie Oak was gone, Jake stood and stretched his six-foot frame, working out the knotted muscles that came from focusing on someone else's problems. Even now, at thirty-eight and after ten years of working with people, he still ached at the end of every session. He was happier than when he'd lived in New York — after he received his PhD from Columbia, he'd worked for two years at an addiction clinic on the Upper West Side, but he hated having to report to a supervisor, and the weekly team meetings wore him down. He preferred to work on his own; in private practice, he never had to explain himself to anyone. He knew he wasn't much of a people person when it came to coworkers.

He'd moved to Halifax after he married Abby, a Canadian enjoying her dream vacation in New York. *Abby.* Jake spun his chair around so he could see the photograph on his desk of Abby and their family. Abby was five years younger than Jake, and bubbled over with enthusiasm about life. He thought fondly of the whirlwind romance, their city wedding, and the move to Nova Scotia. He'd opened his practice in a converted historic stone complex, one of Halifax's oldest breweries, in a prime location on Lower Water Street. He loved the city, loved working right downtown, and he and Abby were enormously proud of their two children, seven-year-old Emily and five-year-old Wyatt.

He let loose a sigh as he leaned back in his leather chair. He always tried to leave half an hour between patients so he could relax, but recently he was finding it hard to concentrate. Recently, the only thing on his mind had been his son, Wyatt. The boy had been complaining of headaches and dizzy spells. Jake and Abby knew something was very wrong.

V

Father McCallum hurried down the sidewalk toward the bus stop. Only one late-morning bus heading for East Haven stopped near the library. He wanted to be on that bus.

He was less than half a block from the stop when he saw the bus pull up. He had to get home right away. He started to run; he couldn't bear the thought of missing that bus.

He didn't. Gasping, he hobbled up the steps and showed his bus pass to the driver, then collapsed into the first empty seat he came to.

When he'd begun working at the library, the Vatican had found him rooms in a house on Henry Street, about a fifteen-minute bus ride from Yale. Today the trip seemed to take two hours. The entire ride he sat looking out the window, nervously playing with the key that hung on a chain around his neck.

Finally the bus stopped at the corner of Elliot and Henry streets, and Father McCallum climbed off and rushed home. He rented the top floor of a traditional Georgian colonial home, and shared the kitchen with his landlords, a retired couple in their late sixties. Like Father McCallum, they were quiet and kept to themselves much of the time. The three had grown to be friends.

The priest hurried to the back entrance of the house. He was about to do something he'd been rehearsing in his mind for more than twenty years.

He went in and started up the stairs. At the top were three rooms: a small living room, a bathroom, and a modest bedroom. The priest entered the bedroom and went directly to the wooden blanket box at the foot of the bed, then unlatched and opened the lid. He lifted out stacks of sheets and blankets and set them aside carefully. At the bottom of the chest was a small metal box with a heavy lock. He pulled it out and set it on the bed, then took the key from around his neck, a key he'd worn every day of his twenty-two years in New Haven. Finally he was going to use it. He unlocked the little box and opened the lid.

Very carefully, Father McCallum pulled an envelope from the box and looked at it in admiration. A large wax seal held the flap of the handmade parchment envelope in place. The seal bore the symbol of the office of the Holy See, one of the most secretive and powerful branches of the Vatican, and the branch that had sent Father McCallum to Yale.

He vividly remembered sitting in the office of Cardinal Espinosa twenty-two years ago. Father McCallum had memorized every word of his sacred mission. The cardinal held up this very envelope and said: "If anyone ever claims the ability to read the Voynich manuscript, you will break the seal on this envelope and follow the instructions. Do not lose this envelope. Do not contact us unless you are sure that the Voynich manuscript can be deciphered. Many scientists and scholars will come to this book but they will find nothing. The manuscript will be read by someone who cannot be recognized by his or her outward appearance. You will know when it happens. Then you will break the seal on this envelope. Keep this secret until that day comes."

The priest slowly broke the wax seal, lifted the flap of the envelope and pulled out a sheet of parchment. He unfolded the weathered piece of paper, his hands trembling, and read:

Do not lose track of the child but do not contact him directly. Under no circumstances must the child be allowed to see the manuscript again and certainly not to read the manuscript aloud. Do not neglect this instruction.
Call this number: 390 (66982) 69.88.35.11 immediately for additional instructions.

The child? How could they have known? Why didn't they tell me I was waiting for a child for the past twenty years? He knew he could follow the first instruction: he had the name of the school the child attended and would go there after lunch to learn more about the boy and try to find out where he lived. He read the second instruction again, then leaned across his bed and picked up the telephone. He carefully pressed each digit. His hands were shaking.

The phone rang only once before it was answered.

A female voice said, "Please hold."

Father McCallum started to speak but realized the woman was gone.

He waited for about five minutes, imagining a series of phone calls and a flurry of activity at the Vatican. The Voynich manuscript must be important if the Holy Church had kept one line, one phone number, dedicated to his call. He tried to calculate what time it would be in Rome. He thought the Vatican was six hours ahead of Connecticut, so it must be around dinnertime there.

And then the phone clicked and a voice said, "Yes?" It was a voice well worn with time and betrayed a heavy European accent Father McCallum couldn't quite place.

"This is Father McCallum. I have been instructed to phone this number."

"Yes, yes, I am well aware. Are you alone?"

"Yes."

"Can anyone hear our conversation?"

"Not on this end."

"Good, good," the voice murmured. "Now tell me who read the manuscript."

"It was a six-year-old boy."

"Yes."

Father McCallum expected another question but none came so he continued, "The boy is autistic and a teacher told me that he has never spoken, but he spoke to me."

"What did the boy say?"

"He said the manuscript was written in the language of the forsaken."

"The forsaken?" the voice asked.

Was it the cardinal? Father McCallum strained to place the accent. "The boy said the forsaken were half angel, half human."

There was a silence. Then: "Tell me, did he read any part of the manuscript to you?" The voice was suddenly sharp.

The priest felt sure it was Cardinal Espinosa. "No," he answered. "I asked the boy to read it but we were interrupted."

"Do not allow the boy to read the manuscript," the cardinal said roughly.

Father McCallum felt uncomfortable. "Yes, of course," he said.

In a more relaxed tone, the cardinal said, "Fine. That is good. And you have told no one but came immediately to this task — to call me?"

"That's correct."

"And you know how to find this boy?"

"Yes."

"Fine. Do not contact this boy directly. Continue to be aware of him and how to find him. I am sending someone to investigate further. When he arrives you will apprise him of the situation and then wait for further instruction from my office."

Father McCallum was taken aback. "You're sending someone?"

There was no reply, and he realized the cardinal had hung up the phone.

He felt let down. He would probably not participate in the investigation of the boy. He was only a watchdog, and now, at the most important moment, someone else would take over, and he, loyal Father McCallum, would end up at a desk job somewhere. He had always hoped solving the mystery of the Voynich manuscript would be life-altering, and that afterward he wouldn't mind leaving his post at the Beinecke Rare Book Collection.

Instead he felt a cold chill. *It is all for the service of the church,* he reminded himself, rubbing his hands together. He had more work to do: he needed to find out about the boy. Where the school was and where the boy lived. When the Vatican representative arrived, Father McCallum would demonstrate his usefulness.

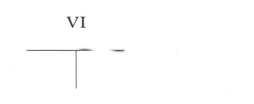

VI

Father Benicio Valori's height made him stand out among the diminutive natives of Cambodia. At just over six feet, he was taller than almost everyone in the tiny village. That wasn't good — his mission was supposed to be discreet.

He stretched and yawned. He was almost forty, but still in reasonably good shape, almost as good as when he'd been in grad school a decade earlier. Benicio remembered defending his dissertation to earn his doctorate in clinical psychology, and he remembered the day he sat in his grad-student office and opened the letter containing an engraved invitation and a first-class ticket to Rome. His Columbia degree had turned into a position in the priesthood under the investigative branch of the Holy See.

And now he was in the back of a hut in Prasat, one of the poorest districts in Cambodia and just east of Phnom Penh, the capital city. He shook his head.

Benicio glanced down. He was wearing nondescript clothes purchased locally: itchy but relatively cool Khmer black shirt and baggy trousers. The heat was oppressive, and his days consisted of a never-ending search for a slightly cooler spot, a bit of shade, a cool drink. The people of Prasat also had to contend with hunger, disease, and roving gangs. The slum was a short distance but a far cry from the capital city. Phnom Penh was rapidly developing into a modern city, with industry and tourism. Not long ago Cambodia would have been completely written off anyone's list of vacation spots, but the city's image was changing as the nation opened up to the world.

Unfortunately, being open to the world brought its share of problems. Benicio rubbed a rough hand through his dark hair as he sat in the back of the ramshackle, dirt-floored hut. The family who owned the hut knew he was a representative of the church. He had tried to explain his reason for coming to their village but he wasn't sure they understood.

The people in the village were outcasts, discarded by a city that had no use for them. They were easy prey for hucksters and thieves. Recently a gang had started selling religious relics in the village, promising the relics conveyed special godly passage away from Prasat.

Benicio knew religious relics were not inherently bad. But he also knew the power of the relic often came from the mythology associated with it.

He had read about relics attributed with miraculous powers. The power to heal disease. The power to free a dead person from purgatory. The power to change a person's destiny. A relic with such incredible powers would be of astronomical value. In the Middle Ages, the church sold licenses so individuals could sell relics to the masses. The church made a lot of money, but Benicio thought the practice was a fraudulent, moneymaking proposition and nothing else.

And someone was doing it again.

The Holy Church had sent Benicio to Cambodia to investigate the selling of religious relics to people who could barely afford to eat. Desperate parents were told the relics would ensure their children would get out of the slums. These days the church frowned on such fraud, but Benicio suspected the relics were being sold by missionaries from the Vatican. Such scams were sacrilege. Given his academic background and previous research on mythology, he was a natural choice for such investigations. He'd recently investigated a suspected case of demonic possession in a rural community in Brazil. An enthusiastic local priest wanted to begin an exorcism immediately but Benicio had quietly gotten the young girl admitted to a psychiatric facility. The church regarded Benicio as a discreet and loyal envoy, so here he was in a Cambodia slum.

He had heard the missionary group would be in Prasat today. He wanted to catch them in the act of peddling the relics.

He watched a young girl move barefoot across the dirt floor of the hut with a broad smile on her lips. He understood why a parent would do anything to make sure a child would survive. It sickened him that his church might be involved in a scam to play on that parental concern.

As he watched her, he heard shouts and cries from the street. Benicio was immediately alarmed. Although his grasp of Khmer was limited, he thought that the commotion was more one of urgency than of danger.

The voices stopped outside his hut, and he heard frantic pounding on the wooden door, then more shouting, before an older daughter turned to look at Benicio.

As he stood, undecided, the girl walked toward him, followed by three local men.

Benicio waited.

When they reached the back room, one of the men pushed forward and gave the priest a gap-toothed smile. He thrust a hand out, and in the hand was a satellite phone.

"You Walt-tory?" the man asked, breathing hard. He'd obviously run some distance.

Benicio regarded him carefully. "Yes."

The two other men, also breathing hard, smiled in an exaggerated, toothy fashion.

The first man spoke again. "Phone."

Benicio took it. "Hello?"

"Father Valori?" The voice crackled with authority and the crisp accent of Rome.

Benicio instantly recognized the voice. "Cardinal?"

"You must go to the United States immediately. It is all arranged. The men there will take you to the airport and I will contact you on the plane."

"Should I retrieve my belongings from the hotel in Phnom Penh?"

"Everything is arranged. Go immediately to the airport."

Benicio said the only thing he could think to say. "Si, Cardinal."

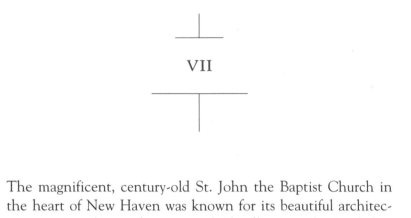

VII

The magnificent, century-old St. John the Baptist Church in the heart of New Haven was known for its beautiful architecture, soaring altar, and an unmatched collection of stained glass in the main sanctuary. The church also boasted a massive organ with more than seventeen hundred individual pipes. Visitors often drifted around the facility, taking pictures and speaking in whispers.

This Thursday afternoon's visitors were anything but usual.

Shemhazai walked purposefully through the front doors into the main chapel. He didn't pause to take in the beauty of the sanctuary but strode towards the nave. He'd been in the church before. Even on the first occasion he hadn't taken any notice of the scale of the building. It wasn't important.

He stopped at one of the huge oak pews, at least fifty feet long. A man with a beard sat about twenty feet along the pew. The church was empty save for a few tourists who kept close to the outer walls, examining the stained glass.

Shemhazai wore his library security guard uniform. He slid silently down the pew until he was next to the heavy-set bearded man who sat, head bowed, hands folded in his lap. He wore a dark green raincoat and a large black fedora. Shemhazai could hear the man praying quietly.

"It is my only intention to provide service to You and bring about closure to the earthly transgressions. Provide us guidance as the days to absolution draw close. Your servant, Azazel."

Shemhazai waited until Azazel turned and made eye contact. "Do you really think God listens to our prayers?" Shemhazai asked.

"Would we really be doing what we're doing if we thought

God wasn't listening?" Azazel asked.

Shemhazai nodded.

"Do you have news?" Azazel asked.

Shemhazai laughed sharply. "Seventy generations spent in purgatory waiting for this moment and you are impatient. If nothing else, I would have thought so many years would have taught you patience."

"Those years taught me only impatience," Azazel said flatly.

"Okay, I'll get to the point. I wanted to meet you because I found the last one."

"The boy? He is here?"

"Yes. He came to the library. He read the book."

Azazel shook his head in disbelief. "It's fitting that the search ends here. Once the boy is gone, all that's left is the book. The final betrayal. We can destroy both."

"There is a complication," Shemhazai announced.

Azazel looked at the altar. "The undercover priest." He sighed.

"Yes. He suspects the boy can read the book."

"How do you know that?" Azazel asked.

"I was watching on the security feed. The boy couldn't have read more than a word or two, but he certainly upset the old priest."

"We should act now," Azazel said and nodded.

"I'm not convinced," Shemhazai argued quietly. "The church is involved. We cannot avoid this fact. If we act with haste we might draw unwanted attention."

Azazel laughed, and a few tourists glanced in their direction. "What do we care about *drawing attention*? We are talking about our very existence."

"Even still," Shemhazai continued. "I would like to control all of the elements. I think we should acquire the book and then take care of the boy after we are convinced of the intentions of the church."

"The intentions of the church are to expose us!" Azazel spat the words.

"The church cannot be our enemy!" Shemhazai retorted. "Let us not forget that the war is only amongst ourselves. All others are innocent — including the bodies we now inhabit."

Azazel grimaced. "Look at this body." He held his arms out, exposing a bulbous gut. "This glutton was hardly innocent when I took him. If not for me he would be a dead glutton — his heart exploded in his chest."

"Even so," Shemhazai said. He didn't want to be reminded of the young body he had taken. The man, Larry Zarinski, was hurt badly in a car accident. By taking the body Shemhazai had helped it heal, but it pained him to think he had replaced a young man's soul with his own. "We should proceed with caution."

"Just get the book," Azazel said. He stood and began shuffling toward the aisle. "Get the book," he said over his shoulder.

Shemhazai nodded.

VIII

Sacred Heart Elementary was located about half an hour away in the small town of Meriden. After he found the school on a map and made a rough calculation of the distance, Father McCallum decided to rent a car. A cab would cost too much, and if he tried the trip by bus, he might get stranded somewhere.

He took Highway 91 north to Meriden and followed the first exit into town — and was immediately lost. He hated driving. He'd stopped to ask directions three times in half an hour. Finally, he found Elm Street and drove past the school. Just looking at the building made him feel intensely guilty, and he decided to park half a block away. He went around the block, then pulled against the curb under the shade of a massive red maple. The street was a swirling maze of colors from the autumn leaves, which helped him feel anonymous.

He looked around before he got out of the car, then felt foolish. *Who would be watching me? I'm the spy.* He took a deep breath and checked his watch: nearing two in the afternoon. *I don't even know what time children get out of school,* he thought, then told himself that even if he missed the kids he could talk to the teachers. They probably stayed longer.

He approached the school and was relieved to see the parking lot still three-quarters full and no signs of any children yet. He headed to the front doors.

It was a beautiful building, new and modern. The sprawling, single-storey facility was bright blue with red trim and lots of windows. The school was in stark contrast to the neighborhood. He saw unkempt yards and paint peeling off the houses, cracked sidewalks and overgrown weeds. He turned to the school again, and he had to look carefully to see the web of steel bars protecting the school's windows. He raised an eyebrow. *I guess this isn't the best area of town.*

He pushed through the double doors, stepped inside, and felt his legs go weak. His plan had included finding the school — and there it stopped. He hadn't thought about what he might say to Matthew's teacher or the aide he'd met at the library. He stood frozen in the middle of the hall.

"Excuse me." A voice broke through his panic. "Can I help you?"

He turned and saw a bespectacled middle-aged woman carrying a large stack of papers. Behind her was a doorway marked Office. She smiled warmly.

Father McCallum brushed a bead of sweat off his forehead. "I'm from Yale University," he began.

The woman nodded, still smiling.

"There was a tour at the Beinecke Library this morning."

"Yes, Ms. Walsh's grade one class."

"Right," the priest said, clapping his hands together. "There was a special little boy in the class — a young chap named Matthew —"

The woman interrupted. "Hold on." She was staring past him. "Sam! Could you come here a minute?" she called.

McCallum looked over his shoulder and saw the aide coming down the hall. As she approached, her slightly confused expression gave way to one of recognition. "Oh, hello," she said, extending a hand to the priest. "You're one of the curators from Yale?"

"Please excuse me," the woman with glasses said. "I need to get these down to a class." She nodded at her stack of papers and walked away.

"Thanks, Deb," Samantha said, then turned to Father McCallum. "What can I do for you? I hope the kids didn't do any damage or anything."

"I'm sorry. No. Nothing like that," he said quickly. "I'm . . . um, Mr. McCallum. I can't quite remember what you said your name was."

"Samantha Neil."

"Ah yes. I'm sorry. I'm dreadful with names."

Samantha nodded, then waited. He realized she didn't know why he was there.

"Listen, I don't want to keep you but I simply had to stop by the school," he continued. "I was positively moved by meeting the young ones and especially touched by meeting little Matthew . . ." He paused, hoping Samantha would fill the silence.

"You mean Matthew Younger. The autistic boy I work with?"

"Yes, little Matthew Younger. What a courageous boy."

She nodded. "He's a good kid. He's got a lot to deal with."

"I can see how that would be true." His face became more serious. "My main job at the library allows some time to help with community projects. I was so taken with young Matthew that I wondered whether there was a way myself or the library could help with his rehabilitation. He seemed so taken with many of the collections we house back at the library."

"I guess he did take kind of an interest, but it's so hard to tell. Matthew's really handicapped. My goal in working with him is to just minimize inappropriate behavior — to help him fit in a little better. He can be quite a handful to work with but his parents aren't well off and can't really afford any special treatment programs like a one-to-one intensive behavioral program. Even my work with him is through a practicum placement. I'm doing a masters in Ed Psych at UNH."

"Well that's just lovely. Good for you," he said. "I don't really know much about disorders like Matthew has. Autism, I mean. It must be quite rare."

"I don't know the exact numbers but it's relatively uncommon. I think it's like four or five kids out of every ten thousand."

He nodded. "Well, if it isn't too bold of me — could you tell me a bit about Matthew? I'm quite interested." This was definitely not a fabrication. Father McCallum needed to learn everything he could about Matthew Younger.

Sam hesitated then replied, "He has a fairly severe type of autism. There are different degrees, like some can talk and some can't. Sometimes they can't even do anything to take care of themselves. Matthew's pretty bad — maybe somewhere in the middle or lower. He doesn't speak, doesn't like to be touched and is very likely mentally handicapped."

He nodded in what he hoped was an understanding manner and then asked, "And don't these children sometimes have special talents such as math or music?"

She smiled. "I think that's more rare. Such children are called autistic savants, but Matthew hasn't shown anything like that."

"Is the disorder genetic?"

"Um, I'm not sure. I don't think people know what causes autism."

"I wonder if I could speak with his parents," Father McCallum said, trying to sound like he was just thinking out loud.

"Foster parents, actually."

"Oh?"

"Yep, I don't know for sure what happened but his biological parents aren't around anymore. He's been in foster care for at least a year."

"Poor little guy."

Samantha nodded.

"Well, if there's anything I could do to help him . . ."

"You know, it was kind of a surprise to see you talking to him," she said thoughtfully.

"Why's that?"

"Well, you were crouched down right next to him at that book display and normally that's one of those things that would set him off and he'd have a screaming fit for an hour."

"Oh my. I had no idea. He showed no signs of being upset when I approached him. In fact, he didn't even acknowledge me."

"That's how he is. You can be shouting right in his ear and

he doesn't even flinch, but then if you touch him or say the wrong word — *bam!* He loses it."

"It must be so difficult for the foster parents. Have you met them?"

"The Youngers?"

Father McCallum noticed that her expression darkened.

"Yeah, I've met them. I guess they have a lot to deal with. They don't come around the school too often."

"Yes, I'd bet it is quite difficult for them." He paused and then added, "Well, thank you for your time. You know how to find me if there is ever any way I could be of assistance."

"The Beinecke Library," she said.

"The Beinecke Library," he repeated. "Speaking of which — I need to get back there." He thanked her and left. As he pushed through the front doors, he exhaled deeply. *Matthew Younger. At least I have the name. Now I need to find out where he lives.*

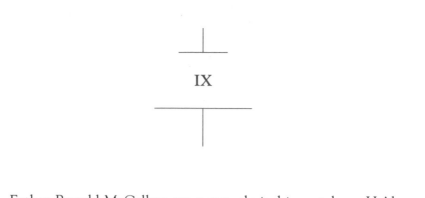

IX

Father Ronald McCallum sat nervously in his rental car. He'd parked where he could see the children filing out of school and heading for the rows of waiting buses. At intervals, teachers helped herd the kids in what seemed to be a well-honed procedure.

He no longer felt like a spy or a secret agent. He felt like a pedophile. He grimaced but continued his vigil.

He was soon rewarded. Matthew Younger drifted out of the school with a group of children. He strained forward, wanting to take note of which bus the boy boarded. Matthew boarded the second bus from the end. He waited nervously until the buses began to pull away from the curb, then started the car and put it in gear, his eyes glued to the back of Matthew's bus. All the buses looked the same. What if he lost track of which one was Matthew's?

Matthew's bus exited the school lot and turned right, rumbling down Elm Street. Only two other buses followed, the rest all turned left.

He breathed a sigh of relief and eased his foot down on the accelerator.

After a few more blocks the other two buses veered off onto different streets, and Father McCallum found himself directly behind Matthew's. He watched the kids through the back window of the bus. One of the children stared at him and made a face. He hit the brake, then heard a screech of tires behind him. He stepped on the gas again.

When the bus turned onto Alliance Avenue and began making stops, Father McCallum panicked. Every time the bus stopped he would have to stop right behind it — but that wouldn't be safe. The kids in the back would surely say something about the old guy who was following them. He tried to slip his jacket off without veering all over the road. He decided he'd turn onto a side street and try to catch up to the bus using a different route. He put the turn signal on, then saw Matthew Younger step off the bus and onto the sidewalk.

He sucked in a breath. A tall, slender woman was waiting for the boy. There were no hugs or smiles. Matthew simply followed the woman when she turned and walked down a side road. The priest pulled up to the curb, and someone honked. His erratic driving hadn't exactly gone unnoticed.

He looked down the side road and saw the boy following the woman — his mother, the priest guessed. *Foster mother*, he corrected, remembering what Samantha had told him. He got out of the car and started following Matthew.

It wasn't long before the pair turned up a pathway and went through the front door of a weather-worn home. Father McCallum waited a few minutes then strolled past the house and noted the address: 55 Union Lane. It was a rough-looking single-storey house in desperate need of repairs. Obviously the Younger family didn't have much in the way of money, but at least Father McCallum knew where the boy lived.

"Thank you, God," he whispered, and headed to his rental.

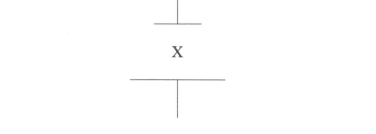

X

When they'd moved to Nova Scotia, Jake and Abby Tunnel had rented an apartment near the Halifax Shopping Centre. It was close to shopping and bus routes that took them right downtown. But there were a lot of people and the roads were busy with traffic, so when they were expecting their first child they bought a house. Now they lived in upscale Perry Lake Estates in Fall River, a suburb just north of Bedford and Lower Sackville. The house, a mixture of brick and dark red siding with white shutters on the windows, was a two-storey rectangular home with a gable roof. It was Abby's dream house. The driveway was paved and the one-acre lot was carpeted with a beautiful lawn and plenty of trees. They'd been there for eight years.

On Thursday evening, Jake sat in the finished basement watching TV. Wyatt played with Legos on the floor in front of him. Jake could hear Emily playing with her wooden Victorian dollhouse somewhere behind him. Abby was doing something upstairs — probably making supper.

"Wanna play Lego with me?" Wyatt offered.

"In a minute," Jake responded without looking at his son. Sometimes it was hard to look at Wyatt without feeling a knot of panic in his gut. Wyatt's headaches, dizzy spells, and occasional blurry vision terrified Jake. Every day when he got home he asked Abby how Wyatt was. He hated hearing that he'd had another spell.

The spells had started a month and a half ago. Last week they had taken Wyatt to the Izaak Walton Killam Children's Hospital, where doctors had performed a series of tests. Jake knew they would get the results sometime on Saturday but had avoided looking at the calendar to find the exact time of their appointment. Abby always wrote appointments on the calendar in the kitchen, but Jake felt sick when he saw the red-ink reminder.

He felt worn and tired. He wished for an easy solution to his son's headaches — Wyatt needed glasses or had an ear infection. The alternatives were too scary.

Tumor.

Cancer.

No. He shook his head. He wouldn't let himself think it. He glanced down at his son. Jake wondered if Wyatt was worried. The boy never let on if he was. Jake smiled.

"*Jake!*" Abby shouted from upstairs.

"Mom's calling," Emily announced without looking up from her dolls.

Jake laughed. "Thanks, I hadn't heard her," he said, smiling.

Emily gave one of her *Oh, Daddy!* looks.

"Coming, dear," Jake yelled toward the ceiling.

"What about Lego, Dad?" Wyatt asked plaintively.

Jake shook his head and stood. "Not right now, buddy, I've gotta go check on Mom and see about supper."

Wyatt turned to his Lego ship and lifted it into the air. With a whoosh the spaceship crashed down into a pile of Legos — a horrendously failed landing. Pieces skidded across the floor in all directions.

"You'd better clean all that crap up," Jake warned as he retreated up the stairs. "I don't want to find any under the TV." He didn't know if he was saying it because it bothered him or because he knew Abby would freak out if she saw toys scattered everywhere.

"You said 'crap,'" Emily informed him.

Jake continued up the stairs.

Something smelled good as he headed to the kitchen. He found Abby stirring something in a skillet. She'd recently taken to making very different kinds of dishes. Exotic things he didn't even know she could cook. He knew people dealt with stress in different ways. He hoped her cooking helped Abby stop worrying.

"Liver and onions?" he asked, smiling.

Abby didn't laugh. "It's called Imam Bayildi — basically just eggplant and tomato. There's also some chicken in the oven. Hope that's okay."

"Sounds good to me. What are the kids eating?" Wyatt and Emily were notoriously difficult to please.

"I don't know. Maybe throw some fries in the oven with the chicken."

Jake tapped at the convection oven. "I'll have to increase the temp to four-fifty. That okay?"

"Sure. By the way, there's a circus at the Metro Centre in a few weeks. Should we take the kids?"

"Did they say they wanted to go?"

"They don't know about it," Abby told him. "I thought I'd better run it past you first."

"Yeah, sure. Want me to get tickets?"

She nodded but didn't look at him, just listlessly stirred the food in the skillet.

Jake paused at the oven, a pan of french fries in his hand. "What's wrong?"

She turned. Her eyes were full of tears. "I think it's getting worse. He was watching TV with Em today and then all of a sudden he was just sitting there, staring. His eyes weren't focused on anything."

"What'd he say?"

"He said he was fine. He's trying to be so tough now because he knows how scared we are. He doesn't want to admit anything anymore. He's so brave." Her voice started to crack.

Jake set the fries on the counter, went over to his wife and put an arm around her shoulders. "We'll sort this out. We've done everything we can. We saw our family doctor. We had Wyatt in emergency twice and we had the hospital tests. He's going to be fine." He wished he believed it.

She turned toward him and put her face onto his shoulder. He could feel her sobs.

"Promise?" she asked.

"Promise," he said confidently.

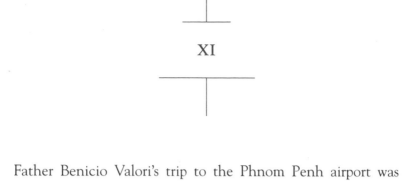

XI

Father Benicio Valori's trip to the Phnom Penh airport was rough and wild. The men who found him in Prasat had excitedly pushed and prodded him through the streets toward a waiting *moto*, the traditional motorcycle taxi of Cambodia, and shoved him onto the back of the bike. The driver turned to him and announced, "I am Mook. I get you airport very fast."

After nearly fifty minutes of hard driving, the bike screeched to a stop in front of the airport, a modern facility full of angles and recessed lighting. Benicio got off the bike and reached in his pocket to pay the bill, but when he looked up Mook and the moto were gone. Benicio shrugged and entered the front lobby, which looked as if it belonged in a hotel. He had been told to go to the Silk Air check-in.

He found the counter and leaned on it heavily as he tried to catch his breath.

"Can I help you, sir?" a beautiful clerk asked. Her voice had the slight clicking of an accent. She'd not bothered to attempt a greeting in Khmer.

"*Si, grazie*, I'm checking in for a flight. My name's Benicio Valori."

"Destination?" she asked automatically as her fingers flicked over a keyboard.

"The United States." He paused, realizing he didn't know exactly where he was going. "I'm sorry but I don't —"

"Oh, my apologies, Father Valori." She nodded and smiled. "We're expecting you — we're actually holding the aircraft. Here is your boarding pass."

Holding the aircraft? He took the pass.

"We also have your passport." She held out an envelope. "We've already cleared you through customs on this end. Please take a seat on the cart behind you. We'll drive you to the departure gate."

Benicio stared at the clerk then took the envelope. He was sure he'd left his passport in the hotel safe in Phnom Penh. He turned and saw an airport attendant in a golf cart. The attendant nodded and pointed at the seat on the back. "I take you."

Within moments Benicio was through the gate and walking down the ramp to the plane. He stopped at the door, where a flight attendant stood, and held out his boarding pass.

After a quick scrutiny the flight attendant said, "Mr. Valori, we're glad you've arrived. Your seat is three rows back on the left. We've already placed your carry-on luggage in the overhead compartment."

"My carry-on luggage?"

"Yes," she said and smiled broadly. "It was all arranged. Have a wonderful flight."

In a daze, Benicio found his first-class seat and dropped into it. *My carry-on luggage?*

Within minutes the plane took off, and Benicio finally breathed a sigh of relief. He'd known the church to act with urgency, but this was extreme. Being pulled off an important assignment and rushed to the airport was a new experience for him. Moreover, the church had obviously used its enormous pull either by way of its status or by paying handsomely. As the plane climbed into the air he reviewed his ticket. He was flying to Singapore then boarding a United Airways flight to Philadelphia, followed by a short hop to New Haven, Connecticut. The total flight time was more than thirty hours.

He couldn't imagine what was going on in New Haven. He knew Yale University was in New Haven, but didn't remember it having anything to do with the Holy Church.

Except . . . He thought for a moment, then dismissed the

idea. *It can't be that.* He vaguely remembered a rumor about a book in the Yale library, a book the church had long suspected was part of a terrible scandal from Old Testament times. It couldn't be that.

The plane finally reached its cruising altitude and the captain switched off the seat-belt sign. Benicio unbuckled and stood, eager to see what was in his carry-on bag. He opened the overhead compartment and found only one small piece of luggage. *Must be mine,* he thought, and opened it. He found some basic toiletry items and a change of clothing — a not-so-subtle suggestion from the church to get cleaned up. If there was one thing he'd learned about working with the Vatican it was that image was everything. He retreated to the first-class washroom to wash away the Cambodian slums.

He squeezed into the tight confines of the washroom, shut the lid of the toilet and set the bag down. He peered into the mirror. Streaks of black stretched across the stubble on his face. The *moto* ride and his work in the slums had left him looking miserable and dirty. He rubbed his rough chin before punching the water on.

He washed and shaved, then nodded at his reflection. *A little better,* he thought. He reached into the carry-on bag for the shirt and pants. He slipped out of his dirty black Khmer shirt and trousers and put on the new outfit, which included a sport coat. He found no traditional religious accoutrements, so he assumed his new assignment was not for broadcast.

He slipped the sport coat on and smoothed down the sides, then felt a bulge in the right pocket. He reached in and pulled out an ID badge and a wallet.

Dr. Benicio Valori, he read. *Yale–New Haven Children's Hospital.* It was an employee badge.

Very interesting, he thought and dropped the ID in the pocket. The wallet contained about a thousand dollars American and a valid driver's license and credit card in his name. He tucked the wallet into his trousers' back pocket. Finally, he gathered up his

Cambodian clothes and shoved them into the bag then left the washroom.

He stretched out in his leather seat, aware only that he had a long flight ahead of him and this might be his last chance for rest.

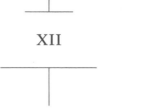

XII

Benicio was sound asleep when he felt a gentle hand on his shoulder. His eyes fluttered open and he saw a flight attendant bending over him.

"Your phone," the flight attendant said, motioning to the armrest next to him.

He blinked and sat up abruptly. "*Grazie,*" he said sleepily as the attendant slipped away down the aisle.

He was on the plane to Philadelphia — the longest leg of the flight — and had fallen asleep again. He wrestled the phone out of the armrest and found the connect button, then put the receiver to his ear. "Hello."

"Father Valori?" It was the crisp voice he'd heard in Prasat.

"Yes."

"This is Cardinal Espinosa. I trust you remember our first meeting."

"Yes, your Eminence. I remember it well." And he did. Cardinal Espinosa had recruited him straight out of grad school. The cardinal had sent a personal invitation for an all-expenses-paid trip to the Vatican, an invitation Benicio couldn't refuse.

He had arrived in the magnificent office of the cardinal and within moments he was convinced he had been called to the priesthood. The cardinal, a charismatic, enthusiastic recruiter, insisted that Benicio's gifts and expertise in mythology and spirituality were crucial to the Holy Church. Benicio's strong Catholic upbringing was also a factor.

Since his recruitment Benicio had learned that Cardinal Sebastián Herrero y Espinosa was the Cardinal Prefect of the Congregation for the Doctrine of the Faith — the CDF — and one of the most powerful men in the Vatican. Many people thought the Supreme Pontiff or even the Secretariat of State were among the most powerful but it was the Congregation for the Doctrine of Faith that held the reins of authority within the church. The CDF, a special branch of the Roman Curia, was responsible for maintaining and ensuring the integrity of the Catholic faith around the world. Benicio also knew Espinosa showed little respect for traditional church boundaries and protocol. He was fanatical about protecting the faith and saw no limit to the means by which he would do that. Twenty years ago he had faced life-threatening cancer but had miraculously recovered. Even the cancer hadn't deterred him from his holy duties.

"Thank you for your immediate loyalty to the one true faith," the cardinal said on the air phone. "Your assistance is urgently required as the eyes and ears of the Vatican. It is in your judgment we trust at the most crucial of hours."

"Yes, your Eminence." Benicio knew the assignment was high priority. After his recruitment and his time in the seminary he rarely spoke with the cardinal. His directives normally came from others well beneath Espinosa. Now, he almost felt nervous.

"As you likely realize from your flight itinerary, your destination is Yale University. We've had a representative there for some time to watch a certain manuscript of importance to the Holy Church. His name is Father Ronald McCallum, and he is expecting you. You will find his address in the pocket of your coat."

A certain manuscript? Benicio wondered. *Could this really be about the Nephilim Bible?*

Cardinal Espinosa continued, "You will investigate a claim made by Father McCallum in regard to a certain child who may have the power to read the manuscript. Father McCallum will explain the details. You must investigate the child and report immediately to me."

The cardinal emphasized the word *me.* Benicio suspected this mission did not have the full blessing of the Holy Church.

"You have been specifically selected for this task because of your proven loyalty and discretion in the service of the Holy Church. In addition, your secular education through your doctorate in clinical psychology will be an asset as the boy in question has psychiatric difficulties."

"Yes, your Eminence." Benicio knew it was not his place to ask questions. Questions, when they were permitted, were always much later.

"Ascertain the validity of Father McCallum's claims. Report to me directly at this number. Do not write this number down." Cardinal Espinosa read off a fifteen-digit number, and Benicio memorized it.

And then the line went dead.

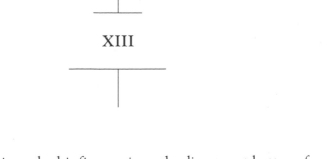

XIII

Cardinal Espinosa let his fingers sit on the disconnect button of his phone for a moment before he dropped the receiver. His office walls were lined with twelve-foot-high bookcases. Every shelf was filled with religious reference books and books about every code and doctrine of the Holy Church. Some of the books dated back centuries, and most were in the original Latin. He'd read all of them, and all in the original language. He glanced around the room, heavy with history, then slowly stood.

"God," he prayed, his arms outstretched, his head tilted skyward, "I want only to serve You. To protect You. To protect the faith.

"I am Your servant. With Your help and guidance I will act. I will act swiftly on Your behalf and erase the source of the poison that might infect the faithful. On my vigilance You can rely."

He sat again and with a trembling hand pulled back the sleeve of his white robe. He opened his top desk drawer, removed a small black case and set it carefully on the blotter. He lifted the lid and revealed an ornate knife with a three-inch blade. He picked up the knife.

The cardinal turned his left arm up and rested it on the desk. The underside was scarred from bicep to wrist. He touched the skin with the knife and carefully drew a straight line. The exquisitely sharp blade slit the skin, and the slit quickly filled with blood. Without hesitation, Espinosa drew a line perpendicular to the first, completing the cross. He struggled to keep his breathing regular as he watched the blood fill the cross.

"For You, God," he whispered.

He set the knife down. "I will call on the forsaken one more time, Lord," he whispered. "I know they are repulsive to You but they will serve this just cause."

He reached for the phone and dialed a number. After three rings someone answered sleepily.

"Do you know who this is?" the cardinal asked curtly.

The sleepy voice snapped to attention.

"Yes —"

"Do not say my name," Cardinal Espinosa interrupted. "You and your brother must travel to New Haven and await my instructions."

"New Haven? Is it the Voynich?"

"Travel, and wait for my instructions. You have my number. Call me when you've arrived."

"Will this be our last mission?" the voice asked. "Will you release my brother and me after we have served one more time?"

"Call me when you arrive in New Haven. Take no action without my authorization."

The cardinal hung up the phone. He was confident in his decision but regretted its necessity.

He picked up a satin cloth and held it against his arm then sat back in his leather desk chair. His mind wandered to when he'd first laid eyes on the two brothers. *Maury and Jeremy*, he thought. *Such unlikely servants of the church.*

Eighteen years ago, as the Cardinal Prefect, Espinosa had eyes and ears around the world. An army of faithful servants who kept watch and reported to the Vatican. Some reported on miracles, religious fraud, or priestly improprieties. Others watched for certain abnormal medical conditions. The cardinal did not provide reasons for his requests. He simply ordered them.

Thus his discovery of Maury and Jeremy began with a phone call.

One of Espinosa's secular agents called to make a report. The agent, a devout Catholic who worked as a hospital orderly in a small town, reported the specific medical abnormality, a skin condition where the body seems to reject its own tissue. The cardinal traveled to North America on the next available flight.

Remembering it now, Espinosa smiled. Hindsight made his actions seem reckless but he had had no other choice. He could hardly imagine taking on the role of an investigator any longer. There were other, more able-bodied people to do such things.

When he arrived in Pigeon Forge, Tennessee, he was amazed that the town existed. Pigeon Forge billed itself as the home of something called Dollywood, a theme park built for a celebrity he'd never heard of.

He got off the plane and went straight to the town's medical center. The orderly had told the cardinal about two recently orphaned children, Jeremy and Maury. Their parents had been killed in a car accident; the boys were showing signs of a serious and possibly infectious condition no one in Pigeon Forge had ever seen. The medical center wanted to transfer the boys to the hospital in Knoxville.

The orderly met the cardinal at the door and escorted him to the director of the medical center.

"Well, it shore is strange to see a man of the cloth all the way from Rome down here in our little neck of the woods. How can I hep you?"

"The church has an interest in the two children. The orphans."

"Yessir, that's a mighty sad case," the director said. "Them boys just got back from Angola or some damn place with their globe-trotting missionary parents when they was in a horrible car accident. The parents are gone but the boys were unhurt — at least by the accident."

"I understand that the children have no living relatives."

"That's right."

"I also understand that this facility suspects the boys have a serious communicable disease."

"Yeah, we got 'em in quarantine until we arrange to get them to Knoxville. We can't handle them here."

"I might be able to help. We have a comprehensive program to deal with boys like these."

The director frowned. "You got what?"

"May I see them?" the cardinal pushed.

"I said they was in quarantine. It wouldn't be much of an idear to go see 'em."

"I understand the risks."

Thinking about it now, Espinosa shook his head. The backward facility was quite lax in its medical precautions. He wondered if it would be the same today. He remembered being allowed to go right down to see the boys, Maury and Jeremy. The facility had only insisted he wear a surgical mask.

Espinosa later told the boys he had known as soon as he saw them that they were Nephilim. Six-year-old Maury and his five-year-old brother were direct descendents of the forsaken line of half-angel, half-human bastard children. He knew because God had given him the power to discern it. It was that simple.

The wheels were immediately set in motion. With his vast political connections and considerable influence, the cardinal arranged for the boys to be made wards of the Vatican. He assured the small-town physicians that he would have the boys' medical condition treated.

Arrangements were made quickly and the boys were ready. By that same evening, Maury and Jeremy were in Rome.

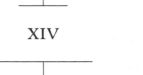

XIV

Shemhazai walked through the library slowly, lost in thought. He was sure of his decision but doubted his resolve. He glanced at the large leather portfolio he carried.

It was closing time and the final security checks were almost done. He headed to the guard station and sat behind the desk, then tapped the three-digit code into the combination keypad and opened the small metal door of the lockbox under the desk. Two sets of master keys were kept there. He pulled one set off the hook and left the box open. Shemhazai knew the keys would open doors but not display cases. It would only be a small inconvenience.

He started toward the display rooms in the back. Soon he reached the climate-controlled room that sheltered the Voynich. He tried the handle; as he suspected, the room was already locked. Shemhazai used the master key to let himself in.

He went to the display case, set down the black portfolio, and looked at the Voynich manuscript. Seeing it now he felt a slight spark of emotion somewhere between fear and awe. He laid a hand on the cold Plexiglas for a moment. He hoped he could touch the manuscript without ill consequence.

He felt beneath the case and lifted the lid, but the case was locked. Only the curators had keys for the display cases. The security guards were expected to protect the books — not handle them.

Shemhazai knew he was about to start a journey from which there would be no return. He breathed deeply, then lifted his arms and spoke. "Father, forgive me my sins."

As he spoke the last word, his body fell like a discarded costume, all life obviously gone before it reached the floor. Almost as soon as it came to rest, the body began to wither; the skin turned dirty brown, then gray, then began sinking into the bones beneath.

In the place where the security guard had stood was now a glowing, golden figure. Without his earthly disguise, Shemhazai stood seven feet tall. He had perfect skin. He reached out and slid his hand through the lid of the Plexiglas case as if it weren't there. He gripped the Voynich, pulled it out of the case, then held it tightly in both hands.

Pain struck Shemhazai. His body burned and throbbed inside and out. His vision blurred. He must find a new host, and fast. He could survive only a few moments in his true form. Then the pain would become overwhelming, and he would cease to exist. Shemhazai hoped he would not need to take a student from campus: he and Azazel had agreed never to take young, healthy hosts.

He picked up the leather portfolio and slid the Voynich inside. Then he left.

Soon he and Azazel would kill the boy and then destroy this book. God would have to forgive their sin.

He hoped.

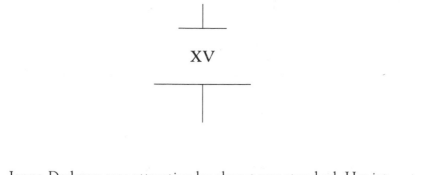

XV

Jenna Dodgson was attractive by almost any standard. Her jet-black hair was cut sharply at her shoulders and hung in a straight line around her face. The contrast with her light skin and pale blue eyes was striking. At thirty-three she was still trim and fit. She'd played women's basketball in college, where she received her degree in pediatric nursing.

She sighed as she surveyed her apartment on this sunny Friday morning. It was okay but sparsely furnished. She referred to it as her "new" place even though she'd been living in it for four months.

Five months ago she'd left Anthony, her husband of two years. She counted him as one of her biggest mistakes. Sometimes she thought it was her biggest disappointment, but that gave him more credit than he deserved. He was just a mistake.

Anthony was a flamboyant, self-involved ass. There was no denying he was entertaining, especially when they were first dating, but entertaining couldn't sustain a relationship. He'd always talked about how their relationship was the most important thing to him. He said they'd always be a team. Somehow, he'd convinced her that he was a man of depth and substance. He wasn't. He was an ass.

But even being an ass wasn't necessarily a deal breaker. The deal breaker was that Anthony thought he could threaten her. She could still remember his exact words. "Why don't you shut the fuck up before I shut you up?"

Just plain nasty.

And not something she would allow him to repeat.

So she had moved out. At first she stayed with a girlfriend, Maria. Anthony tracked her down and whined and complained.

He promised he'd never threaten her again. He said he'd really learned his lesson and he was going to get help. When that didn't work, he told her how he couldn't live without her. She still wanted no part of him.

After a few weeks at Maria's she'd found this apartment. It was a great building, right next to Mic Mac Mall in Dartmouth, but it wasn't what she wanted. She and Anthony had had a house in the south end of Halifax, and she could walk to the children's hospital where she worked. Now she lived across the harbor. When she'd moved, her commute had changed from a ten-minute walk to a forty-minute bus ride. She hated riding on the bus. She would have driven but knew she wouldn't be able to park anywhere near the hospital, not without paying an arm and a leg.

And it nagged at her that she lived in Dartmouth. She knew it was silly but there had always been a rivalry between Halifax and Dartmouth. Haligonians, the snobs, always stuck their noses up at the working-class Dartmouth side of the harbor. There was nothing to that old rivalry any longer but it did feel like a drop in status to go from South End Halifax to Dartmouth. She blamed Anthony for that too. *The bastard.*

She picked up her backpack from beside the bed. Her shift would start soon, so she needed to get to the mall and catch her bus. As she moved through the apartment she stopped to look at a photograph she'd found in a box in the closet the night before.

She held it and smiled. Benicio, her boyfriend from her days at Columbia University. She wondered how he was doing. The idiot had left her to go into the priesthood. That was always a great story to tell her friends — how she'd driven a man to celibacy.

She set the picture on the counter and turned to leave, but the phone rang. For a moment, she debated not answering and then relented. She picked up the cordless receiver and checked the built-in call display. It wasn't Anthony, it was her friend Maria.

"Hello Maria," Jenna said.

"You're still coming after work, right?"

"Yes," Jenna said, rolling her eyes.

"Just making sure," Maria said. "I don't want you backing out. We're just going to the Old Triangle — it's not the Liquor Dome. You better be there."

"I will," Jenna promised.

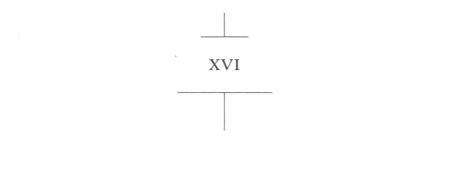

XVI

"Please return to your seats, fasten your safety belts, and place your trays and seat backs in their upright position," the attendant announced. "We are beginning our descent into New Haven. If you have a connecting flight in the Tweed terminal, one of the agents will be waiting to assist you. Thank you for flying US Airways. We wish you a safe and happy journey."

Benicio was already belted in. His tray and seat back were in the upright position. He was ready for the plane to land.

A few minutes later he was off the plane and in the small but busy New Haven airport. Benicio walked toward the exit, his mind set on getting a taxi and finding Father McCallum.

Then he saw something that stopped him in his tracks. Standing at a Budget rental counter were two men he'd seen before. Two men he'd seen walking in the corridor of the Congregation for the Doctrine of the Faith at the Vatican. Benicio knew that tourists didn't have access to that wing of the Vatican.

One of the men, pale and smooth-skinned, was rubbing his forearm obsessively. The other man was wearing an eye patch. Benicio noticed he had his baseball cap pulled low, as if to hide the patch.

When he'd seen these men at the Vatican, they'd been in civilian clothes. Civilian consultants inside the Vatican, especially in the office of the CDF, were people to avoid. Period.

Looking straight ahead, he walked to the exit and out to a row of waiting taxis.

***

"Can we please just get the fuckin' car and go?" Jeremy whined. He shoved the bottle of lotion in his pocket and pulled down his shirtsleeves. "This air is hurting me."

Maury was bent over the rental car counter. "Just a second." He signed the last form and pushed it toward the clerk, then straightened his hat and self-consciously felt his eye patch.

"Thank you, sir," the clerk said as she reclaimed the form. Maury saw her nose wrinkle. He knew he and his brother emitted a slightly foul odor even at the best of times. "I'll get your keys and you'll be on your way. The lot is just through those doors." She pointed down the terminal.

"Fine," Maury said flatly. He wasn't fooled by her courtesy. He knew most people thought he and Jeremy were sickening.

"My feet," Jeremy whispered to Maury. "I want to get somewhere and put the lotion on my feet."

"Shut the fuck up," Maury whispered. "What do you want me to do? Steal a car?"

Jeremy shifted nervously. "I better not lose another toe."

"There you go," the clerk said, dropping a set of car keys on the counter rather than putting them in Maury's outstretched hand. "Please don't hesitate to call with any questions or concerns. There's an attendant out in the lot to help you find the vehicle. It's a red Honda Civic."

Maury stared at her with his good eye then slowly picked up the keys. He kept staring at her until her fake smile disappeared.

"Let's go," Jeremy urged.

Maury grabbed the keys. "Thanks," he said, and then left with his brother.

XVII

Father McCallum awoke to the sound of his phone ringing. He glanced at the clock on his bedside table. It was barely six in the morning. He'd had a restless night, not knowing when the Vatican representative would show up, not knowing what would happen next in the great mystery of the Voynich.

He wanted more sleep. The night before, he had thought about going in to work late. Today was Friday, after all. The phone rang again and he reached for it.

"Hello?"

"Mr. McCallum?" a terse voice barked.

Father McCallum was immediately awake. "Yes, sir." It was Garrett Eastman, assistant director of the Beinecke Library. Mr. Eastman had never telephoned him before.

"There's an issue. Can you come down to the library?"

It sounded like a question but the priest knew it wasn't. "Of course, of course," he started. "What's going on?"

"I'd rather discuss it with you once you arrive. Thank you."

"I'll be right there," he said, his heart planted firmly in his throat. He hung up the phone and took a deep breath. He was sure something had happened to the Voynich manuscript.

He showered and checked his beard briefly to make sure it wasn't too unkempt. He dressed in record time, then headed downstairs. Good thing he'd kept the rental car — he was too keyed up to wait for a bus this morning. He found the car, unlocked it, got in, and drove.

As he approached the library, his fears escalated. There were three police vehicles parked right outside. His first irrational thought was that the library had discovered he was a spy. Should he drive right past? But he couldn't do that — he still had a job to do for the church. He pulled up against the curb, turned the ignition off, took a breath, and got out of the car.

He made his way through the crowds gathered in front of the main entrance of the Beinecke, then saw an officer stationed at the door.

"I'm sorry, sir," the policeman said, "the library is closed."

"I work here," the priest managed to say. "I was called down."

"Got some ID?"

Father McCallum showed his badge, and the officer held the door open for him.

The priest stepped into the Beinecke, expecting a flurry of activity, but the library was quiet. Too quiet.

"Hello?" His voice echoed in the cavernous area.

Garrett Eastman came through the doorway behind the security station. "Mr. McCallum," he snapped. "Come in here, please."

"Where is everyone? Why are there police outside?"

Garrett Eastman waited for the priest to join him behind the security desk then ushered him into the back room, explaining, "The police are searching the building, looking for clues or whatever it is that they do in such situations."

"But what is the situation?" Father McCallum asked.

"Someone has stolen the Voynich manuscript."

The Voynich! I knew it! "What? How?"

"*How* is what we want to know. As the curator of the ancient collections you know all about our security in the Voynich display area. I believe you are one of the few who even had keys to the cases."

He started to protest. "But I didn't —"

"Oh, stop," Garrett interrupted. "You aren't a suspect. At least not yet."

Father McCallum had been in the library's security nerve center only once, during the compulsory tour on his first day of work. The two men stopped near a control panel. A library security guard sat at the panel, and two police officers stood next to him. Above the controls were rows of monitors showing different views of the library.

"Roll the tape," Eastman said without introducing Father McCallum to anyone.

The security guard punched a few buttons, and they all watched as a uniformed security guard walked into the library.

"You can see he's carrying something to put the Voynich in — look right there." The guard pointed to a large black portfolio visible on the screen.

The view blurred into fast forward and then switched and Father McCallum watched the guard on the screen walk to the main security desk, reach under, and pull out a set of keys.

"That's where Larry gets the keys to the Voynich room. He knows what he's doing," the library guard announced.

"Larry?" Father McCallum asked.

"Larry Zarinski," Eastman said. "He's been with us for only a few months but came with a stellar résumé, which included other posts at the university. He'd been in a car accident and was off on medical leave but made a miraculous recovery and decided to keep working. That's when he applied here at the library."

"The car accident must've rattled this guy's brains loose," one of the officers quipped.

The camera view blurred and switched again as the guard fast forwarded, and they all watched Larry walk through the library to the Voynich room. He used the keys to enter, and the camera view switched again.

On the screen, Larry set the portfolio down then moved to the case and started to rattle the lid. Then he stepped away from the case and held his arms up.

"You can see his lips moving here." The guard again pointed at the screen. "I wish we had audio on these cameras."

The screen went blank.

"What happened?" Father McCallum asked. "Where's the picture?"

"That's all we got," Eastman said glumly. "For some reason the camera went dead, and all we have for the next ten minutes is static."

"What about when he leaves? Do we see him leave?"

Eastman nodded at the monitor. The static stopped, the guard slowed the film to normal speed, and Father McCallum saw the hall outside the Voynich display room. There was a slight blur of motion, as though the door was opening, and then the picture went fuzzy.

"It's like that all the way back to the entrance," Eastman said. "It's as if someone or something left, but we couldn't tape it."

"Something?" Father McCallum exclaimed. "What are you talking about? It was this Larry guy. The security guard. Did you find him yet? Do we know where he went?"

"Oh, we know where Larry is," one of the police officers said.

"What?" Father McCallum yelled. "Well, get him. We need to get the Voynich back!"

"Come with me," Garrett Eastman said and took Father McCallum's arm. He led him through the library to the Voynich room. A policeman stood in front of the door.

"Forensics is still in there," he said to Eastman. "Do you need to go in?"

"I just want Mr. McCallum to have a look."

Father McCallum stepped to the doorway and looked in. Two men in white paper suits crouched near a library security guard uniform. The priest frowned. There was something else, something inside the uniform. He gasped and turned away.

"What is that?" he asked weakly.

"That," Eastman said, "is what's left of Larry Zarinski."

XVIII

Jake stood in the doorway of his waiting room looking at nothing in particular. He was listening. Gladys Warbeck had just left after her appointment and should be reaching the staircase soon.

Bang!

He heard the heavy crack of the fire door, which meant Gladys was on her way out. Jake's third-floor office was one of only four on this top floor, and all were connected by a dark, granite hallway. There was only one way on or off the floor and that was via the large staircase at one end. Without physically watching his patients leave, Jake gauged their departure by the slam of the staircase door.

And in the case of Gladys Warbeck he wanted to make sure she was gone. He couldn't bear the thought of running into her in the hallway. She'd come to his office about a month earlier on a referral from the Workers' Compensation Board Return to Work program. Gladys had hurt her lower back on the assembly line at the Hershey's chocolate factory in Dartmouth. She'd been off work for nearly six months, and although her physical injury was healed, she still complained of debilitating pain.

Jake's role, paid for by the WCB, was to help Gladys live in spite of her pain. He met with her weekly to review her activity levels, teach cognitive reframing strategies around the pain, and mentally prepare her to get back to full-time employment. Working with Gladys was regimented, straightforward, and boring. Jake hated it.

Now that Gladys was gone, he could make a coffee run before his next appointment. It was still early on Friday morning but he already needed more joe.

He walked slowly down the stairs, not wanting to catch up to his patient. Her chronic back pain made her a fairly slow mover.

He didn't see her when he exited the Brewery Market and headed west up Salter Street away from the harbor. He normally went to Tim Horton's on Barrington or, if he was short on time, up the hill to Cabin Coffee on Hollis. Today he was short on time.

He jogged up the street and pushed through the front doors of Cabin Coffee to inhale the rich aroma of fresh coffee. The place was rustic and friendly, full of worn furniture and extra-large coffee tables. Lots of people wasted entire afternoons settled deeply into the leather couches and sipping lattes. Jake had never sat in the place; he'd go in, get a coffee, and be gone. Time was precious. To him, maybe the most precious thing.

He waited at the counter until the server came over. She was an extremely attractive young woman. "What can I do for you?"

He laughed but suppressed the urge to answer with something suggestive. "Just a coffee. Large."

"House blend?"

"Sure." She turned, and he let his eyes wander down her back. Between her cropped shirt and low-cut jeans he could see a tattoo on the small of her back. He liked the young woman even more.

"Dr. Tunnel?"

The clerk had distracted him. He turned to find one of his patients standing right next to him. "Harold! What are you doing here?"

"I saw you come in and just wanted to say hi."

Jake turned to the counter where the server was setting his coffee down. He handed her a two dollar coin and asked for a receipt. Without looking around, he asked, "You aren't following me, are you, Harold?"

"Oh, no, Dr. Tunnel," Harold said earnestly. "I just saw you go in here."

"But our appointment isn't for another hour." The barista tried to give him change but Jake accepted only his receipt.

"I don't want to be late. I always come down early and just walk around."

Jake nodded. "That's great. I'll see you later, then." He started for the door.

"Yes, Dr. Tunnel. Thank you."

In the past few days, Harold Grower had been popping up at odd times. He said the encounters were accidental, but Jake wasn't sure. Harold was a vulnerable man who needed constant reassurance from others — especially Jake. Jake knew that soon they would have to discuss the encounters in therapy. When unhealthy attachments couldn't be fixed, it often meant terminating the therapy sessions and referring the patient elsewhere. Jake tried to keep a professional distance to avoid feeding into Harold's dependence.

But the frequency with which he showed up was increasing. Jake and his family would be at Mic Mac Mall and see Harold. They'd have dinner at East Side Mario's and Harold would be sitting somewhere nearby. Jake thought the guy was becoming a pest — a smiling, enthusiastic, appreciative pest.

As he headed back down Salter Street he pushed Harold out of his mind and focused on his next client, a guy whose treatment-resistant schizophrenia made for some bizarre sessions.

It just never ends, he thought, and rolled his eyes as he pushed open the doors of the Brewery Market.

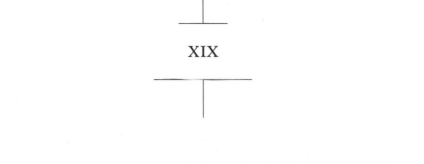

XIX

Father McCallum sat on his bed. His head ached. His body felt sick. He had waited much of his life to understand one book, and now that book was gone. Some lunatic had stolen it just when the mystery was going to be solved. Everything was ruined.

He'd run from the library as soon as he could, and driven the rental car home, wanting only to crawl into his bed and pull the covers over his head.

But he knew he wouldn't be able to sleep.

All the questions the police kept asking him swirled through his head. *Who'd want to steal it? Why? How much is it worth? Who'd pay for it?* He'd been able to give only half-answers. He couldn't tell them the value of the book — he didn't know its value. And if he told them the Vatican had been watching the Voynich for years, they'd never believe him.

So he ran home.

He felt light-headed. Should he have some breakfast? He wasn't sure he had the strength to go downstairs. He lay down on the bed and closed his eyes.

***

"Ronald!"

Father McCallum bolted awake. "Yes?"

"Ronald!"

The sound came from all around him. He opened his eyes, his head in a fog. *How long have I been sleeping?*

But he wasn't in his room.

Nothing looked familiar.

Except it *was* familiar. He was lying on the steps by the

communion rail. It was dark, but he could just make out the altar and the first row of pews.

"Thou are not of this Church," the voice boomed. "There is no welcome for thee in my house."

"Where am I?" He could hear his voice shake.

"Thou shalt not address that which is and has always been, world without end. Thou hast become an abomination in my sight. A horrible mistake. A blight on the world. Thou wilst be removed."

"What are you talking about? How did I get here?" Father McCallum felt a surge of panic. He wanted to stay calm and focused. *Just take a deep breath*, he told himself. He stood, using the communion rail to pull himself up. His eyes were adjusting to the darkness. He was definitely in a church, a familiar church. Then he recognized it.

It was the church he had been baptized in. Our Lady of Grace, in West Babylon, New York. Why was he here?

"Thou hast brought shame to the order of things. The balance is lost," the voice said.

The voice seemed louder, more commanding. He couldn't place it.

"And behold I bring a flood of waters upon this holy place to destroy thy flesh. I will take thine own breath of life and thou wilt be lost. I will destroy all that I have created. The mistakes of an unholy union will be hidden."

"What?" Father McCallum asked. He didn't have time to say more. There was an enormous crack, as though the church had been struck by lightning. He turned toward the doors to the sanctuary and felt a current of air strike him.

Then, without warning, he felt a surge of water flow around his legs. He yelped. The water was cold and dark, and was rising quickly. His back was to the massive crucifix on the wall. He had no place to go.

"Help!" he screamed, although he knew it was futile. He was going to die here.

The water swirled past his hips.

"Die!" the voice boomed. "Die!"

"No!" Father McCallum begged. He saw a door and tried to swim toward it. But the water rose faster and the swells grew more violent. They pushed at him, slamming him against the pulpit, the back wall, the crucifix.

He strained and strained, but the water lifted him and tossed him around like a rag doll.

A swell brushed over his head, and he fought to find the surface, then broke free and gasped for air. Before he could take a breath another swell forced him down.

I'm going to die, he thought.

"Ronnie?"

I'm going to die.

"Ronnie," a pleasant voice called again, "are you up there?"

He opened his eyes. The voice was different — a female voice.

His face was slick with sweat, and as he rolled over he realized the bed was also soaked in sweat.

My bed! I'm in my bed. It was just a dream.

He listened.

"Ronnie?" It was Evelyn, calling from downstairs.

"Yes," he answered.

"You have a visitor," she sang up the stairs.

Father McCallum shook the dream from his mind and tried to focus on the present. *The Vatican is here about the Voynich!*

"I'll be right down."

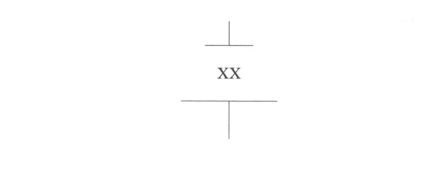

XX

"Remind me again why we're staying in a shit motel," Jeremy said. It was Friday morning and he was lying on one of the double beds in a small room in the Roadside Motel. The yellow wallpaper and its bright flower border smelled of years of smoke and dirt. The twenty-inch JVC was securely bolted to an aged dresser, and Jeremy had almost given up trying to get the remote to work.

Maury pulled the heavy drapes closed on the second small window and turned to his brother. "We're staying here because this shit motel is a short drive from Yale and the Beinecke Library. We're staying here because it's right on the highway. And we're staying here because shit motels like this let you pay in cash. Places like these never care about anything."

Jeremy seemed unconvinced. "You'd think the Vatican would have a better system. Can't they get fake credit cards or set up some hideouts around the country?"

Maury flipped open his suitcase. "Maybe the church doesn't want to waste any money on a dead ass like you."

Jeremy laughed and tried the remote again. He desperately wanted to get something out of the piece-of-crap television — something to keep his mind occupied. He pressed the buttons carefully. He'd lost almost all feeling in his fingers, and didn't want to snap one off.

Maury held a bottle of pills up and shook it. "Did you take your ten-in-the-morning pill?"

Jeremy kept pushing buttons on the remote. He held his other hand out, and Maury dropped a large purple pill into his palm. Jeremy popped it in his mouth.

Maury also took a pill then set the bottle down. "I'm going

to call the church. Keep the volume down."

Jeremy looked at him with disgust and held the remote in the air. "I can't even change the volume with this piece-of-shit remote."

"Whatever." Maury pulled a large phone out of his suitcase. It looked like an antique cell phone. It was really an untraceable satellite phone with a dedicated line. From anywhere on the planet they could flip the phone open and be directly connected to Cardinal Espinosa. Maury turned the phone on, waited until the signal-strength bar showed, and pressed SEND.

The line rang three times before a voice answered. There was no greeting, no small talk, just the accented voice of the cardinal. "You have arrived?"

"We're here," Maury told him.

"Keep this phone on and do not stray far. I will contact you very shortly. Do you have a vehicle?"

"We rented one at the airport."

"Thank you." And the cardinal hung up.

Maury pushed END and dropped the phone into his suitcase.

"And how is the old fart today?" Jeremy asked, grinning.

"He's great. He sends his love."

"Let me guess — he said for us to just sit around with our fingers up our asses until he calls again."

Maury shrugged. "What else?"

"Fine." Jeremy stood up. "I think I'm starting to stink. I need the cream — you got some there?"

Maury dug around in his suitcase and pulled out what looked like a large bottle of shampoo. He handed it to Jeremy who headed into the bathroom. Maury called after him, "Let me know when you're almost done and I'll put the stuff on your back."

"Thank you, sweetie," came the singsong reply.

Maury shoved the suitcase to one side, dropped onto the bed and stared at the ceiling, barely listening to Jeremy whistling in the bathroom. His eye patch dug into his forehead, and he pulled on it to relieve the pressure. He'd only started wearing it recently, because his eye had become infected. Then it rotted out. Maury felt as if things were getting worse and worse.

He marveled at his younger brother's ability not to take anything seriously. All of life was a game to Jeremy. He didn't worry about the long-term; he didn't worry about the church's control over them. Maury did. He wanted out, even if it meant the end of them both. He just wanted out.

What really bothered him was that he and his brother had never had a choice. No one had ever asked them if this was the life they wanted. The church had capitalized on their vulnerability when they were young, and never gave them a choice.

That was going to end — Maury would make sure of it. This trip to Connecticut was the last time they traveled anywhere for the great Cardinal Espinosa.

Jeremy didn't know, but almost a month ago Maury had confronted the cardinal. He had shown up, unannounced, in the office of the Congregation for the Doctrine of the Faith and demanded a meeting. He knew the cardinal wouldn't refuse — he couldn't risk a scene.

Maury demanded that the church release him and his brother. The cardinal had smiled and nodded.

"Stop fuckin' grinning at me," Maury demanded. "Living like animals with our bodies falling apart is no laughing matter."

"My son," Espinosa said. "You misunderstand. Your life has been a tremendous gift. Every second you continue to breathe is a miracle."

"It's no goddamn miracle to me."

The cardinal winced at the sacrilege, especially in his office. "Please don't take the Lord's name in vain."

"Why?" Maury raged. "We are God-damned, aren't we? You told me yourself many times."

The cardinal spoke slowly, patiently, as though talking to a child. "You are forsaken. Both you and your brother are born in the line of Nephilim. That is true."

"And only you can keep us alive with your potions and medications. I know that. But I want out."

Espinosa raised an eyebrow. "Out? My son, I know you feel you have suffered a lifetime of pain, but I assure you that you have been spared a suffering you couldn't imagine. I smile only because I knew you would be in my office to request this thing. I knew you would come to me."

"Then give us our medication and let us go. No more missions."

"It is not my release that you seek. You must pray for God to welcome you back. It is the heavenly Father who has declared your lineage an abomination."

"To be quite honest, your Eminence, I don't give a fuck about God's opinion."

The cardinal sucked in a breath. "Not in His house. You will not profane in His house again."

They glared at one another.

Finally, Espinosa spoke. "There will be one more mission. The last and most important one."

"One more?"

"Yes," Espinosa said. "Wait for me to contact you, then complete this one last task. After that you will be free."

"No more missions?" Maury asked.

The cardinal smiled and nodded.

And this is it, Maury thought. The last mission.

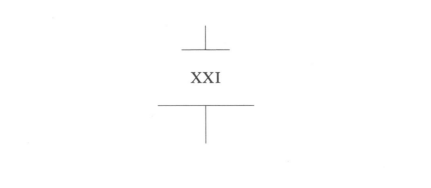

XXI

Father McCallum stared at his reflection in the bathroom mirror. His face was streaked with red from the panic of his dream. He splashed cold water against his skin and gave a heavy sigh. He had to meet the man who would take over the investigation of the Voynich manuscript.

Worse yet, he would have to admit that the Voynich manuscript was gone.

Stolen.

"Under my watch," he whispered. "I'm so sorry."

He pressed a towel to his face and then headed down the stairs. He tugged at his beard slightly, hoping to compose himself mentally and physically.

He found Evelyn near the bottom of the staircase standing in the kitchen with a tall, bronze-skinned man who looked like he was in his mid- to late thirties. Father McCallum had wondered if the Vatican would send an old cardinal from a local diocese. This man looked so ordinary, and wasn't even wearing a priestly collar. Maybe he wasn't the Vatican representative.

"Hello," he said tentatively.

Benicio smiled. "Mr. McCallum? My name is Dr. Benicio Valori."

"Doctor," he said, and nodded, still unsure.

"Oh, a doctor," Evelyn blurted breathlessly. "How wonderful."

"My training is in clinical psychology. I'm not a medical doctor," Benicio offered.

"How lovely," Evelyn shot right back. It was obvious she didn't realize there was a difference between a medical doctor and a psychologist. "That must be so rewarding."

Dr. Benicio Valori nodded. "It has its moments."

Father McCallum felt beads of sweat on his forehead. He didn't have the strength to endure small talk. "What can I do for you, Dr. Valori?"

Evelyn frowned. He realized his abruptness had surprised her, and he tried to smile.

Benicio smiled, too. "Business, actually. We share some acquaintances, and I've come with a number of matters to discuss."

"Library business, no doubt," Evelyn said. "Mr. McCallum is an important person at Yale."

"*Si*, he is indeed," Benicio agreed.

"Evelyn," the priest said. "I shouldn't want to bore you with our business. Shall I invite Dr. Valori upstairs to my flat?"

"You may do whatever you like," she answered. "But I'm going to put on some tea and bring out my special gingersnaps." She turned to the counter and pulled off a colorful cookie jar.

"Please don't go to any trouble," Benicio said.

"It's proper," she said. "Besides, I need to head out. I'm meeting Henry at the mall after his doctor's appointment. So I'm going to go. I'll put the water on but leave Ronnie to get the tea ready." She filled a kettle from the tap and set it on a burner before turning to Benicio.

Dr. Benicio Valori took her hand and gave it a quick kiss. "It was an absolute pleasure to make your acquaintance."

Evelyn giggled and blushed. "Oh, you really are a gentleman. It was quite wonderful to meet you, too." She turned to Father McCallum. "You must invite Dr. Valori over more often."

There was a moment of silence after they heard the front door close behind Evelyn, then Benicio put his hand out. "Allow me to reintroduce myself. I'm Father Benicio Valori. I work with the CDF and was sent here by Cardinal Espinosa."

Father McCallum shook his hand. "Father Ronald McCallum. Pleasure to meet you." He motioned to the small kitchen table, and both men sat.

"So you're not a doctor?" McCallum asked.

"I am — I graduated from Columbia with a doctorate in clinical psychology. I joined the church right after graduation."

"Are you an investigator?" The older priest knew investigators were the Vatican's religious police and went around the world investigating church-related matters. It was never a pleasant experience to have one show up at a parish.

"Yes, I've been assigned in that capacity ever since I was ordained," Valori said.

"Your accent sounds Italian," McCallum suggested.

"I was born in Sicily but my family moved to the U.S. when I was a teenager."

Father McCallum watched the younger man, not sure what to think of him. Benicio's face was difficult to read. Just then the kettle began to whistle. He stood and moved to the stove.

"So you've been stationed at the Yale library for some time?" Benicio asked.

"The Beinecke Rare Books collection. Yes. Quite some time. A good twenty years." He dropped tea bags into two mugs and filled them with hot water before returning with them to the table.

"Wow, that's quite a commitment."

"It is," the older man agreed. "But I love it. It wasn't what I expected after entering the priesthood, but I do love it. I could see where scholarship might even have been my vocational path if I hadn't entered the church."

"That's great," Benicio replied. "And now you've finally got something to report on, eh?"

McCallum frowned, noticeably troubled.

"What is it, Father?" Benicio asked gently.

"It's the reason you're here. The Voynich manuscript. It was stolen."

"So it is the Voynich," Benicio said.

McCallum looked up. "You didn't know you were coming about the manuscript? They didn't tell you? They didn't tell you that I'd found someone who can read it?"

Benicio shook his head. "I wasn't in a good place for a briefing. The church mentioned you were watching over a manuscript. I thought it was probably the Voynich. I was told you'd fill me in when I got here."

"I can try."

"Did you tell the church about the theft yet?"

"I haven't had a chance."

"How was it stolen?"

The older priest shook his head in disbelief. "Someone just kind of walked in and took it."

"Walked in?"

"Yes, the security tapes show a man going to the Voynich display case but then he just sort of drops down, and next thing, the Voynich is gone."

"And the person?"

"It was a security guard. Someone who worked at the Beinecke."

"And they can't find this man?"

Father McCallum sighed. "They found him, all right — his body was left in front of the display case. Sort of decomposed, or something."

"*Non capisco.* I'm not following this. Maybe we should back up. I know a little about the physical manuscript, but why don't you assume I know nothing and walk me through this thing."

The older priest settled back on the wooden kitchen chair. "An American antiques dealer named Wilfrid Voynich discovered the manuscript in 1912. He found it in Villa Mondragone, near Rome, among a large number of ancient manuscripts owned by the occupant of the villa. The Jesuit College inherited all the papers when they took over the villa."

"*Si,*" Benicio said. "I know the Villa Mondragone. It is still used for conferences and special events. I was recently at a retreat there."

"I've heard it's a magnificent building."

"Beautiful. But *scusi* — go on with your story."

"Wilfrid Voynich discovered the manuscript when he was examining the volumes at the Mondragone. He immediately thought he had something special, something unique, even though the book was written in a language Voynich didn't recognize. He took it to the United States and made copies, which he distributed widely, hoping someone could identify the language. He sent it to linguistic experts, historical scholars, theologians, everyone he could think of."

"And no one could read it?" Benicio asked.

McCallum nodded. "No one had a clue. Even then, people said it was a hoax. One scholar said it was a book of meaningless gibberish. But Voynich kept searching. After he died and the book changed hands, people continued to search for the truth of it. But no one has ever decoded a single word."

Benicio smiled. "An entire book written in a language we can't figure out, even with all the computers and decryption technology these days."

"It is a fantastic story. Even more interesting is that linguistic analysis of the manuscript shows it has all the features and characteristics of a real language. In other words, it isn't gibberish. The words have an order and rhythm that suggest a real language."

Benicio shook his head. "Wow."

"Voynich's wife inherited the manuscript when he died, and before she died she left it to a dear friend, who had once worked for her husband. The new owner sold the manuscript — already known as the Voynich — to H.P. Kraus, a book dealer, for about twenty-four thousand dollars. Kraus was convinced the book was valuable and he harbored great expectations of its sale but was met with skepticism and disinterest. It seemed the general public had written the manuscript off as a hoax. As a result, Kraus finally gave up and donated the Voynich manuscript to Yale in 1969. Shortly after the donation, the Vatican sent a representative to work in the Beinecke Library."

"Does anyone else know about the Vatican's interest?" Benicio asked.

"It seems not, even though it's no secret that the Vatican once possessed the book."

"I hadn't heard this part. The Vatican used to own the Voynich? Not just the monks at Mondragone?"

"The Vatican used to own it. Kraus purchased the manuscript in about 1963, then set about researching it so he could place a value on it. At some point he met a representative of the Vatican library, a Monsignor José Ruysschaert, and discreetly inquired about the Voynich. Ruysschaert fully believed the book was in the possession of the Vatican. Kraus, crafty soul that he was, asked to have a look. Ruysschaert went to the inner vaults but returned empty-handed. This was no surprise to Kraus, who told Ruysschaert *he* had the manuscript. Apparently, the Vatican had lost track of it in the distant past. Kraus made no secret about the church gaffe, but the Vatican played it down."

"So what *is* the Voynich manuscript, exactly?" Benicio asked.

Father McCallum shrugged. "It's a bound collection of parchment paper leaves, handwritten in a continuous flowing script, language unknown. There are more than two hundred and thirty pages, roughly broken into five sections — the sections are based on the crude drawings that appear throughout the manuscript. The herbal section features a number of drawings of plants, all unknown, of course. The second section is astronomical or cosmological and contains drawings of star systems and representations of what might be the zodiac. Next there is the biological section, with odd drawings of veins or blood vessels and portly, naked women. Then the pharmaceutical section, which has drawings of small containers and samples of medicinal plants and herbs. At the end is the recipe section — mainly lines of text, each starting with a drawing of a star. That's the literal description of it, but what it *is* — no one knows."

There was a long silence in the room. Finally Father

McCallum spoke again. "Do you know what the Voynich actually is?"

Benicio shook his head. "No."

"You don't?" McCallum asked in surprise. "I assumed they would send an expert."

Benicio laughed. "I only knew about half of the story you just told."

"I'm confused," McCallum said. *Why has the Vatican sent this man to take over my life's work? A man who knows less about the Voynich than I do?* Father McCallum composed himself and asked, "What kind of cases do you normally investigate?"

"Events and puzzles related to mythology and biblical lore. When I was a graduate student, I researched the effect of myth on psychological well-being and social practice."

"Myths," the older priest said.

"Listen," Benicio said gently, "obviously this is your project. I don't plan on taking anything away from you. I want to help investigate whatever's going on — that's all. I want to put your mind at ease. I'm here to help *you*."

Father McCallum immediately felt better. As much as he wanted to dislike this young priest, he couldn't. The man was so respectful.

"Now," Benicio continued, "do you have any idea why the church has been interested in the Voynich for all these years?"

"No," Father McCallum said, deflated. "I was hoping you were here to tell me."

"All I know is a rumor I heard once."

"A rumor?"

Benicio grinned. "It's a bit of strange one."

The old priest leaned forward in his chair.

XXII

Benicio took a moment to compose himself before he started. "Do you know anything about the Nephilim?"

Father McCallum thought about it. "It rings a bell. Something Old Testament."

"Yes," Benicio said, "an Old Testament myth. The Nephilim are briefly mentioned as the half-breed children born of angels who had relations with women."

Instantly, the color drained from Father McCallum's face.

"What is it?" Benicio asked, alarmed.

"The boy," the old priest said. "The boy who can read the manuscript. One of the things I heard him say was, 'half man, half angel — God's secret.'"

Now it was Benicio's turn to be shocked. "The cardinal told me there was a child who could read the manuscript — but that's all he told me. Did the boy really say that?"

"Yes."

"How did you find this boy?"

"There was a school tour at the Beinecke. I found the boy staring at the Voynich display."

Benicio whistled.

"So, what does it mean? Why can the boy read the book?" Father McCallum asked.

"I don't know for sure."

"What about the rumor you mentioned?"

Benicio nodded. "Right. The rumor is that the Voynich was the Nephilim's story. The story is, God hated the Nephilim, and He hated the angels who disobeyed him by having relations with women. He wanted them all destroyed. That's why God sent the floods to wipe out the world. But the world wasn't wiped out. The Nephilim survived — a few of them, anyway. And they managed to memorize their history. It was passed down from one generation of Nephilim to the next until they could record it, in the pages of the Voynich manuscript."

"Why can't we decipher it?"

"It's written in the language of the Nephilim, the half-breeds. A language we cannot read — by God's command."

"So God doesn't want us to read it. It's His secret."

"Yeah, that's part of the story."

"You know," Father McCallum said thoughtfully, "the very first thing the boy said was, 'the language of the forsaken, the tongue of the dead.'"

"The word *nephilim* means *the forsaken* or *the dead ones*," Benicio said slowly. "In ancient times, anyone thought to be Nephilim was considered dead already."

"The Voynich is written in the tongue of the dead," Father McCallum mused. He paused and then added, "That means the boy —"

"— is Nephilim," Benicio finished.

XXIII

Jake quietly opened his office door. Harold Grower was sitting in the waiting room. He'd been sitting there for the last twenty minutes. Early for his appointment as usual. Jake never started sessions early — boundaries were a big issue. He closed the door silently and went to his desk. He had another minute before the session started.

On top of a pile of mail was a letter from Blue Cross, the health insurance company that would be paying for Harold's appointments. Jake had sent Blue Cross an invoice for Harold's first four sessions; this should be the check to cover them. He opened the envelope and pulled out a sheet of paper. After Jake's name, Harold's name, and some dates, stamped at the top in bold capital letters was: CLAIM DENIED Beneath that there were strings of numbers and codes that inevitably described why the claim was denied. Jake shook his head and read no further. This happened frequently with insurance companies. A doctor might forget a signature or date on a claim form, and the claim would be denied. Sometimes claims were denied because the coverage in one calendar year had run out. Jake dropped the letter on his desk. He'd deal with it later.

He looked at his watch: eleven-thirty. Harold was his last appointment before lunch. He wished it were quitting time — he wanted to get home and see his family. He wanted to unwind. He wanted to see how Wyatt was doing.

Jake opened the door to his waiting room again, this time more noisily. Harold's face lit up, and he jumped to his feet.

"Dr. Tunnel!"

"Come on in, Harold."

The older, slightly overweight man came quickly into the

office. His manners and agility suggested a man younger than the graying hair and glasses suggested. Harold immediately settled on the couch as Jake dropped into his leather desk chair.

"What's on the agenda today, Harold?" he asked casually.

Harold looked concerned. "I'm worried about you, Dr. Tunnel."

Jake preferred not to be formal in speaking with clients and normally operated under first names. Some of his clients insisted on referring to him as "Dr. Tunnel" anyway — especially the older ones. Harold insisted on the title. "You're worried about me?"

"I think you're unhappy. I think you're missing something."

Jake shook his head. "You know what, you're probably right, but I can't let you use the session to help me. This is *your* time. It wouldn't be fair." Jake used the classic therapy line to get out of talking about himself.

"Oh, I don't mind. I think it's important."

Harold had been referred to Jake by the military base. Jake had a steady stream of patients from CFB Halifax, which housed a large segment of Canada's naval fleet. The base had its own psychiatrists and psychologists, but management often sent personnel to private doctors for ongoing therapy. Harold's therapy was definitely ongoing.

Six months ago, Harold Grower, a Navy helicopter pilot, was sent to help locate the crew members of a fishing boat that had capsized during a bad storm. Harold had gone to the back of the chopper to bring a rescue diver and a fisherman up on the winch while the co-pilot flew the chopper. Somehow, Harold fell out of the helicopter and dropped fifty feet into the cold, thrashing waters of the Atlantic in the pitch dark. He was in the water for almost twenty minutes before the co-pilot found him and he was winched onboard. Harold Grower had been off duty for five months, and talked constantly about how God had saved him that night.

"Are you happy?" Harold asked intently. "I mean are you

really happy, deep down inside?"

It was a bad time to ask that particular question. Jake was tempted to say he wasn't the slightest bit happy. He was tempted to say his son was sick, and all Jake wanted was for Wyatt to be better. He knew he couldn't say any of those things: the psychologist must seem invulnerable. If he showed his flaws, Jake would not be convincing as a healer. Clients need to borrow from the strength and resolve of the therapist. "I'm fine — how have you been feeling?"

Harold looked at him sadly. "God reaches out and touches all of us with a message. We just have to listen."

"What message did God give you?" Jake asked quickly. One way or another he was going to get these sessions focused on Harold Grower.

"God wants me to lead."

Jake smiled slightly. "To where?"

"To the answers we seek," Harold replied without a trace of a smile. "God wants me to provide the guidance when the path is lost."

"Do you talk to God? Can you hear Him?" Jake wondered if Harold was slipping into a psychotic disorder. His focus on being saved by God was outside the realm of a normal reaction to an abnormal event, and could indicate post-traumatic stress disorder. But if Harold thought God had given him special powers, Jake would have to try a different approach.

Harold looked even sadder. "Of course I can hear Him. God talks to all of us. We have to choose to listen."

"How do we do that? How do we make that choice?"

Harold laughed. "I can't answer that."

Jake didn't know how far to push it. He wanted to ask more questions, to search for a psychotic element, but he didn't want to suggest he believed in Harold's delusion. He decided to use another classic therapy technique, reflection. He restated Harold's perspective.

"So, God communicates with all of us but we have to choose

to hear the message. The problem is how and when we make that choice."

"That's right," Harold said. "The curious part is how God talks to us. Sometimes it is directly, in our dreams or in things we see. Sometimes it's indirect, like events that happen in the world. Sometimes God communicates to us in tragedies that affect us."

"Tragedies like when you fell out of the chopper?"

Harold laughed loudly. "I wasn't talking about me, but I see why you'd say that."

Jake really didn't want to go there. He didn't want to talk about God communicating through tragedies. Just thinking about it flooded him with anxiety about Wyatt. He wanted to get off the topic.

"You certainly are a man of faith," he said.

"You are, too, Dr. Tunnel. You are, too."

Jake waited, but Harold just smiled.

"So let's get started for today," Jake finally said. He opened Harold's folder to signal they needed to get to the business of therapy. "Let's —" He looked at the unsigned release-of-information form, right at the top of the papers in the folder.

It was fairly routine for psychologists to contact close family members to get different perspectives; it helped the doctors assess patients and monitor treatment. Jake wanted to talk to Harold's wife, and any other relatives, if he had them. Harold had never talked about his family, and he refused to sign the release form.

"Oh," Jake said. "Before we get started, I wonder if I can get you to sign this thing now."

"Actually, Dr. Tunnel, I don't think that'd be helpful."

"Oh come on, Harold. I just want to talk to your wife and see what she thinks. I don't need to say anything about our sessions. They're confidential."

Harold shook his head. "No, not yet."

"Maybe next time?"

"Maybe. You'll get to speak to my wife soon enough."

Jake relented. He didn't want to push: it could damage rapport. "Did you bring your schedule?" Harold was keeping a weekly schedule of his activities so they could make sure he had sufficient structure and social opportunities.

Harold kept smiling. "We are all people of faith. We all believe in something, even if we believe in nothing at all. Faith separates us from animals. Those of us who don't possess it shrivel up and die."

"Right," Jake said. He really wanted to use the appointment for therapy. "Do you have your schedule for last week?"

Harold looked serious. He somberly reached into his coat pocket and brought out a piece of paper.

"My schedule for the last week," Harold announced.

"Great, let's have a look."

***

Twenty minutes later, Jake set Harold's file on his desk and stood — a signal that the session was over. Harold also stood, and they walked slowly to the door, where Jake patted his patient's shoulder and wished him a good week. Harold, who seemed lost in thought, nodded.

Jake watched him slowly cross the waiting room toward the door, then stop. *Uh-oh.*

Harold turned, his expression intense. "Oh," he said. "There's something else."

Jake didn't have time for *something else*. He wanted to eat lunch. He spoke cautiously. "Yes?"

Harold held his hand out. "You need to have this. It will be your exit when you're trapped. Look to the church."

Jake hesitated but opened his hand, and Harold placed a heavy, old-fashioned key in Jake's palm. It looked as if it could have belonged to a 1930s jail cell, made of thick, dull copper in need of polishing. Jake stared at it then looked at Harold.

"What is this?"

He shrugged. "Please. Just keep it."

Jake knew he shouldn't accept gifts from patients — gifts blurred the professional nature of the relationship. He looked at the key again. "Okay," he said, "thanks."

Harold smiled but didn't leave.

"Anything else?" Jake asked patiently.

"I just wanted to say I'll be praying for your family."

Jake nodded. "Thanks."

"And especially for your little boy. Everything will be fine."

Jake was stunned. He'd never mentioned Wyatt. "Uh, okay." *How does Harold know about Wyatt?*

Harold left.

For a long time, Jake stood and stared at the doorway, a small bubble of anger slowly forming. Harold must have been following his family. He knew about Wyatt.

XXIV

Shemhazai and Azazel stood across the street from Matthew Younger's house.

"The Nephilim boy lives here?" Azazel said.

"Yes."

"This is it, then," Azazel said with some satisfaction. "The end of our torture."

Shemhazai was silent.

"Let us do God's will."

"And then destroy the Voynich?" Shemhazai asked.

"Yes, then it will be finished."

"We will be welcomed back into God's house?"

Azazel nodded. His beard itched, and he reached up to scratch it. His heavy frame made every motion tedious, and he was always sweating. "I, for one, cannot wait to be done with these earthly bodies."

Shemhazai shifted uncomfortably. He'd been forced to inhabit the first person he'd met after discarding the body he used as the library security guard. Tonight he looked like a young, athletic university student. It had been unavoidable. Shemhazai could live outside a host for only a few minutes; then he would wither and soon disappear. It was part of God's curse.

"Let's go," Shemhazai finally said.

"Wait!" Azazel put a hand in front of Shemhazai's chest.

The two men watched as a car slowed to a stop in front of the Younger residence. A gray-haired man and a younger, olive-skinned man sat in the car, looking at the house.

"Who is that?" Azazel asked.

Shemhazai squinted. "The librarian priest." He looked again. "I don't recognize the other."

"What are they doing here?"

Shemhazai shook his head. "Following up on the boy, I imagine. They aren't going to just let this go."

"But we have the book. The boy cannot help them without it."

"Maybe they don't know that."

"Let's move," Azazel whispered angrily. "I don't want to be seen here."

They started walking away.

"What do we do now?" Shemhazai asked.

"I don't know. I wanted to do this quietly. I didn't want the church involved. It's too complicated if they get in the way."

"It might be unavoidable."

"I realize that. I'm prepared to make that decision when it is necessary. Right now, it is not necessary."

"I agree."

They kept walking.

XXV

Father McCallum looked at Benicio. "I've noticed you aren't wearing a collar."

Benicio nodded.

"Does this mean you're undercover? You aren't going to tell the boy or his parents what's going on?"

Benicio laughed. "I don't know what's going on! I can't exactly spill the beans to Mom and Dad, can I? What would I say? 'Hey, we think your autistic son can read a thousand-year-old book and, oh yeah, we also think the boy might be half angel'?"

"Five-hundred-year-old."

"What?"

"The Voynich manuscript has only been dated back five hundred years. You said a thousand."

Benicio laughed again. He couldn't help himself. "You're absolutely right. *Scusi.*"

There was silence in the car.

"You're a very difficult man to dislike," Father McCallum finally said.

"*Permesso?*"

"I don't like that the church sent some hotshot to investigate the child. It's an insult that they don't believe I can handle it."

Benicio nodded, his face somber.

"As a result, I expected to dislike whomever arrived to take over."

"Understandable," Benicio said. "And it was my intention to be thoroughly dislikable."

McCallum smiled. "You see, there you go again." He placed a hand on Benicio's shoulder. "You may try to be unlikable, but I see through it. You actually strike me as a genuine, caring individual."

Benicio smiled.

"Why don't you go talk to the parents? I'll wait here."

"No, no, no. We will do it together. You can help me."

"I don't want to jeopardize the investigation. Maybe I can be of more help once we get to the school to see the boy. It might be best if only you went in."

Benicio considered. The church hadn't given him instructions, but they had provided the hospital ID badge. That would allow him to be subtle. He needed the parents' agreement if he was going spend time with Matthew.

"But you've never spoken to the parents yourself? They wouldn't recognize you?"

"It's his foster parents, and no, I've never met them."

"Foster parents," Benicio said, nodding. "Right. Okay. You're coming with me."

**

Down the block, Maury and Jeremy sat in their red Honda Civic. With one hand Maury held a small receiver to his ear. He had his other hand out the window, pointing a miniature parabolic dish at the old priest's rental car.

"What are they talking about? Why don't they go in the house?"

"Shut up. I can barely hear anything. I think they're whining and bitching about who's going in." The small microphone picked up every sound from the street, and he had to strain to hear the two men's voices. "Wait," he announced. "I think Benny's going in."

"Is he leaving the old man?"

Maury looked through the windshield. "Nope. They're both heading in."

Jeremy perked up a little. "Wanna go search the car?"

Maury stared at his brother. "For what? Man, you're an idiot."

Jeremy frowned. "Fuck you."

"You just stay here and be ready to roll. I'm going to get closer to the house and see what I can find out."

"Let me go do it," Jeremy pleaded.

"Fuck off," Maury spat back and got out of the car, closing the door carefully. He headed down the street.

Jeremy frowned. "Good luck, you and your one eyeball," he muttered. He watched Maury slip into the backyard of Matthew's house.

As he watched his brother he felt his own hand twitch. He brushed the fingertips of both hands together. Nothing. No feeling. He reached into his coat pocket and took a small atomizer out. He slid his arms out of his jacket and sprayed a liberal mist up and down both.

XXVI

Benicio stood nervously on Matthew Younger's doorstep. He wasn't accustomed to lying, but there was no way he could stretch the truth far enough to make his visit believable. He looked at Father McCallum and smiled. He rang the doorbell.

"*Exitus acta probat,*" he whispered. *The outcome justifies the deed.*

Through the curtained windows of the door he noticed movement, then the door opened. Benicio saw a rough-looking man in his early forties, with thinning hair and wearing glasses that were slightly tinted. A heavy beer belly protruded from a stained white T-shirt.

"What?" the man said abruptly.

"I'm terribly sorry to bother you," Benicio began. "I'm Dr. Valori. I'm a clinical psychologist. This is Mr. McCallum from Yale University. We wanted to speak to you about your son."

The man looked surprised. "My son? You mean Matthew?"

"Yes, Matthew."

"Are you from the school? Is it because he didn't go today?"

"I'm sorry," said Benicio. "You mean Matthew's home?"

"Yeah, he's home. He freaks out sometimes and won't go to school."

"Oh," Benicio said, taken aback.

"So, what's this about? Did the kid break something? I ain't paying for shit."

"No, no," Benicio reassured him. "I'm here on behalf of the Yale–New Haven Children's Hospital. We're running a new experimental treatment program for severe autistic disorder. We're recruiting children to participate in the program. It's completely free of charge."

The man held his hand up. "I don't know what the hell you're talking about. Couldn't you have just called or sent a letter?"

Benicio nodded, as though he'd expected this response. "I feel very awkward about just showing up like this. I realize it's an inconvenience, but your son's name came to us in an unexpected way and left us in a bit of a time bind."

"What the hell you talking about?"

"Your son's class recently toured the rare books collection at Yale, and Matthew made quite an impression on Mr. McCallum, here. Knowing about the ongoing research, he was kind enough to contact me directly and inquire about adding your son's name to the list. Meanwhile, the research team has completed the selection of participants, and we're going to start next week."

"That's right," McCallum jumped in. "I didn't want Matthew to miss out on this opportunity so I sort of insisted Dr. Valori meet you. The school provided your address."

"Fuckin' school," the man mumbled.

"Pardon me?" Benicio said.

"What ya say your name was again?"

"Dr. Valori," Benicio said, and began searching his jacket. "Oh, I'm terribly sorry — I didn't even show you my hospital ID. I could be anybody standing on your doorstep." He found his wallet and retrieved the employee card for the Yale–New Haven Children's Hospital.

"And I'm Ronald McCallum." He pointed to the ID clipped to the outside of his jacket, then extended his hand, but the man ignored it.

"Fine, whatever. Step in here for a second." He turned and moved into the house.

Benicio looked at Father McCallum and gave a silent whistle. They both stepped into the entranceway.

"Hey Carol," the man shouted. "There's two guys here about the boy."

"What?" The response came from somewhere in the house.

"Get down here!" the man screamed.

He turned to Benicio and Father McCallum. "You can talk to her about him." He walked away, leaving them standing at the front door. Benicio looked at his companion and mouthed, "What's going on?"

The house stank of cat urine and something else Benicio thought might be alcohol and vomit. He found it difficult to breathe.

A minute later, a woman in her late thirties rounded a corner and stood before them. "Whatcha want?"

She was barely five feet tall and had short, spiked brown hair with streaks of blonde, which Benicio thought were probably her own attempt at highlights.

"Good morning," Benicio started. "I'm Dr. Valori and this is Mr. McCallum. We want to talk to you about having your son join an experimental treatment program at Yale–New Haven Children's Hospital."

"I ain't no Morman and I don't want to become no Morman."

"No, I'm with the children's hospital, and Mr. McCallum is with Yale University."

"We ain't got no money."

"Ma'am," Father McCallum interjected. "What we wanted to talk to you about is a program that's free of charge. The people in the program would like to work with Matthew."

"In fact," Benicio added, "there might even be an opportunity for financial reimbursement for you and your husband."

Suddenly the husband was back. "Honey, what's with your manners? Invite these important men in and get them a coffee." He pushed her away and waved the priests into the living room. "Take a seat, gentleman. I'm most curious about this program."

The living room, which was at the front of the house, was small and dirty. There was an old TV set in one corner across from a floral-print love seat. Along the third wall were two chairs. None of the furniture looked comfortable. They both remained standing.

"Would you like a coffee or anything?" the wife asked.

"No thank you, Mrs. Younger. I'm fine," Father McCallum said.

"Go get them some coffee," the husband barked, and she turned and left the room. "That's Carol," the man said. "I'm John Younger."

***

"Son of a bitch," Maury muttered. He couldn't find a good position from which to watch the house, and there were no trees or bushes he could hide behind. He ended up flat against the wall under the kitchen window at the back of the house — in plain sight of the neighbors. He knew he couldn't stay there long.

He held the parabolic dish up to the window but heard only static. He went to the front of the house, but realized he couldn't risk listening through the living room window. He was sure that's where they all were. He went around the house again and looked into the kitchen.

The mom was right there. He dropped down and squeezed against the house, hoping like hell she hadn't seen him. After a few minutes he decided it was safe to try the parabolic microphone again. He twisted it this way and that and finally heard part of a muffled conversation, something about the boy. Benny wanted to talk to him. *That'd be fun*, he thought. *Trying to talk to a retarded kid.*

***

"So, your son is here?" Benicio asked.

"Um," John started awkwardly. "Yep, I'm sure." He shouted. "Carol! Bring the boy in here."

"I think he's upstairs," she called.

"Oh, he's up in his room? It would be very helpful to meet him on his own territory," Benicio said. As Carol came out of the kitchen he started to follow her.

"Oh no," John exclaimed and moved toward Benicio. "She'll bring him down."

"Excuse me," Father McCallum said, blocking John Younger. "I'd like to ask a few more questions to get an idea of the financial compensation you'd qualify for."

Benicio stayed right behind Carol, who took the stairs by the front door. The parents didn't want him upstairs, and his instincts told him something wasn't right in this house.

The stairs ended in a small corridor. Carol turned to him sharply. "Just wait here and I'll get him out of his room."

She opened one of three doors in the hall and stepped in. Benicio was right behind her.

The boy's room contained a tiny box spring and mattress pushed against one wall and a nearly empty bookcase. There were no toys, no stuffed animals.

Matthew stood facing the wall next to the bookcase. With one finger he slowly traced a circle on the faded wallpaper. Benicio realized he must have been doing this for quite some time because there was a line worn into the wallpaper.

"Matthew," Carol said in a slow, patronizing way. "There's someone here to see you."

"That's okay," Benicio said. "I'll just talk to him right here."

She turned and frowned. "No, I'll bring him down."

"I'd like to speak to him alone. You go downstairs. I'll be right there," he said firmly.

She glared at Benicio. "He don't speak, you know. He's a retard."

Benicio nodded and stood his ground.

She faced him, hands on her hips. "It ain't anyone who'd take a orphan retard, you know. He's damn lucky."

Benicio felt his face redden in anger but said nothing. He waited patiently, and she finally left. There was a strong smell of urine in the room, and he noticed a wet patch on the boy's pant leg.

He knelt next to the child. "Matthew," he said softly.

The boy continued to trace the circle on the wall.

"I'm Dr. Valori. I want to talk to you. I want to talk about that special book you saw at the big library."

The boy didn't acknowledge him. He continued to trace the circle.

Benicio was silent for a moment then looked at the wall. "What are you drawing on the wall?"

There was no answer.

"You drawing a circle?"

The boy's finger stopped on the wall. Benicio watched as he carefully lifted his finger, touched the top of the circle then tapped the bottom of the circle. Then he touched the left side of the circle, and moved his finger across to the right side.

It was the sign of the Cross.

Matthew resumed tracing the circle.

"What was that?" Benicio asked, his voice shaking. "Did you just draw the Cross?"

The boy didn't respond.

"Matthew?" Benicio urged. "Can you draw that again?"

Nothing.

Benicio tried to slow his breathing and heart rate. "Matthew, what can you tell me about God's secret? About the forsaken ones?"

Matthew's finger stopped.

Benicio held his breath.

The boy turned slowly to face the kneeling man. Their eyes were level. "The fathers have returned from exile. The forsaken must tell the story."

Benicio held very still. "Who are the fathers? Who are the forsaken?"

Matthew turned to the wall and began tracing the circle.

"No," Benicio whispered. "Talk to me. I'm here to help you.

I'm here to help the story be told."

Matthew continued to trace the circle.

"Please," Benicio urged.

Nothing.

Benicio sighed. "Okay, buddy. I'll be back. You hang in there." He put his hand gently on Matthew's back as he stood.

And Matthew screamed.

Benicio pulled his hand away. He had touched the boy for less than a second.

"I'm sorry," he said quickly. "I didn't mean to upset you."

The boy shrieked.

***

Maury could hardly make out the conversation. He twisted the volume dial right to the top.

Suddenly there was a high-pitched scream from inside the house. He knocked the earpiece from his ear and bit his lip to keep from yelling.

He didn't need the dish to hear the father asking what happened.

Maury scrambled up and began running. As he passed the front of the house he heard pounding footsteps from inside. He ran to the car.

***

Benicio's stomach leapt into his throat. He knew autistic children sometimes had strong reactions to physical touch, but Matthew had taken him completely by surprise.

"What the hell?" John Younger yelled from the boy's doorway. "Get out of here."

"My apologies," Benicio started. "I just was saying goodbye and touched his back."

"He don't like to be touched," Younger announced. "Just get

out of here. Just let him alone." Younger hurried him down the stairs; Father McCallum and Carol waited at the bottom.

"Dr. Valori?" Father McCallum asked.

Benicio shook his head at the old priest, then addressed John Younger. "Thank you for your time. We'll get the paperwork together and return shortly. I think there'll be sizable compensation for you."

They reached the front door and Father McCallum opened it, then stepped onto the porch, Benicio right behind him. "Thanks. And once again, I'm sorry if I've upset Matthew."

"Does that all the time," Carol announced flatly. She closed the door without another word. The two men stared at the door for a moment. Finally Benicio spoke. "*Dio li aiuta*," he said. "*Dio li aiuta*." God help them.

XXVII

"I think you're right about the boy," Benicio said. He and Father McCallum were in the rental car, which was still parked outside Matthew Younger's house.

Father McCallum's pulse quickened. "Really?"

"There's something different about Matthew. He traced the sign of the Cross on the wall. He said, 'The fathers have returned from exile. The forsaken must tell the story.'"

"What does that mean?"

Benicio put his hands on the steering wheel. "Let's get out of here and go somewhere we can talk."

Father McCallum agreed.

Benicio started the car and pulled away from the curb, then drove them to the highway and headed toward New Haven. Neither man spoke until Father McCallum pointed out a bill-board advertising the International House of Pancakes.

"That'll do," Benicio agreed. He took the next exit, found the restaurant, and parked. They went in and sat at a booth.

A friendly waitress in a tight brown apron appeared next to them with a pot of coffee. "You boys need some joe?" she asked.

McCallum nodded. "Thank you."

Benicio pushed his mug toward her.

She poured the coffee, said, "I'll give you boys a couple of minutes," and was gone.

Father McCallum finally asked, "Why was Matthew scream-ing?"

Benicio sighed and ran a hand through his dark hair. "I don't know. I had pretty much decided I wasn't going to get anything else out of him and was leaving. Without even thinking, I put a hand on his back as I said goodbye. That was it. He started screaming as soon as I touched him, and he wouldn't stop."

"You just rested your hand on his back?"

"Yep. I didn't startle him or anything. Just gently placed it there and he started up."

McCallum looked concerned.

"It isn't an uncommon reaction for autism," Benicio explained. "Frequently, people with autism are extremely sensitive about physical touch. They just can't bear it."

"And so they scream like that? The kid sounded possessed."

"I know. It freaked me out, too. I hardly ever worked with kids when I did my doctorate, so I'd never seen anything like that before. I can't even say if that's a typical autistic reaction."

"But the boy talked to you before he started screaming?"

"*Si.* He said the fathers have returned from exile and the forsaken must tell the story."

"And the forsaken are probably the Nephilim?"

"Well, that's one interpretation," Benicio agreed. "*Nephilim* literally means the ones forsaken by God."

"What will you do now?"

Benicio was solemn. "I need to report back. I'll give my impressions to the church and see what they want me to do. I'll have to tell them about the Voynich being stolen. I don't know what impact that will have. I was thinking I'd take the boy to the Beinecke to read it, but I can't do that now."

"There's other copies of the book."

Benicio frowned. "You have a copy?"

"No, no, no," McCallum said. "I mean that the entire manuscript has been scanned, and there are copies of all the research that's been done over the years."

"That's great!" Benicio exclaimed. "Where can we get them?"

"Anywhere. Every single page of the Voynich is on the Internet." But suddenly he frowned.

"What is it?" Benicio asked.

"I'm not sure the copies are any good. I asked the cardinal why I had to watch the Voynich manuscript when all the pages were available online, and he said only the original can be read. The copies are useless."

"What? Why?"

"He just said that eyes will look directly on the manuscript and read. I never asked for more of an explanation."

"I know there is a legend or myth about the Nephilim that they can only read the language written by the hand of another Nephilim. Obviously, a copy isn't written directly by a descendent."

"Perhaps that is it," Father McCallum said.

The waitress slid up next to their table. "Orders, guys?"

They both scooped up plastic menus. Benicio ordered an egg and ham crepe wrap and McCallum ordered pancakes. She thanked them, topped up their coffee, and spun away.

"Have you ever investigated anything like this before?" Father McCallum asked.

Benicio shook his head. "Nope. This one is completely out there."

"Could this boy really be Nephilim?"

"I don't even want to speculate. Not yet."

"Maybe he can read the manuscript because he's autistic."

"I don't really see how — it doesn't make sense that a child would not develop speech but then be able to talk specifically about the Voynich."

"Because if he can't talk, he can't talk," Father McCallum said.

"Right. Even in the cases of savants I don't think this fits."

"That's when the child has a real talent for something."

"*Si*, like when an autistic child has incredible math skills or can play the piano like a virtuoso."

Both men were silent for a moment. Then the old priest asked, "Do you miss it?"

"Miss what?"

"Clinical psychology. You did your doctorate and then entered the church, where you haven't exactly practiced as a psychologist."

"Well," Benicio said slowly, "That's true, but I use my training every day. I investigate issues around the world. When I meet new people I have to establish rapport quickly and efficiently. I often have to help people through a crisis just to ask them what's wrong. I use a lot of psychology without actually hanging up a shingle that says I'm a psychologist."

"I can see that. I never meant to imply you don't use your training. I was just curious whether you ever regret the path you took. You must have given up a lot to serve the faith."

"You get a lot back though," Benicio said. "You probably know that more than I. How do you manage being so isolated out here? You aren't working in a church at all."

Father McCallum's face lit up. "I couldn't be happier. I love the library and I love my job there. And I know I'm serving a higher purpose. I know there is a great secret hidden in the pages of that book, and we're finally so close to it. I can't believe my good fortune. This has been a mystery for hundreds of years and I may be here when it's finally solved. I couldn't be happier."

The food arrived and they began to eat. Benicio knew Father McCallum wanted to talk about the Voynich, to speculate about the mysteries it held and the Vatican's role, but he was too tired to listen. The effort of the last few days was rapidly catching up with him. He also found himself thinking about grad school. It had been a great experience: the work, the classmates, and the practical experiences.

When he'd joined the church he'd left behind more than a career. His calling also meant leaving his girlfriend. Seeing Father McCallum growing old chasing the Vatican's mystery gave Benicio a glimpse of his own future: he would grow old alone. He would have no one.

He missed Jenna.

"What are you thinking about?" Father McCallum asked.

"Nothing," Benicio said, shaking his head. "Just wondering what's going to happen next."

XXVIII

As they walked to the car, Benicio said, "I'm exhausted. I think I'll grab a cab and head to the hotel. The Vatican put me in the Holiday Inn Express. I need to get some sleep. It's been a real whirlwind recently."

"Listen," Father McCallum said. "Why don't you drop me off at my place and then keep the car. You'll need it more than I will. That way I know you'll stay in touch with me."

Benicio smiled. "No, you don't have to do that."

"Really, I insist."

Benicio nodded. "Okay."

They headed for the older priest's house. When they arrived, Father McCallum said, "Would you try and keep me in the loop?"

Benicio frowned. "Of course. Why do you ask?"

"Once you report and they find out the Voynich is gone, my usefulness might be at an end. I'll be disappointed if I can't follow this thing through. I'd like to help."

Benicio knew Father McCallum was right: if the CDF saw no further use for the old man he'd be reassigned and forgotten. "If there's any way I can swing it, I'll make sure you stay involved. I won't leave without saying goodbye."

Father McCallum smiled broadly. "I was right about you. You're a hard man to dislike." He got out of the car and walked toward his house.

Benicio watched him walk around the house to the back before he put the car in gear and headed to his hotel.

***

Father McCallum hung his coat on a hook at the back door and walked through the kitchen. He went upstairs without calling a greeting to Evelyn and Fred. Then he remembered it was late Friday morning — they'd be out grocery shopping until after lunch.

He felt tired and sad. No, not sad — dejected. His energy completely drained.

He knew why. Father Valori would call the Vatican and report on the child. *The church isn't going to need me any longer. My job was to watch over the manuscript, and now it's gone. I'm no good to them any more.*

He tried to wash those thoughts from his mind. It was the exhaustion talking. He should just take a nap.

Ronald McCallum walked into his bedroom. He kicked his shoes off, sat heavily on the edge of the bed, and then dropped over sideways. He had to talk to someone.

The Most Reverend Thomas O'Regan, in the archdiocese of New Jersey.

The old priest thought of his dear friend, a respected figure in the Roman Catholic church. *I'll just call him up for a chat.*

He sat, reached for the telephone, and dialed the number, thinking about what he would say. Thomas knew he worked at the Beinecke Library, but Father McCallum had been careful not to divulge the exact nature of his work. The CDF had insisted on secrecy even with other church members. It seemed too clandestine to Father McCallum, but a part of him enjoyed the top-secret feel of it.

"Office of the Archbishop."

"Yes, could I speak with the archbishop please?"

"Who can I say is calling?"

"Ronald McCallum — an old friend." This was true in every respect. Ronald and Thomas had attended seminary together years before and remained friends ever since.

"One moment."

There was a pause and a clicking sound, then Thomas said, "Ronnie?"

It was good to hear his voice. "Hey Thomas. How are things?"

"Wonderful. Wonderful. What about you? Still guarding the books?"

He hesitated. "Yes. Still here."

"Everything okay?"

Father McCallum heard concern in Thomas' voice. Again he hesitated, then said, "Sure. I guess. Just reaching another milestone and feeling my age, I suppose."

"What's the milestone?"

"Well, I think that my job here at the library might be getting close to an end."

"Why? What happened?"

The old priest weighed his words carefully. "I'm not sure. I really feel like I need to talk to someone. My world is getting turned upside down and I've never felt so disoriented, so disconnected."

"Ronnie," Thomas said, "why don't I come visit you. I have some time in my schedule and could pop down there for the day."

"No, no. I wouldn't hear of it. I didn't call to try and pull you away from your work. I just wanted to hear a friendly voice, I guess."

"Can't you tell me some of what's going on? I might be able to help."

"Well, the short version of the story is that I've been watching a certain manuscript for all the years I've been here."

"Right."

"No one has been able to make sense of the manuscript in fifty years, and then yesterday along comes a child who can easily read it."

"That's good, isn't it?"

"I thought so but I don't know. The CDF sent someone to look into it and that person is reporting to the Vatican right now. I think the CDF is going to take things over. I'm worried I'm going to be out."

"What was the manuscript?" Thomas asked.

Father McCallum bit his bottom lip. "Um, I'm not sure I — maybe I'd better not say."

Thomas didn't comment.

"I think it's better if I don't give any specifics."

Thomas still didn't speak.

"Hello? Thomas? You there?"

Still nothing.

"Hello?" the old priest repeated.

The line clicked again, and Ronnie McCallum heard a distant hum of static. He was about to hang up when a heavily accented voice spoke softly. "Your betrayal is noted."

Then the line went dead.

XXIX

After he settled into his room Benicio contemplated the phone call to the Vatican. He knew he wouldn't be able to relax until he called. He was worried, though. Once he made the call he could be forced into immediate service without having a chance to rest. He was tempted to put it off, if only for a few hours.

But that was not the Vatican way.

He picked up the hotel phone and hit zero to connect to the front desk, then gave the operator the fifteen-digit number he'd memorized on the plane. He dropped into a moon-shaped chair next to a tiny table. It was a clean, comfortable room, but small.

One ring.

"Hello?" It was the accented voice of Cardinal Espinosa. Benicio realized the cardinal had been sitting by the phone. Good thing he hadn't waited until morning with his report.

"Your Eminence," Benicio began. "I have made contact with the boy."

"And?"

"There is something unusual, no doubt. I haven't had a chance to observe the child reading the manuscript because —"

"No!" the cardinal said sharply. "The boy is not to view the manuscript again. You are only to determine the credibility of Father McCallum's claim. You are not to let the boy read the manuscript."

"Well, I was going to say that the Voynich manuscript has been stolen, so I —"

"Stolen? Already?"

Already? "I can't verify the boy's abilities without letting him see the manuscript. Should I be looking for the manuscript?" Benicio asked.

"That book is not your concern. You were to evaluate the claims of Father McCallum. That is all."

"Yes, your Eminence."

"Is there credibility to Father McCallum's claim? Yes or no?"

"I would like more time to investigate, but right now I would say there is a chance of it. The boy said the fathers are free and the forsaken need to tell the story. Unfortunately, that's all he said, but it's quite remarkable given that he is not supposed to be able to speak at all."

"The fathers are free?" Cardinal Espinosa asked. "What does that mean?"

"I don't know."

"Can you get the boy?"

"*Non capisco.*"

"Can you get the child?" Espinosa said again. "Bring him to me." It was an order.

"Your Eminence," Benicio began, his mind racing. "I don't think I could convince the parents to let me take the child."

"So don't convince them. Just take the child."

"By force?"

"If need be, yes."

Benicio didn't know what to say. There was a very uncomfortable pause.

Finally the cardinal spoke again. His voice was calm and carefully measured. "My son, I have misspoken. Forgive me. My enthusiasm impaired my reason. Ignore what I said. We must discuss the matter more thoroughly. Return to the Vatican immediately. I will have a ticket waiting for you at the airport."

Something is going on here. "What about the child? I think it would serve the church better if I —"

"Don't tell me what would serve the church. As of this moment, the boy is no longer your concern. And he is certainly not the concern of Father McCallum. Your assistance to the Holy Church has ended in regard to this matter. Speak of it to no one, and return to the Vatican."

Benicio wanted to ask questions but never had a chance. He heard a click. The cardinal was gone. He slowly placed the receiver on the cradle.

The cardinal had said some exceedingly strange things. Benicio didn't believe Espinosa wanted him in Rome to discuss anything. But he knew why the cardinal was calling him away. There were other men here. The men he'd seen at the airport. If the cardinal wanted Matthew Younger, he'd send those men. *The hired hands of the Vatican. Wonderful,* he thought. *I'm sure those guys will be real tactful.*

He shook his head as he remembered Father McCallum's concern. *Well, Ronnie,* he thought, *they are going to cut you out. Unfortunately, they're going to cut me out of this one too.*

He sighed heavily. Sleep was no longer an option. He might as well break the news to Father McCallum. He would keep his promise, tell the man what was happening. It was the least he could do.

***

Cardinal Espinosa's body gave an involuntary shake. He drew his hand away from the receiver he'd just hung up and stared at his forearm. Fresh trails of blood glistened in the sign of the Cross.

The truth is known. Father McCallum cannot be trusted. The boy can read the manuscript. God's secret is vulnerable to the world.

He turned his gaze to the ceiling. "My Father, I had not chosen wisely in allowing that man to be involved. I will correct the mistake. And I will not allow the book to be read. You can count on my service, God, to prevent the lies of the forsaken from being told."

The cardinal lifted the phone and dialed, then waited.

Jeremy answered.

"Are you aware of the situation?" the cardinal asked without any greeting.

"We saw Valori and McCallum at the boy's house."

"What did they find out?" the cardinal asked.

"Don't know. They weren't in there long before the kid was screaming."

Silence. "Do you know what Father Valori told the parents?"

"We think they made up some story. They were showing badges at the door."

"Go see Father McCallum. He has betrayed the church. I need to know if he has spoken of this matter to anyone other than Valori. He must be silenced."

"Silenced?"

"And then get the child. You must bring him to me. If you cannot obtain the child, make sure he cannot hurt the church. He is a threat to us. He is a threat to you."

"So, if we can't bring the kid back to the Vatican —"

"Then there is no boy," the cardinal said curtly. Then he hung up.

XXX

Father McCallum paced in his room. *It's the CDF*, he thought. *The CDF is monitoring my phone calls. Now they think I've betrayed them. I was never going to tell Thomas anything. I just needed to talk to someone.*

He thought about calling Cardinal Espinosa to explain or apologize, but he knew it was too late.

So he prayed. He asked for guidance. He asked for forgiveness. He asked for hope.

Evelyn and Fred would be home soon from grocery shopping. Maybe he should go out, take a walk. Something. He didn't want to stay in his room.

He nodded. A walk would clear his head. He went to the bathroom, turned the tap on and leaned heavily on the counter while he let the water run. Sometimes it took a while for the old plumbing to push hot water up to the second floor.

Did I really betray the church? Is it my own pride and vanity that make me feel so upset?

"Hello, Father McCallum," a voice said.

The old priest turned and saw a large, rough-looking man with an old-fashioned eye patch standing in the doorway. "Who are you? What are you doing here?"

"Come on out. Let's have a chat." The man spoke casually, as though they were greeting each other on the street. Old friends.

"Get out. Get out of here right now."

"Grandpa," scolded Jeremy from behind his brother. "That's no way to talk to us. We're all part of the same big, happy family." He moved so Father McCallum could see him. He had the same leering grin as the one-eyed man.

"Let's just go have a seat," Maury said, and turned to look across the hall. "This your bedroom over here? Mind if we sit in there?"

Father McCallum was too shocked to respond. Who were these men?

As if in answer to his question, Jeremy said, "Cardinal Espinosa sent us. You don't have to freak out."

"The cardinal?"

"Yep," Maury said. "Came here directly. On orders right from the horse's mouth."

"For what?" Father McCallum asked. The situation still felt wrong and dangerous.

"We're here to help on the whole book thing. You know, the Voynich manuscript," Jeremy said. Both men were in the bedroom now. Jeremy waved for the priest to follow, then Maury motioned him to sit on the bed. "We're going to have a chat with you and then go visit the little retard kid."

"Matthew?" Father McCallum said with concern.

"So who else have you talked to about the Voynich?" Maury asked.

"I'm sorry?"

"It's a tough secret to sit on all these years," Jeremy offered. "Who else have you told?"

Father McCallum was aware of a strong smell, a sickly, sour odor like rotting food, but with a hint of perfume, as if someone was trying to mask it. "I didn't tell anyone. I wasn't even going to tell the archbishop."

"The archbishop, eh?" Maury said and raised an eyebrow. "What'd you tell him?"

"Nothing. Just that things were coming to a head."

"You gave the archbishop head?" Jeremy blurted out and then laughed.

Maury glared at him then turned to the priest. "Did you write down your thoughts about the Voynich anywhere? Do you keep a diary?"

"No. Nothing."

"Just so you know," Maury said. "We're going to search this place. We're going to rip it apart, so you might as well tell us if we're going to find something. It'll make things much easier."

"I never wrote anything down. I never told anyone why I was in New Haven. I've been loyal."

Maury and Jeremy stared at the priest. Then, "Why don't you get started," Maury said to Jeremy.

Jeremy turned to the dresser, pulled a drawer out, and overturned it. He kicked at the contents.

"Hey! That's not necessary." Father McCallum noticed that the younger man was missing fingers on both hands. He turned to the one-eyed man.

"Who did you say you were?" Father McCallum asked.

"We didn't say."

"Tell him," Jeremy said over his shoulder as he pulled the dresser apart.

"Tell me what?" the priest asked. Fear rose in his throat like bile.

Maury slowly moved a hand up to his eye patch and lifted it to reveal the ruined eye socket. "We're the bastard children of the angels," he said. "The forsaken. The Nephilim. We're the reason you've been guarding that book all these years. It's our secrets that are recorded there."

"What? I don't understand."

Maury shrugged.

"Nothing in this dresser," Jeremy announced, and kicked the contents of the last drawer across the room. "You wear some really fucked-up underwear."

Maury nodded then addressed the priest again. "Roll your sleeve up," Maury ordered.

"Why?"

"Just do it, old man," Jeremy said, and stood next to his brother.

"No." The priest stood.

"Grab him!"

The younger man lunged, and Father McCallum raised his arms defensively. As they struggled, a voice called from downstairs. "Ronnie, that you?"

Evelyn and Fred. "Get out!" Father McCallum screamed. "Call the police!"

"Shut him up," Maury barked and took a step toward the bedroom door.

"Get —" McCallum began, then Jeremy hit him hard right on the nose. The priest stumbled. As he fell, the back of his head slammed against the corner of the bedside table with a sickening crack.

"Ronnie?" a voice called from downstairs.

Jeremy crouched beside the fallen man and touched his neck. "Nothing."

"Fuck!" Maury announced. "Let's go. We have to take care of the lady and her husband. We can search in here later."

They ran down the stairs.

XXXI

Benicio pulled the rental to a stop in front of Father McCallum's house but didn't get out. Ronnie was a good guy. It would break his heart to learn the Vatican was pulling them off the Voynich.

He glanced at his watch. His flight left later in the afternoon. He had a few hours.

He got out of the car and looked at the house, then headed for the back entrance. He knew from earlier that this was the door Father McCallum used. As he rounded the house, he saw that the back door wasn't completely closed. He knocked loudly and waited.

No answer.

He knocked again and saw fresh marks on the door. They looked like a crowbar had made them.

He pushed the door open all the way.

"Hello," he called. "It's Father Valori. I'm here to see Mr. McCallum."

No answer.

He moved into the house, still calling. Then he heard a moan. He started through the rooms and found an old man curled on the floor and Evelyn on the couch. The man's thinning gray hair was matted with blood. Benicio dropped on his knees next to Evelyn, who was groaning softly.

"Ma'am, can you hear me?"

Her eyelids fluttered. He felt her pulse. It was steady.

"Can you hear me? Can you tell me what happened?"

She didn't answer. He turned to the old man and felt for his wrist. He found a very weak pulse.

Benicio stood. "Mr. McCallum?" he called. "Ronnie?"

He went into the kitchen and saw a cordless phone on the wall. He grabbed it, hit the talk button, dialed emergency, and started up the stairs.

"Fire, police, ambulance. What's your emergency?"

"There are people hurt. Send the police and an ambulance," he shouted. He took the steps two at a time.

"Sir, what's your location?"

He gave it, then said, "Please hurry." He lowered the phone and called to Father McCallum again.

No answer.

He put the phone back to his ear.

"Sir, what's your name?"

"Send the ambulance and the police. I need to go." He turned the phone off and set it on the hall floor, then called to Ronnie again.

No answer. No sound.

It occurred to him that whoever did this might still be in the house. He no longer felt like rushing.

"Hello?" he called.

He tiptoed to Father McCallum's door and peered in. The room was torn apart — clothes everywhere and furniture upturned. There were fist-size holes in the drywall.

He took a few steps into the room and saw Ronnie lying on the floor near an overturned table. Benicio rushed in and knelt beside the old priest, then saw blood under the man's head.

"Ronnie!"

Father McCallum moaned softly.

He was alive.

"Ronnie. Hold on. The ambulance is on its way."

Father McCallum raised his arm and touched Benicio. "You need to go."

"I'm staying right here with you. You're going to be okay."

"Not me. The boy. Help the boy."

"Forget that. Let's get you to the hospital. We'll take care of everything else later."

Father McCallum's eyes opened wide and he squeezed Benicio's hand harder. "It's too late for me. They're going after Matthew. You have to help him. No time." The old man's arm slid to the floor.

"Ronnie?" Benicio said softly.

No answer.

He stood and crossed himself. He heard sirens. The ambulance would be here soon. Benicio had to find Matthew Younger.

XXXII

"I apologize for the short notice," Maury said. He was sitting in the Youngers' living room. John and Carol were on the couch, and Jeremy was next to him in the other chair. "We need to leave now."

John looked skeptical. "I don't know. I thought the other two guys were going to come back. The doctor guy, what was his name, honey?"

"Valori."

"Right," John said, nodding. "Valori. And he said something about money."

Jeremy smiled. Maury had come up with a story to explain why they were taking the boy, but before he could bring it out, the parents had offered up Father Valori's line about a special treatment program. It was easy to build off that story — but the parents weren't convinced yet.

"We work for Dr. Valori. He sent us," Maury said. He felt the capped syringe in his pocket. They would take the boy, one way or another.

Carol yawned. She wore an off-white robe. "Don'tcha have any papers or brochures we can look at?"

"It's a brand-new program. We don't have any promotional material yet. And as for money, we are prepared to reimburse you in the amount of ten thousand dollars."

"Ten grand?" John blurted.

"Yes," Jeremy said. "Your son needs to join the residential program right now. We'll send you the reimbursement fee."

Maury pretended to cough to cover his mouth. He didn't want the parents to see him grinning. *Idiots.*

"John? Do you think we need to check with the foster service?"

John Younger didn't even look at his wife. "How soon do we get the, ah, the money?"

"When Matthew registers at the program the check goes out automatically."

"John!" Carol said more loudly.

"Not right now," the husband said.

There was a knock at the door.

"Goddamn," John grumbled. "Carol, get the damn door. We've never been so damn popular." He smiled crookedly at Maury and Jeremy.

The brothers braced themselves. Jeremy leaned back in his chair, hopeful that he could see the front doorway. He couldn't.

***

Carol opened the door. "Oh, Doctor. I didn't know you were coming, too. The other men are just —"

Benicio Valori's face was a mask of urgency. He put a finger to his lips, then whispered, "Say nothing. The men in your home are not with me. They are not associated with Yale University or the hospital."

"What?" she whispered, the color rapidly draining from her face.

"Who is it?" John called from the living room.

"Tell him it's the paperboy and you'll be right back," Benicio whispered.

"It's — it's just the paperboy. I'll be right back," she called to her husband.

"Listen," Benicio whispered, "We need to take Matthew out of here. Those men are not who they say they are. I imagine they are trying to convince you to hand him over."

"They said they're taking him to your treatment program.

They said they're going to pay us. It's just what you were talking about this morning."

He nodded. "I know. They say what they need to. Where's Matthew? Is he upstairs?"

"I don't understand," she said. "If they're not working for you, what's going on?"

"Those men think Matthew knows things. Valuable things. They might be planning to hurt him."

"Matthew doesn't know things. He's retarded."

"I'm sorry — there isn't time to explain. Can you help me? Can you go back and keep talking to them while I try and get Matthew out?"

"I don't know. I —"

"Hey Father. Whatcha doing here?" Jeremy was standing in the hallway.

Carol looked at Benicio. "Father? This is your son?"

Benicio kept his eyes on Jeremy. "Hello. I can't seem to remember your name, so you have a bit of an advantage."

Jeremy nodded. "Guess so."

"Honey?" Carol called, her voice cracking. "Honey?" She turned and walked toward the living room.

"I think you've really fucked things up for the church, Father," Jeremy said, then turned and followed Carol.

"What's going on?" John asked as Benicio stepped into the room behind Jeremy. "What are you doing here?"

Maury jumped to his feet, his eyes fixed on Benicio.

Carol was crying. "Get them out," she begged her husband. "Get them all out."

"What the hell is going on?" John demanded.

Jeremy pointed to Benicio. "He's just here to make sure things go okay. There's no problem."

"Bullshit. Someone better start talking."

"I can explain," Maury said, then stopped. "No, actually, I can't."

"I want all of you out of my house," John ordered. "Now!"

"Just hold on," Jeremy said. "We can figure this out. There's no problem here."

Maury slipped the syringe out of his pocket. "We can figure this out," he echoed.

Benicio saw the syringe. "Look out! He has a weapon!" he yelled, and lunged at Maury, knocking him over. Benicio grabbed the hand holding the needle and slammed it to the floor as Maury fell.

Jeremy pulled a gun from his jacket. "Get the hell off him."

Benicio didn't see the gun; he continued to struggle with Maury. The men rolled against the coffee table and knocked it over.

Jeremy kept the gun pointed at Benicio. "Stop it!" he screamed.

No one noticed John slip out of the room. No one noticed until Jeremy felt something cold and hard against his temple. "Stop this fuckin' bullshit right now," John snarled.

Maury and Benicio stopped rolling long enough to notice Jeremy and John.

"Drop your fuckin' gun," John said.

Jeremy complied.

"And you two shits stand up."

Maury and Benicio stood.

John shoved Jeremy toward them and pointed his twenty-two caliber in their direction.

Benicio raised his hands.

"This is ridiculous," Maury said. "Put your little gun away."

John slowly moved his gun from one brother to the next. Carol stood at the back of the room, watching. She looked shocked.

"Carol," John said, "call the police and tell them to get over here."

"You don't want to do that," Jeremy pleaded. "The money is real. You'd be giving up ten grand."

Benicio saw movement out of the corner of his eye. Matthew was standing silently at the front door.

"We don't want the police here," Maury said. "Let's just finish talking."

"I'm done talking to you shitbags."

Carol came into the room holding a cordless phone. "You want me to call the police, John?" Her fingers hovered over the buttons.

"Don't do that, Carol," Maury pleaded.

"What the hell did I tell you to do, Carol?" John shouted and turned to look at his wife.

Maury jumped toward John, who swung the gun out of the way. There was a loud crack, then Maury fell. Jeremy flew at John, punched him in the mouth, and as he staggered, snatched the gun from him.

Carol screamed and started dialing. Jeremy spun and hit her in the face with the gun. She fell backwards in an explosion of blood.

Benicio didn't wait to see what else was going to happen. He turned and ran to the front door, scooped Matthew up, and bolted out of the house.

The boy kicked and struggled but Benicio held on to him and kept running until he got to the rental car, then climbed in, still holding the boy. He started the car and sped away.

As he drove he realized that there was a sickening smell on his clothes. An odor that must have rubbed off on him during his fight with Maury. *Somehow,* Benicio thought, *it smells like death.*

XXXIII

Azazel and Shemhazai watched two men run from the Younger house and get into a car. The men pulled away from the curb and raced down the street.

Azazel frowned. "Things have grown more complicated."

"Let's go."

They walked up the path to the Younger residence. The door was open. They went inside.

Azazel covered his nose. "This place reeks of death."

Shemhazai nodded. "Someone is definitely unclean."

Azazel pointed to the floor. "Blood?"

"Someone is wounded, certainly."

They moved into the living room. John and Carol Younger lay on the floor. Azazel crouched near John. "This one is still alive. Possibly drugged."

Shemhazai was beside Carol. Her eyes were wide open, her face a mess of blood and skin. "She is not."

"Curious," Azazel said and stood. "Shall we search for the boy?"

Shemhazai also stood. "He is not here."

"But those men didn't have the child."

"That's true," Shemhazai said slowly.

"Do you think the priests have the boy? The ones we saw earlier?"

Shemhazai nodded.

"Given the lack of co-operation between the priests and these other men, I would have to assume that only one of the groups is working at cross-purposes to our own efforts."

"Possibly. What are you suggesting?" Shemhazai asked.

"It would seem that we should attempt to establish an

alliance with the men who are unclean. They might lead us to the priests and the boy."

"Very well, let's find them. If they agree to help us find the child, fine. Otherwise, they are an impediment to our mission."

Azazel said, "And I shouldn't like to have additional impediments. Not when we are so close to bringing this matter to a close."

XXXIV

Matthew sat motionless in the passenger seat.

Benicio had been driving for more than an hour, wanting to put distance between himself and the Vatican goons. Now he felt like he was driving aimlessly. They'd circled Meriden a number of times, staying on side streets and back roads. Benicio felt sorely inexperienced at getaways.

He'd realized quite soon that Matthew would sit by himself. Benicio had helped the boy into the passenger seat. Since then, Matthew had sat, motionless. Not glancing out the window. Not humming to himself. Nothing.

Benicio felt sorry for the boy. He seemed trapped in a body he was unable to control. The priest imagined a vibrant young child deep inside wanting to get out. Autism was cruel.

Benicio also felt sorry for the foster parents. They were hardly the most caring, concerned people he'd ever met, but he still felt sorry for them.

He was thankful the boy wasn't screaming. His vague knowledge of autism from grad school had taught him that screaming fits weren't uncommon. Being grabbed and carried to the car should have set him off. It hadn't. Benicio thanked God for that.

He wondered what had happened in the house after they left, then he willed the thought from his mind and kept driving.

A few miles later he saw a sign for Interstate 91. Going north would take them to the Connecticut border. He took the ramp.

"Might be best to get out of the state for a bit," he said.

Matthew didn't respond.

Benicio figured that the Younger residence was swarming with police. Until he figured out what was happening and what danger the boy was in he didn't dare go back to the house. He would call from the road   preferably far down the road   just to let the family know Matthew was safe.

He felt a flood of panic at the thought of Father McCallum. Was he dead? Were there people hurt or dying at the Younger house? And here he was on the run with Matthew. Was he kidnapping the child? *God*, he prayed, *I hope I'm making the right decision. Please help me know what You want me to do.*

He drove north through Connecticut toward the Massachusetts border, checking his rearview mirror for the flash of pursuing police. So far, they seemed to be safe. He wondered if he should have gone straight to the nearest police station when he left with Matthew. But how would he have explained his involvement? Could he say, "Hello, I work for the Vatican and we think this boy is half angel, so I took him away from his parents"? And that wasn't the only problem. Benicio knew that even in police custody Matthew would not be safe from the Vatican. He knew he'd eventually have to go to the police but not yet. He needed time.

He looked at the boy "I wish you could understand what I'm saying I wish you knew I only want to help you."

The boy didn't answer.

Benicio sighed. "It's going to be okay. I promise you that." He reached over and patted the boy's knee gently.

And Matthew screamed.

He didn't shift. He didn't move. He just opened his mouth and screamed.

Benicio jerked in alarm. "I'm sorry! I'm sorry! I forgot."

Matthew closed his mouth. He didn't acknowledge Benicio.

"I'm sorry," he repeated. "I won't do that again. I just wanted to tell you I'm trying to help you. That's all." He wasn't sure the boy understood.

He focused on the road.

***

Benicio drove through Connecticut, Massachusetts, and New Hampshire and was speeding through Maine when he spotted a gas station with an old-fashioned pay phone at the edge of the parking lot. He pulled the car up to the phone and stopped.

Matthew didn't react.

Benicio wanted to watch the boy while he was on the phone. He turned the engine off, removed the key, opened his door, and climbed out, then went to the phone. He checked his watch. Midafternoon here; early evening, Vatican time. He pushed in his calling card and dialed.

It took a moment, then he heard the familiar ring. He watched Matthew, who remained motionless in the car.

Finally, someone answered. "*Allô?*"

"Father Lumière?" Benicio asked.

"*Oui.*" The word was an urgent whisper. "Is it Father Valori?"

"Jacques," Benicio spoke quickly, "I think I'm in trouble."

"Something is stirred. Something very big."

"What's going on? What have you heard?"

"Were you contacted by the CDF?"

"Yes."

"By Cardinal Espinosa?"

"Yes. What's going on?"

Father Lumière knew secrets. He was a head chef and had the run of Vatican City. Everyone knew him, so conversations rarely stopped when he entered a room to deliver meals. Benicio considered him a close friend.

"There is fury. I know little more. Espinosa is, how you say, on the warpath. He has spoken to Cardinal March about someone. He means to have the someone excommunicated. Is it you?"

"Me?" Benicio asked in surprise. Would the cardinal know of his actions so quickly?

"What have you done?" Jacques asked.

"Have you ever heard of the Voynich manuscript? Has anyone been talking about it?"

"*Oui.*" A tentative answer.

"What's the matter? You have heard of it?"

"Is that what this is about?" Jacques' voice betrayed alarm. "Why do you ask of this book?"

Benicio looked at Matthew and decided the boy didn't need to be kept secret. "I've found someone who can read it."

"*Merde!* Benicio! Do you have the manuscript?"

"No, I —"

"You are in great danger," Jacques warned. "Do not interfere."

"Why? What's the book about?"

"God's sin. His great mistake. The Grigori. The CDF would do anything —" He stopped speaking.

"What?" Benicio asked. "They'd do anything to what?" Benicio knew the Grigori were the fallen angels God had originally sent to Earth to help man, and that they had eventually lusted after women and had children. The children were the Nephilim.

The connection clicked with static. Father Lumière was gone.

"Hello? Hello?" Benicio said.

"My son," came another voice, a familiar voice with an Italian accent. "What do you hope to accomplish?" For a brief moment, Benicio allowed the shock and fear to run through him. Then he forced it back down again.

"Cardinal Espinosa," he said.

"Stop. You don't know what you are dealing with."

"Tell me then."

"Of course. Jeremy and Maury will come and meet you. You should all return to the Vatican with the boy."

"Why did you send them?" Benicio's voice betrayed his distrust.

"Certain jobs require certain people. This job required them."

"What was my job?"

"You were to confirm the truth of the boy's gift. Now, Benicio, come home."

"What is it that the boy will read?"

"This is not a conversation for the phone," Cardinal Espinosa said. He sounded irritated. "Give the boy to my men and return to the Vatican at once. That is an order."

"I can't," Benicio said quietly.

"What?"

"I don't know what's going on, but I intend to find out."

"You are risking your life," Espinosa spat. "You are risking your soul."

"Maybe." He hung up.

He stared at the car. The boy was sitting still. Benicio felt a pang of guilt and picked the phone up, dialed information, and asked for John Younger in Meriden.

The phone rang once. "Hello."

"Hi, is this John?"

"Who is this?"

Benicio wasn't sure he had the right number. "Is this John Younger?"

"Yes, who is this?"

"I was at your house earlier when all the commotion happened. How are things now?"

"Do you have the boy?"

The boy? That's an odd way for a father — even a foster parent — to phrase the question.

"Do you?" the man asked, more forcefully.

"He's fine," Benicio answered. "I was concerned for his safety and —"

"Where are you now?" the man demanded.

Benicio wasn't sensing any actual concern for the child. Something wasn't right.

"He's safe," Benicio repeated. "What happened there after I left?"

"Just bring him back," the man said impatiently. "Bring him back and we won't charge you."

"Is everything okay there? You sound strange."

"Benicio," the voice said calmly, "just bring that kid back here. You are in a world of trouble already. Cardinal Espinosa doesn't appreciate your little stunt."

It wasn't John Younger, but it didn't sound like Jeremy or Maury either.

"Who is this? Where are Matthew's parents?"

"Don't be an idiot. Bring us the kid. We'll be waiting at the house."

The phone went dead.

The Vatican had sent more people to clean up the situation. That was bad news. This thing was getting bigger by the second. Bigger and deadlier. Maury and Jeremy were probably pursuing him right now — assuming they hadn't been shot by John Younger.

He looked around the service station, wanting inspiration. He needed a plan. He needed to get away from Jeremy and Maury long enough to figure out what was going on. He needed help.

Then he had an idea. It would mean driving right through the night, but if Matthew slept that would be fine.

He slid into the car and looked at Matthew. "Have you ever been to Canada?"

XXXV

Jake stepped into the old-style Irish pub and inhaled happily. It smelled of beer and food.

After his last appointment, Jake had looked out the window and seen Friday afternoon gridlock on Lower Water Street. He had turned the radio on: a three-car pile up on the Macdonald Bridge had backed traffic up everywhere. Jake had two choices — sit in traffic or let the traffic sort itself out. The Old Triangle was a five-minute walk from the his office.

A visit to the pub served another function. It allowed him to unwind after a day full of patients. He refused to take home the tension and stress of his job. Better to take a thirty-minute break at the pub, avoid the traffic, and get home in a good mood.

Especially now.

Especially with Wyatt being sick.

Jake took his usual seat at the bar and ordered a Rickard's Red.

"Hard day, boss?" the bartender asked. Even though he recognized Jake, they weren't on a first-name basis. Jake had never offered his name. He didn't like amateur psychologists.

"Same thing over and over." Jake hated this kind of small talk. Sometimes, he felt like his entire job consisted of forcing small talk. Some sessions were so difficult. After work, the last thing he wanted to do was have an awkward conversation with the bartender.

"You must work around here," the bartender concluded. "I've seen you in here a few times."

It was hard for Jake not to roll his eyes. "Yep."

The bartender had expected more. The guy obviously took it

as a challenge to figure out his customers when they didn't want to share.

"What do you do?" he pushed.

"Stool samples," Jake said without cracking a smile.

"What's that?"

"I work up in the hospital lab. I analyze stool samples. I sift through them and look for parasites and other abnormalities."

The bartender obviously wanted to laugh. He wanted to share in the joke but was waiting for a sign that it actually *was* a joke. Jake looked completely serious.

The silence stretched until the bartender spoke again. "What kind of work is that? I mean, how do you like that?"

Jake looked at him, still not smiling. "I can honestly say it's a shitty job most of the time."

The bartender snorted but Jake just stared at him and nodded thoughtfully. Then he turned his attention to his beer, and the bartender slid away. *I hope Wyatt's going to be okay.*

***

Jenna, Maria, and Karen sat in a booth at the back of the Old Triangle. There was a half-full pitcher of Alexander Keith's beer on the table.

"You need to get back on the horse," Maria announced.

"And hope he's hung like one, too," Karen giggled.

"You guys," Jenna said. "Behave yourselves. We're supposed to be respectable nurses."

"Only when we're on duty," Karen answered. She took a pull from her mug.

"Do you have any prospects?" Maria asked.

"Honestly," Jenna said, "I don't want to talk about me all night. Let's just have fun."

"Talking about you is fun!" Karen laughed. She finished her beer and reached for the pitcher.

Jenna shook her head. She didn't need pep talks. She'd matured past the point of needing to be in a relationship. She just wanted to be her own person for a while. She wanted to do her own things and not have to negotiate with a *partner*. She really wasn't in the mood to have these two convince her she needed a man.

"What about a fling or two?" Maria asked with a curious smile.

"What makes you think I haven't?"

"Oh." Karen perked up. "Do tell."

"I'm not saying I did and I'm not saying I didn't."

"Then you didn't," Karen said flatly.

"I don't think you're a fling kind of person," Maria said, squinting at Jenna.

"Well, why'd you suggest the fling, then?"

"Ooh," Karen breathed. "What about him?" She was looking at the bar. The restaurant was busy, but the bar was clear except for one lone man. "He's kind of hunky."

Maria and Jenna looked.

"I can't really see his face," Maria said.

"But he has nice hair," Karen said. "And look at that butt."

"You guys," Jenna said, embarrassed.

A waiter set a large plate of chicken wings on the table. "This side is mild and this side is hot," he said. "Do you ladies need anything else?"

Karen, grinning, motioned the waiter over. He bent toward her and she whispered, "We might need you to invite that sexy stranger at the bar to our table."

The waiter straightened and laughed. "I'm afraid I can only get you what's on the menu. Just let me know if you need anything else." He headed to another table.

"You tit," Jenna said, scowling at Karen.

"Yeah," Maria said as if agreeing with Jenna. "Don't invite him over until we get a look at his face." She laughed.

"No problem," Karen said. "Keep your eyes on him."

The three women looked at him. "What are you going to do?" Jenna asked nervously.

"*Hey guy!*" Karen shouted, then looked away.

Maria and Jenna were still looking at him when he turned. They turned their heads quickly.

"You tit!" Jenna said again, trying not to smile at her friend's brazenness.

"Well?" Karen asked. "Is he cute?"

Jenna said, "I think I know him."

"What? Who is he?"

"I think he was a friend of someone I used to date a long time ago."

"Who?" Maria and Karen asked in unison.

"Just a guy, back at university."

"Not *the* guy?" Maria asked.

Jenna didn't answer. She was pretty sure it was Jake.

"Is it the friend of the guy who left you to be a priest? That guy?"

It was. Jake Tunnel, Benicio's best friend at Columbia. She knew he'd relocated to Nova Scotia but she'd never bumped into him. She wasn't sure he'd remember her after all these years. And just this morning she'd been thinking about Benicio. *What are the odds? Next thing you know I'll be running into Benicio.*

XXXVI

"How's your stomach feel?" Jeremy asked, grinning.

"Asshole," Maury snapped. "You know I'm going to have to change bandages all the time. It's going to slow us down."

Jeremy just smiled.

The two were traveling north in their rental car. For a Friday evening, traffic was light. After they left the Younger house they'd contacted the church, and the cardinal ordered them to pursue Benicio and the boy, who were traveling north. The brothers had no idea how Cardinal Espinosa got his information, but they had never known him to be wrong. *Exitus acta probat*, the old priest had mumbled on the phone. It meant nothing to them. They just did what they were told.

The satellite phone beeped on the backseat. Maury reached over and grabbed it.

"Hello."

"Where are you?" Cardinal Espinosa barked.

"Headed north, out of Connecticut," Maury answered.

"They may be heading to Canada. Stay on a direct path to the border. Contact me once you near the crossing. I will ascertain that they have crossed the border."

"Yes sir." He hesitated, then added, "Sir?"

"What?"

"What about Benicio?"

"He no longer serves the best interest of the faith. He stands in the way of your freedom and the continued health of the church. You may deal with him accordingly."

Maury was surprised. Benicio was a highly trusted agent. "Should we speak to him first? Do you want us to find out his intentions?"

"I don't wish him to further complicate the directives of the church, but if he will cooperate then so be it." Cardinal Espinosa hung up.

Maury listened to the dead line for a moment then pushed the off button. He tossed the phone into the back.

"What's up?" Jeremy asked, grinning. "Wrong number?"

"We're supposed to head to Canada."

"And?"

"And I doubt we'll be bringing Father Valori back."

Jeremy's smirk faded but he nodded in resignation. They followed orders. That's all they did.

XXXVII

The Izaak Walton Killam Children's Hospital strategic plan included Saturday appointments — Jake had heard something about a commitment to reduce wait times and increase sensitivity to consumers. The strategic plan didn't make it any easier to be sitting in a pediatric neurologist's office on a Saturday morning.

"Thanks for seeing us today, Dr. Merrot," Abby said as she took a seat.

Jake sat next to her, and they both looked across a wide desk at the gray-haired doctor. His round features and the reading glasses perched at the end of his nose gave him a slightly comical appearance, as if he were a caricature of the aging country doctor.

"Not at all," Dr. Merrot said, his expression serious.

"So?" Abby asked. She wanted to get straight to business.

"And where is young master Wyatt today?"

"He's at home with his sister," Jake said. "We got a babysitter."

Dr. Merrot nodded. "Fine, fine."

"The tests?" Abby prompted. "What'd you find out?"

The doctor frowned. Jake felt as if he had a knife in his heart. He held his breath.

"Well, Wyatt's going to need surgery," Dr. Merrot said. "There's no easy way to tell you. We're going to need to do a little investigating."

"Investigating what?" Abby asked. Her voice trembled, and Jake could hear the panic sneaking in. He put an arm across her shoulders.

"There's no reason to think Wyatt isn't going to pull through everything and be fine, so let's stay positive," Dr. Merrot said, and offered them a weak smile.

Jake knew the worse the news the more preparation there was. He wished the doctor would blurt it out.

"Wyatt has a tumor. We aren't entirely sure about the size or the kind. It was difficult to find on the CT scan."

"A tumor," Abby whispered.

Jake gave her a little squeeze. *Tumor* was one of the words they didn't want to hear. He bit his lip; he didn't want to get emotional. He knew if he let Abby see him cry he would be useless to her.

"Yes, but that doesn't mean a whole lot just yet," Dr. Merrot added quickly. "We need to take a biopsy and have a better look at its exact location."

"What did you mean it was tricky to find?" Jake asked.

Dr. Merrot took a deep breath. "Well, not all tumors are encapsulated. Sometimes they branch out slightly and so aren't as easy to detect. Wyatt's tumor was spread thinly enough that it was difficult to find."

"Will that make it more difficult to remove?" Abby asked quietly. Tears ran down her cheeks.

Dr. Merrot nodded. "There is that chance. With tumors that branch it is sometimes more difficult."

"What's the next step?" Jake asked. He wanted to keep the conversation moving forward so they could stay focused on action.

The doctor leaned his elbows on the desk. "We'd like to admit him as soon as possible. That will give us first crack at the next operating suite. We're going to make Wyatt one of the hospital's top priorities."

In all likelihood, every doctor at the children's hospital said this to every parent, but it still made Jake feel a little better. He wanted to think there was a team of doctors devoted to Wyatt, working around the clock to make him better.

"You mean today?" Abby asked. "Should we bring him down today?"

"Tomorrow would be fine," Dr. Merrot said.

"How long will he be here?"

"I really can't say. You should probably plan on at least all of next week. Possibly longer."

The room was silent for a moment. The news was a weight that sank through Jake and kept pulling him further and further down. He was afraid to look at Abby. His eyes filled with tears as images of Wyatt played in his mind. Images of his son laughing and playing with his big sister. Images of him sitting on the couch playing video games.

"What are the risks?" Abby asked.

"There's the normal risks associated with this type of surgery. Whenever you are dealing with the brain there are serious risks."

"Brain damage? Death?" Abby asked. Panic was creeping into her voice. "Could he die?"

Dr. Merrot's expression didn't change. "Little Wyatt's sick," he said calmly. "We'll need to do some surgery to help the guy get better. I'm afraid there aren't any other options."

Abby nodded, sniffed, and blew her nose.

"As you leave you can register Wyatt for his stay. That will make it quicker when you come tomorrow," Dr. Merrot added. "The nursing station is just down the hall, and the nurses can help you. When you come tomorrow I hope to have a surgery time arranged. They'll know at the desk."

"Thank you, Doctor," Jake said. "Thanks for everything." He stood and looked at his wife.

Abby also rose, and they left Dr. Merrot's office.

XXXVIII

Benicio stood beside the car and watched the traffic moving through the customs booths. There was a steady lineup of cars going in and out of Canada.

He'd driven through the night, stopping only for gas, the washroom, and snacks. Matthew had had only a bag of Doritos and a small carton of chocolate milk. The rest of the time the boy slept.

Benicio wasn't sure how they would get across the border; if the customs official asked for identification, he and Matthew would be detained.

They probably don't even allow rental cars across the border without some special permit. They'll probably stop us and search the vehicle.

Then Benicio noticed a lane dedicated to truckers, extra-wide and almost hidden by a parade of semitrailers. It gave him an idea. Not necessarily a good idea, but an idea nonetheless.

He turned to the car, opened the passenger door and crouched down.

"Hey," he said quietly, "do you want to get out for a bit? Stretch your legs or go for a bathroom break?"

Matthew didn't answer.

Benicio looked around. They were at the far end of the parking lot near the duty-free shop. The last chance to buy before crossing the border. He didn't want people watching when he tried to deal with Matthew.

"Do you want to get out for a bit?" he asked again.

Matthew turned stiffly and swung his legs out of the car. Benicio backed away to give him room, and the boy stood on the pavement.

"There you go," Benicio said warmly. "That must feel better."

Matthew began walking toward the front of the vehicle.

"Do you want to use the washroom?" Benicio asked.

Matthew stopped in front of the car and undid his pants. He began urinating on the ground.

"Whoa," Benicio called. "*Che fai?* What are you doing?"

A motor home pulled up near them, and a middle-aged man poked his head out the driver's window. "Hey buddy, do you know a good place —" He stopped abruptly when he noticed Matthew. "Is that kid taking a leak right there?"

"I'm sorry. He's a little different."

"I'd say he's a lot different," the man said. "That boy's too old to be pissin' out here when the facility is just right on over there."

"My apologies. My son is autistic."

The man didn't have a response to this. From somewhere inside the motor home, a voice yelled, "Leave the poor man alone and let's get going!"

The motor home driver gave Matthew a disapproving frown, and the big vehicle drove away.

Matthew was doing up his pants. Benicio ran a hand through his hair. *I need to find a phone*, he thought. *Time to call Jake.*

XXXIX

Jake paid Becky, a shy fifteen year old and one of their best babysitters. She lived only a few doors down the street. Wyatt and Emily always reported having a wonderful time with her.

On the way home from the hospital, Jake and Abby agreed to be strong for the sake of the kids. It wasn't fair to allow grown-up concerns to filter down to them.

But everything went out the window when Wyatt ran up to his mother. Abby scooped him up for a hug then started crying. Jake immediately sent Abby upstairs to collect herself, then dealt with the sitter.

Becky was a bright kid. She knew enough not to ask how the visit to the hospital had gone. She thanked Jake for her babysitting money and left.

Jake closed the door behind her then walked into the living room. Emily was sitting on the couch reading.

"Where's Wyatt gone?" Jake asked.

"To his room. Playing video games, I think."

"How're you doing?"

"Good. What's wrong with Mom?"

"Mom's okay. It's just tough sometimes."

"What happened at the hospital? What's wrong with Wyatt?"

"Oh, just some routine stuff. Some more tests and things. Wyatt'll have to stay at the hospital for a bit. Nothing for you to worry about." Jake wondered how much he should tell a seven year old. Emily was perceptive beyond her years, but it wasn't just a matter of understanding; it was a matter of carrying a burden. A seven year old shouldn't have to contemplate losing her little brother.

"He's going into hospital?"

"Yep, but don't worry about it. Everything is going to be fine."

She made a funny face. "You're the one who keeps saying I'm worried. That makes me more worried than anything."

Jake grinned. *She's so smart.* "Are you being sassy with me?" he asked in mock anger. "Do you want to suffer the wrath of the tickle monster?"

Her face lit up. Jake hunched over, wiggled his fingers menacingly, and moved close to her.

"Dad!" she screamed. "No!"

Jake kept wiggling his fingers. "I can't stop it!"

Emily dropped her book and jumped to her feet. "No!" she pleaded, laughing.

Jake lunged at her. "Must . . . tickle . . . sassy . . . girl."

She ducked away and ran behind the couch. "Help!" she yelled.

Jake took a step toward her, and Wyatt came flying into the room. He had a sixth sense for commotion.

"I've got him!" Wyatt yelled and tackled one of Jake's legs.

"Noooo!" Jake screamed, pretending to be in pain. "You've got me!"

Emily ran over and pushed at Jake until he fell onto the couch. Both kids jumped on top of him, trying to pin him down while avoiding his writhing fingers.

"You can't stop me," Jake hissed through clenched teeth. "I will have my revenge on you."

"No you won't, butthead," Wyatt answered as he wrestled with one arm.

Jake stopped fighting and became serious. "Wyatt, buddy?"

Emily sensed the change of tone and stopped struggling.

Wyatt's eyes met Jake's.

"Wyatt," Jake started again, "what did we say about calling people butthead?"

"Not to."

"Right. You're saying that way too much. Can you please

stop?" Butthead had become one of Wyatt's favorite words. Abby and Jake still hadn't figured out where the boy had picked the word up.

"Yes," Wyatt said reluctantly.

Jake noticed that Abby had come out of the bedroom upstairs and was standing on the staircase watching them.

"Thanks, buddy," Jake said. Then he smiled broadly. "Now you two stop being such *buttheads* or I'm going to have to really get you."

Emily gasped then laughed. Wyatt squealed, and the fight was on again.

Over the din of Jake and kids the phone started to ring. Abby went in and grabbed the phone in the kitchen, and a few seconds later held the receiver out to Jake.

"Jake," she called urgently. "It's Benicio!"

He frowned. When they'd talked a few weeks ago, Ben was headed to Cambodia. He never called when he was on one of his exotic assignments. Jake took the phone.

"Kids, let Dad talk on the phone now," Abby said. "It's Uncle Ben, and I think it's long distance."

"Hey, Ben!" Jake said.

"Hi, Uncle Ben!" Wyatt and Emily screamed.

Benicio laughed. "Say hi to the kids for me. How are you doing, Jake?"

"I'm okay."

"How's Wyatt?"

Jake paused. "Probably should talk about that later. Abby and I just got back from the hospital. Wyatt has to be admitted tomorrow."

"*Sono spiacente.* I'm sorry. If there's anything I can do to help you just name it."

"Thanks buddy. We'll get through it. So what's going on? I thought you were in Cambodia?"

"I was but I'm back. I'm actually just at the border going into New Brunswick."

"You're kidding. Are you headed this way?"

"Jake," Benicio said, "I think I'm in trouble. I may need your help."

"What's going on?"

"It's something I'd much rather talk about in person."

"Sure," Jake said. "You're always welcome here."

Benicio hesitated.

"What is it?" Jake pressed.

"I think I'm in trouble with the church. It might be pretty big."

"Whatever it is, you can handle it," Jake said. "And you can count on me to help."

"I really appreciate it. *Grazie*."

"When are you going to be here?"

"I would guess we could be there tomorrow night or Monday at the latest."

"Monday's a whole lot better for me," Jake said, thinking he had to take Wyatt to the hospital on Sunday. He hadn't even noticed that Benicio had said "we." "Why don't you come by my office? You know where it is."

"Okay. I'll see you then."

Jake slowly walked to the kitchen and dropped the phone in the wall cradle. He couldn't imagine what trouble Benicio could be in. Then he noticed Wyatt and Emily hovering, just waiting for the action to start again.

Jake bent over slightly and adopted his most menacing expression. He wiggled his fingers at them and said, "Okay, who wants some of me?"

***

Benicio hung up and stared at the phone. He felt horrendously guilty for calling Jake. The Tunnel family was having such troubles with Wyatt that imposing on them was unforgivable. Not only that, but Benicio hadn't told Jake what was going on. He hadn't even mentioned Matthew.

He looked at the rental car. Matthew was in the passenger seat, staring out the window. Benicio turned and looked down the road at New Brunswick. He decided he better get moving.

XL

"This is so fuckin' stupid," Maury moaned. He and Jeremy stood in the cramped washroom of a service station. They'd stopped in Houlton, Maine, near the border crossing into New Brunswick. Maury was unwrapping bandages from his midsection while Jeremy leaned against the door.

"Stop whining."

Maury glared at him. "No one shot you in the gut," he spat. "Now I have to change these bandages all the time and I'm gonna use up a hell of a lot more of that decelerator cream. I'm screwed."

"You baby." Jeremy grinned. "Most people would be happy that they got shot in the gut and it didn't kill them. You? All you can do is whine."

Maury turned away from him and looked in the dingy mirror. He could see a blackened wound just over his navel. A brownish, thick fluid seeped from the hole. He grabbed a handful of paper towels, wiped the fluid away, and dropped the towels onto the floor. The plastic squeeze bottle of lotion was on the edge of the sink. Maury liberally doused his abdomen then rubbed the lotion on. He was careful to smooth some of it right into the bullet hole. When he finished he turned and tossed the bottle to Jeremy, who caught it and slid it into one of the large pockets of his jacket.

Maury felt weak and dizzy, an unexpected sensation. The bullet had hurt him more than he wanted to let on to Jeremy. He realized that didn't make sense. Both he and his brother were forsaken — soulless — and could not be killed by ordinary means. They would live until their flesh rotted off their bones. If that was living.

There was a heavy knock at the door and a voice yelled, "What the hell's going on in there?"

It was the gas station attendant. He'd given them a strange look when they'd both gone into the washroom — a one-person washroom.

"Get lost," Jeremy yelled.

"I want you two freaks out of there," the attendant shouted, and banged on the door again. "And what's that stink? What the hell are you doing in there?"

"I said get lost!" Jeremy yelled, and banged the back of his boot against the door.

"If you shits aren't out of there in five seconds I'm calling the cops."

"Fuck you!" Jeremy said and laughed.

Maury ignored them and was wrapping bandages around his midsection. He pulled tightly as he rolled the cloth all the way around. When he finished he motioned to Jeremy, who brought a pair of scissors out of a pocket, then cut the bandage. Maury pulled out some surgical tape and fastened the bandage.

"We might as well get out of here before Bozo calls in the posse," Jeremy said.

Maury shrugged, and the two men left. The gas station attendant was standing just outside the door swatting a baseball bat against his open hand.

"Get the fuck out of here and don't come back," he snarled.

As they walked past him, Jeremy noticed the man recoil at the putrid scent of them. Jeremy paused, leaned over, and snapped his teeth at the man's face. The man stumbled backward, banging into a stand full of potato chips. Then the brothers left.

In the car, Maury said, "We need to check in and make sure we're going in the right direction."

"Fine." Jeremy nodded.

Maury reached to the backseat for the satellite phone. He flipped it open and hit the auto dial.

The phone buzzed as the first ring sounded. It buzzed again and then a third time before a male voice with a slight Italian accent answered. "Hello?"

"Put him on," Maury barked.

"He will not speak to you at present. Your instructions are to follow the target into Canada. We have been provided information that the father and the boy have passed through the border."

"You have information, do you?"

"We received a report that a vehicle with Connecticut license plates rushed past the customs booth. Apparently, the border is quite vulnerable, and the Canadian agents have no ability to take chase."

"You're kiddin' me," Maury scoffed.

"Additional information suggests that Father Valori may have a contact in Halifax. You should pursue a Dr. Jacob Tunnel."

"Dr. Tunnel?"

"Yes. A psychologist."

Maury took the phone from his ear, cupping it with his free hand. He leaned toward Jeremy. "They think the priest is going to see some psychologist in Halifax."

Jeremy rolled his eyes.

Maury returned the phone to his ear. "Anything else?"

There was no answer. Cardinal Espinosa's personal assistant had hung up.

Maury punched the *End* button. "Asshole."

XLI

Sunday morning.

Benicio yawned. He'd driven almost all night. Only once had he risked stopping at the side of the road to catch a few winks. Matthew had slept through most of the trip. He would sit, staring straight ahead, until fatigue caught up with him, then he would slump to the side and snore. Benicio was relieved to hear the soft purr, but the way Matthew slept made him look dead. Spooky.

The priest looked at the road. New Brunswick was a pretty enough province. Lots of trees. Good highways. He smiled.

Then he frowned. For a moment he had felt like a tourist on a jaunt. But he was a rogue agent from the Vatican with a kidnapped child in the car. *I really need to take a break*, he thought. *I'm losing it.*

A billboard announced something called an Irving Big Stop at the next exit. He figured it was time for another stop. He wanted to get something to eat and clear his head.

He drove down the ramp and saw a restaurant and gas bar right next to the highway. He parked on the far side of the lot, away from the pumps. There were quite a few cars. He hoped the restaurant wasn't too crowded.

He looked at Matthew. The boy had woken up when the car stopped.

"Hey guy," Benicio said softly. "We're going to go in here and get a bite to eat."

No answer. No acknowledgement.

"You hungry?"

Still nothing.

Benicio reached out to pat the boy's shoulder but stopped in time. Physical contact was an important part of how Benicio communicated. A tap on the knee. A hug. Touching someone's arm. He was Italian, after all. It was difficult to restrain himself with Matthew.

He got out of the car. By the time he walked around the car, Matthew stood waiting.

"*Bene*," he announced. "Let's go see what's for breakfast."

They had to wait in line to be seated. Matthew had walked slowly alongside Benicio, without resistance.

The Irving Big Stop was a pleasant, clean place. A big, happy hostess welcomed Benicio and Matthew with a heavy French accent.

"We have only de booth open?" she said. "You and your son like de booth?"

He nodded, and she led them to a booth by the window overlooking the parking lot. Matthew sat across from Benicio. The hostess dropped plastic menus in front of them and then pulled a paper place mat from her pocket and set it in front of Matthew.

"You like coloring, little man?" she asked, although she didn't wait for a reply. She reached into a pouch on the front of her apron and pulled out a handful of well-used crayons. She set them on the place mat. "*Voilà!*"

She turned to Benicio. "Your waitress will be right with you." She spun and was gone.

"She's friendly," Benicio said.

Matthew didn't look up.

"What's that you have?" the priest asked, leaning over. The paper place mat was covered with activities. Mazes. Animals to color. A simple word-find puzzle.

"That looks like fun," Benicio said. "Can I help color?"

Matthew didn't move.

"I'd really like to color that moose. I think I should make his head orange."

Matthew lifted a hand from his lap and picked up the orange

crayon. He held it up to Benicio. His eyes stayed down.

Benicio's hand shook slightly as he took the crayon. He couldn't believe Matthew had responded. He wanted to hug the boy. Just color, he told himself. Don't overreact.

He started coloring the moose.

"I could really use some help," he announced. "I bet this moose would look funny if someone colored his legs green." He kept working on the head.

Matthew picked up the green crayon and started, very slowly, to color the moose's legs.

Benicio wanted to laugh out loud.

"*Bon matin*," a singsongy voice interrupted them. "Good morning." The waitress had appeared, holding a coffeepot.

"Good morning," Benicio said, sitting up straight.

"Coffee?" she asked.

Benicio turned his mug up, and she filled it in one dramatic pour.

"You ready to order?"

"What do you say, Matthew? Shall we get something?"

Matthew continued to color the moose.

"What about some pancakes? Do you like pancakes with lots of syrup?"

Matthew stopped coloring for a second and nodded slightly.

"Pancakes it is! Make it two orders," he told the waitress.

She wrote on a pad and swept away. Benicio looked around the busy room. Every staff person in the restaurant was constantly on the go. Coffee being poured. Huge plates of food being whisked to tables. It was a wonder they weren't careening into each other.

Benicio and Matthew continued to color until the food arrived. Huge stacks of buttermilk pancakes perfectly browned and sending off curls of steam. A pitcher of real maple syrup. Benicio had never realized there was a difference. He silently vowed never to buy fake maple syrup again.

To his surprise, Matthew began eating the pancakes right

IN TONGUES OF THE DEAD

away. Benicio realized the boy must be very hungry. The road-side food hadn't been nearly enough. No wonder Matthew had been so compliant on the way in here. He was plowing his way through the pancakes quickly. Benicio hoped he didn't burn his mouth.

"Go easy, buddy," he said. "We have time. I'll get you some more, too, if you want them."

Matthew kept eating.

Soon they were both nearly done. Benicio felt much better with a few good cups of coffee in him, and he'd connected with Matthew in a way he'd never thought possible. He felt slightly optimistic for the first time since he'd walked into Father McCallum's home and found that violent scene.

Matthew finished his last bite and carefully set his fork on his plate.

Benicio smiled at the boy as he finished counting out money to leave on the table. "Well, buddy," he said. "What do you say about hitting the road again?"

"What's your hurry?" a gruff voice said from next to them.

Benicio turned to find Maury and Jeremy standing at the end of the booth.

XLII

Jake slowed and turned into the parking garage for the children's hospital. He felt a knot in his stomach but tried to ignore it. He didn't want to risk looking at Abby. If there was even so much as a tear in her eye he might lose his composure.

"Here we are!" he announced.

Emily and Wyatt were in car seats in the middle row of the minivan. Jake preferred driving his Volvo but the minivan was better for family use.

He found a parking space near the entrance, and everyone unloaded.

As they trekked through the bright corridors following the purple trains painted on the walls, Jake marveled at Wyatt's strength. The boy marched bravely wearing his Incredible Hulk backpack over both shoulders. Wyatt had insisted on packing his own special bag with a few books and toys.

They reached a nursing station, and a nurse escorted them to Wyatt's room. Jake had called before they'd started out and requested a private room. He knew it would be a lot easier on Abby and Wyatt, and his health insurance would pay for it.

The nurse showed them to room 205 and told them to make themselves at home. The resident would visit, then there were education sessions for Wyatt in the afternoon. This was the hospital's presurgery prep, designed to help the children adjust. Jake felt numb. He wondered if he looked like a zombie just standing there and nodding as the nurse talked.

As soon as the nurse was gone, Abby started fussing around the room. He knew his wife wanted to stay busy so she wouldn't think about where they were and what was going to happen in the next few days. It was easier for her to pretend they were just getting sorted out in a hotel room.

Emily wandered around looking at the buttons and switches. "Don't touch anything, sweetie," Jake warned.

Emily glared at him as though his suggestion was ridiculous.

"Not a bad room, hey guy?" Jake said to Wyatt.

Wyatt stood on a ledge next to the window. The room looked out toward Dalhousie University. "I guess."

"What're you looking at?"

"Nothing."

There was a whirring noise, and Jake turned. Emily was standing at the foot of the bed. "Sorry," she announced. "Found the controls for the bed."

Jake laughed. "Don't worry about it."

Abby finished putting books out on a table next to the bed and went to stand behind Wyatt. She put her arms around him. "What do you say, big guy?"

Wyatt shook free and jumped from the ledge. "Do we have to stay in the room?" he asked.

Abby put her hands on her knees and bent over to talk to him. "Well, I was thinking that we should probably take a trip down to the gift shop. We should check it out and see what kind of stuff they have."

"That sounds like a plan," Wyatt said brightly.

Abby looked at Jake. He nodded his approval.

They left the room and started down the hall. As they approached the nursing station Jake whispered to Abby, "You go with them. I'll be right down. I'm just going to check something here."

She nodded, and the kids raced ahead to push the button for the elevator.

Jake stopped at the nursing desk. A pleasant-looking nurse came over.

"Hi," Jake said. "We just got here with Wyatt Tunnel. Dr. Merrot thought you might have a date for his surgery. He's in room 205."

"Sure, let me check." She looked at a computer terminal and hit a few buttons. Her finger traced a line down the monitor. "Yep. Tuesday. He's on a special list for the next available, but he's booked for Tuesday morning."

"That's great. Thanks." Jake suddenly felt like he might faint. Hearing the date of his son's brain surgery was like a blow to the stomach. He put a hand on the desk to steady himself.

"Are you okay?" the nurse asked.

"I'm okay," he said.

"Wyatt's going to be fine," the nurse said softly. "We're going to do everything for him. Don't you worry."

Jake looked at her. She smiled and put a hand over his on the desk. He nodded. "Thanks."

"Now get down to that gift shop and buy Wyatt whatever he wants."

He laughed. "I will."

XLIII

"Move over, brat," Maury ordered.

The boy slid over.

Benicio also slid over, to allow Jeremy to sit next to him. He wrinkled his nose at the smell.

"You're pretty slick, aren't you?" Jeremy asked.

Before Benicio could answer, their waitress was back. "*Bon matin,*" she announced, then frowned, her nose twitching. "Good morning," she said less cheerfully. "Coffee?"

"Nothing right now," Maury said. "We just need to talk to our friends for a minute."

The waitress left.

Benicio looked at Maury. The man's good eye was glazed, as though he were sick or stoned, and his skin was very pale. The guy wasn't doing very well.

"Why are you here?" Benicio whispered.

"We're just following orders," Jeremy said. "Like you should have done. We wouldn't need to be here if you weren't such a fuckup."

"What does the church want with this boy? He's done nothing wrong."

"We don't care about the kid," Maury mumbled. His words slurred slightly as though he had trouble speaking. "What the church does is the church's business."

"You can't believe that. You can't just do what they say and not worry about the consequences."

"Just watch us." Jeremy grinned. "That happens to be one of our specialties."

"You're animals."

"Watch your temper, priest boy. You don't want God getting mad at you."

"Don't talk to me about God. You two know nothing about God."

"Don't be so damn righteous," Maury retorted. "We know more than you've ever known. We're God's bastard children. It's your damn God that's made us suffer our whole lives."

"What are you talking about?"

"We're Nephilim," Jeremy said. "Half angel, half man."

Benicio's surprise was obvious. "Why would you say that?"

"Say what?"

"Why would you say you're Nephilim?"

"Because we are," Maury said.

Benicio glanced at Matthew. He felt as if the whole world was going mad. First there was the suggestion that Matthew was Nephilim, and now these men. "The Nephilim are a legend — a myth."

"It's not a fuckin' legend. We're the proof right here. God has forsaken us and our bodies have rotted away since the moment we were born. Only the church has fought to save us."

"And so we do the odd job for them," Jeremy finished.

Benicio shook his head. "They've done it again."

"Done what?" Jeremy demanded.

"You aren't forsaken by God. You aren't Nephilim. There's no such thing."

"What the hell are you talking about?" Maury sneered. A line of spit dripped from his mouth and clung to his shirt.

"The church used the myth of Nephilim to ostracize many groups of people over the years. There's no such thing as Nephilim. Angels never had sex with women."

"Our bodies are fuckin' falling apart!" Maury yelled. "Look at my goddamn eye." He pulled the patch up to reveal the deformity beneath.

Benicio looked concerned. "Listen to me. The church must

have found you at a young age, right? Likely it was a church mission that found you in a third-world country. Probably somewhere in Africa. They raised you in secrecy and treated you with special medicine. Am I close?"

"The cardinal found us in the U.S.," Jeremy said, smirking.

"Right after our parents came home from Africa," Maury added.

The smile left Jeremy's face.

Benicio took a deep breath. "You aren't forsaken. You guys have leprosy. It's treatable. You don't have to live like this. You don't have to be slaves to the church."

"Bullshit," Jeremy said.

"God never forsakes anyone," Benicio continued. "You can get help. Real help."

Maury opened his mouth then closed it. His head drooped toward the table.

"Maury," Jeremy said. "What's wrong?"

"Got to go," Maury whispered. "Got to go." He slid out of the booth and tried to stand, but his legs wouldn't support him. He stumbled, then crashed into a neighboring table, bringing all the dishes down with him. The two women at the table screeched, and staff came quickly to Maury's side. Most of the patrons turned to watch but didn't immediately move.

Jeremy moved to his brother's side. "Maury?" he cried. "What's going on?" He rolled his brother over. A reddish-brown stain spread across his shirt. "Maury?"

"Let's go," Benicio whispered to Matthew. He and the boy moved quickly to the doors and stepped outside.

Benicio glanced back to see if Jeremy was following them. The commotion continued inside the restaurant and he couldn't see Jeremy. He turned to the boy. Matthew was standing silently next to him.

"Let's go, Matt," he said, and they ran toward the far end of the parking lot.

XLIV

"Get back," Jeremy screamed and waved his arms to shoo people away. Staff were still crowding around Maury. "He's fine!"

A large bearded man in a white shirt and tie came over. "I'm the manager. What's going on?" He had no hint of a French accent.

"This guy just dropped and fell over the table," a waitress said.

"Call an ambulance!" the manager barked.

"No!" yelled Jeremy. "We don't need an ambulance." He bent over Maury. "Come on. Snap out of it. We gotta get out of here."

Maury's eyelids flickered.

The manager spoke again. "Is your friend okay?"

"He had a seizure. He has epilepsy. He's fine. He just needs a second."

Another waitress tapped the manager on the arm. "I had a cousin with epilepsy," she said. "It was the weirdest thing. He'd just drop and shake all over for a minute or two and then it would be like nothing happened. The family hardly even reacted to it after a while."

The manager turned and gave her a look that instantly shut her mouth. He turned back to Jeremy. "You need anything?"

"Space."

The manager held his arms up. "Okay, people. Everything's fine here. Keep enjoying your meals. Everything's taken care of." He told one of the busboys to start cleaning up the mess.

"Maury!" Jeremy whispered. "We gotta go."

Maury put an arm around Jeremy's neck. Together they stood, and Jeremy helped his brother to the door.

"Sorry about everything. He's okay now," Jeremy told the manager, who held the door for them.

"Hope so. You're sure you don't want me to call an ambulance? Your buddy looks pretty rough."

Maury held his jacket over his stained shirt. "I'm fine. I just need to rest."

The manager was happy they were leaving. "Okay then," he said. "Take care."

The brothers hobbled to the rental car, and Jeremy helped Maury into the passenger seat. As soon as he was in the driver's seat, he turned to his brother. "What's wrong?"

"It's the gunshot," Maury said. "It really messed me up."

"But the cardinal always said we couldn't be hurt by stuff like that. We're forsaken."

Maury shook his head. "I don't know. I'm not sure."

"Not sure about what?" Jeremy demanded. "Are you starting to believe what that priest said? You think we really are just a couple of lepers?"

"Jeremy," Maury shouted, then winced. "Goddamn it. Look at me. Look at us. Our bodies are falling apart. What makes more sense? That we are bastard children with angels and humans as ancestors and forsaken by God to rot in our own skin? Or that we got leprosy when our parents were in Africa doing their missionary work?"

"But the cardinal —" Jeremy started.

"I need help," Maury said quietly.

A knock on the driver's side window made Jeremy jump. Two men were standing next to the car. He rolled the window down halfway. "What?" he snarled.

"I am Shemhazai, and this is Azazel," the younger man said. "We can help."

XLV

It had been a long few days. Benicio stood beside the rental and stretched. He'd parked on the top floor of a garage in downtown Halifax. They'd finally made it.

Traffic had been reasonably light all the way into town. He was glad it was Sunday evening. Downtown Halifax was notorious for its narrow one-way streets, and he wouldn't want to be driving in rush hour. The few times he'd been here Jake had always done the driving, which had suited Benicio fine.

He looked at the car. Matthew sat motionless in the passenger seat. Benicio needed to coax the boy out. They'd made a small connection at the restaurant, but Benicio thought it had been ruined by the appearance of Maury and Jeremy.

The Halifax Casino garage was a multi-storey facility, always open and always busy. The twenty-four-hour casino made sure of that. Benicio chose the top level, thinking there'd be less traffic, though a few cars were parked in the dimly lit level.

Out of the corner of his eye he saw movement and froze. There was someone here, watching them. Benicio stared into the dark corner where he'd seen motion.

And waited.

Nothing.

He slowly scanned the rest of the level, watching for movement.

Nothing.

He felt foolish. *I'm freaking myself out. I've got to calm down.* He shook his arms and legs and jumped up and down to get his circulation going. Then he crouched down near the passenger door. "I'm going to open the door," he announced as he looked at the boy.

Matthew didn't acknowledge him.

He pulled the door open. "We need to get going. There's a hotel up the street. We can rest for a bit. It's just a little walk." Benicio planned to leave the car in the parking garage and hoped it wouldn't be noticed for a while. He didn't like Halifax traffic, and he didn't want to drive a car with Connecticut plates.

"Can you get out of the car?" he asked quietly, moving a little closer to the boy. "Maybe when we get to the room we can do a little coloring together. Would you like that?"

The boy didn't move. Benicio looked around. It was going to be dark soon. They needed to go.

"Okay, I'm just going to help you out. I'm not going to hurt you." He wished that he'd paid more attention to the child psychopathology classes in grad school. Benicio had only taken the minimum number of child-based courses because he didn't think he'd ever work with kids.

He reached in and put a hand on Matthew's shoulder. The boy instantly reacted, pulling back and yelling — screaming — in a high-pitched shriek.

Benicio moved back. "Whoa, whoa," he said, holding his hands out. "I'm sorry. *Scusi. Scusi.*"

The boy kicked and flailed his arms, all the while keeping up his high-pitched scream.

Benicio looked around nervously. He didn't want anyone coming over to see what was going on.

"What do you want?" Benicio asked. "What can I do?"

The boy stopped and stared straight ahead.

"I want to help you. We need to get out of here and find a safe place."

No response. Benicio thought about something he hadn't brought up with the boy in a while. "If we're going to figure out that Voynich book together, then we need to get going. I really want to learn about it. I want to know about the language of the forsaken."

The boy turned and looked at him. His expression sent a chill down the priest's spine. To Benicio, Matthew's eyes seemed vacant, lifeless.

The young priest spoke again. "Yes, the language of the angels. Only you can help me with that."

The boy stared. It was difficult to tell if he was looking at Benicio or straight through him.

"Is there something you want to say? Is there something you can tell me about the language of the angels?"

"I am . . ." Matthew's voice was deep and hollow.

"Yes? You are what?"

"I am . . ."

Benicio moved forward slightly.

"I am Nephilite. I am forsaken."

"What? Why do you say that?" Benicio wondered if Matthew was repeating what'd he heard Maury and Jeremy say at the restaurant. The boy couldn't know what he was saying — he wasn't Nephilim. Benicio put his face in his hands. It was getting harder and harder to think. After a moment he looked up. Matthew was standing in front of him. "Guess you're ready to go."

Matthew didn't say anything.

Benicio shrugged. "Well, for a Nephilim you sure can be quiet sometimes." He started walking.

Matthew fell into step behind him.

PART II

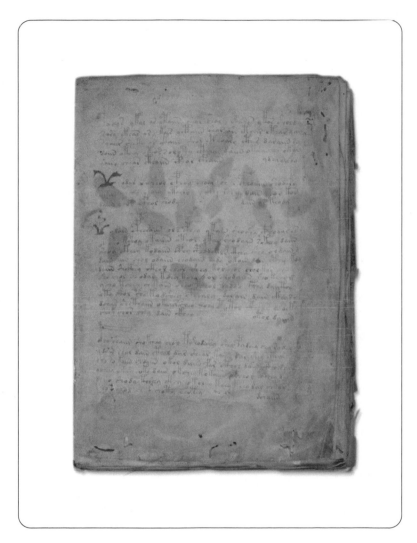

XLVI

Jake balled up the last fast-food wrapper and dropped it in the garbage. On the way home from the hospital he and Emily had stopped at McDonald's. Emily usually only got to eat fast food as a treat, on special occasions. Today Jake was too tired to cope with anything more complicated.

It had been hard to leave Abby and Wyatt at the hospital. He felt he should be spending every second with his son, but Abby was right when she said it made more sense for him to take Em home and let her keep her routine. Their daughter had school tomorrow, and Jake had to see a few patients before he could cancel the rest of his week.

Once home, Emily went off to her room and Jake wandered into the kitchen to tidy. He contemplated pouring a rye and Coke but didn't. He decided he'd have a celebratory drink when Wyatt came home. That'd be a much better reason.

Emily had been quiet on the way home from the hospital. He asked her if she had any questions or wanted to talk about anything but she'd said no. She'd always been a smart but quiet kid.

He left the kitchen and headed down the hall. There was faint music coming from her room, and he found her crouched over Wyatt's video game, watching the screen intently and pushing buttons. He thought it was odd because she rarely played it.

"What're you doing?" he asked her.

"Playin' a video game."

"Yeah," Jake said, "but why? You never play that."

She kept pressing buttons. A bouncy little tune emanated from the small, gray-plastic rectangle. "Wyatt never lets me play when he's around."

"Oh," Jake said in a comical voice, as if she had just solved a great riddle.

"Dad!" She sounded exasperated. "I just wanted to, okay?"

"I'm not saying there's anything wrong with you playing. I think it's kind of nice."

She glanced at him but kept playing. "Why?"

"Well, I know it's weird not having Wyatt here, so playing that game probably makes you feel closer to him."

She didn't respond.

Jake figured his analysis was a little heavy for a seven year old. He sat next to her, trying to see the screen. "What game are you playing?"

"Mario versus Donkey Kong," she said. "It's Wyatt's favorite."

"What do you have to do?" To Jake the screen was incomprehensible. There were little men, ladders, fireballs, and multiple floors in a building. He had no idea what was happening.

"See that present?" Emily asked, her eyes on the screen and her fingers dancing on the buttons. A little Mario character suddenly backflipped through the air and snatched a tiny square. "I need to get it and then find the key and open the door."

Jake nodded. "And then what? You fight Donkey Kong?"

"No," Emily said, shaking her head as though that would be ridiculous, "then I have to find the Mario toy in the bubble."

"The bubble?"

"Once I get all the Mario toys, I lead them through a room and put them in the toy box."

"Okay," Jake said slowly.

"And *then* I fight Donkey Kong," she announced as though that idea finally made sense.

Jake watched the Mario character jump over gaps, lift up massive gold keys, and run past moving black bombs. He couldn't tell how Emily was doing.

There was a sad little noise, and the Mario character crumbled to the ground, then disappeared. "I'm not as good as Wyatt," Emily announced. "He can double jump somehow and get past stuff. I don't know how he does it."

"Yep, he's pretty good at it, isn't he?"

"Yep."

"Maybe after school tomorrow we should take the game to the hospital."

She nodded but Jake could sense some reluctance. It was probably hard for Emily to think about her little brother being at the hospital. For kids it was easier to just pretend someone is at a friend's house or down in the basement. Being reminded that Wyatt was at the IWK waiting for surgery must have been difficult.

Jake wanted to distract her, keep her thinking positive thoughts. "I think tonight would be a good night to buy a movie on one of the movie channels. What do you think about that?"

She looked up, her face alight. "Really? But it's a school night."

"I won't tell Mom if you don't."

"I won't," she promised.

"Get your pajamas on, I'll grab some pop and chips and bring them down, and I'll meet you in the family room." Jake stood to leave.

Emily clicked the game off and snapped the screen shut, slid off the bed and bolted to the dresser. "Can I pick the movie?"

"You bet!" Jake said.

XLVII

Benicio and Matthew stood at the corner of Lower Water and Sackville streets. It had taken them fifteen minutes to walk from the parking garage. The boy silently followed Benicio, stopping when he stopped, walking when he walked.

Benicio could see large block letters on the roof of an old, dark-brick building, white paint on black shingles: BREWERY MARKET. Jake's office was in that building. He was tempted to take a trip down there right now and see if his friend was in. He knew it was unrealistic. Jake had a lot to deal with at home with his son being sick.

He looked at Matthew. Benicio wasn't sure he was doing the right thing. He wasn't sure he should have taken the boy. He wasn't sure he should have come to Canada, and he was very unsure about getting Jake involved.

But who else will help? And where else can I go?

He sighed. "There's a hotel just up the street. Let's go get checked in."

They walked up Sackville Street to the hotel, then pushed through the revolving door into a modern lobby. A young man in a white dress shirt with a tight green vest and matching trousers stood at the registration desk. His name tag said Jimmy.

"I'd like a room for the night," Benicio said.

"Certainly, sir. How many in your party?"

"Just me and the boy." He wondered how that sounded. Did they look suspicious? He was pretty sure they did.

The desk clerk didn't seem to notice. "Smoking or non?"

"Non."

"We have a deluxe suite on the tenth floor."

"Perfect," Benicio said.

"Credit card?" the clerk asked and held out a hand.

Shoot. All Benicio had was what the church had provided. He knew there was a credit card in the wallet, but if he used it the Vatican would know where he was within moments. "Hold on a second," he said, and pulled the wallet out. Still lots of American cash.

"You know, I'd much rather pay cash."

Jimmy frowned. "Unfortunately," he said slowly, "we do require an imprint of a valid credit card."

"We just need a place to sleep for tonight. We have an appointment tomorrow morning. My son is sick."

Jimmy nodded. "I appreciate that, sir, but it is our policy to only provide rooms to individuals with a valid credit card."

"But a man in your position *can* make an exception." Benicio laid a hundred dollar bill on the counter. "That's why you're working the desk alone."

Jimmy looked at the bill for a moment before he responded. "I'm really sorry, sir. Without a valid —"

Benicio set another hundred on the counter. "Now, how much did you say the room was? I'll pay cash right now."

Jimmy's hand moved, and the two hundred disappeared. "One seventy-five plus tax."

***

The suite was beautiful, with two queen beds and dark oak furniture. Matthew stood just inside the door.

"You pick your bed," Benicio said as he dropped the key card on the bureau next to the TV cabinet. "Come on in, Matthew. It's okay. This is our room. We're going to sleep here and then get going in the morning."

Matthew didn't respond.

"Are you hungry?"

No answer.

"Do you need to go to the bathroom?" Jake saw Matthew's

head move slightly. "The bathroom's right there. Do you need to go?"

Matthew turned and started towards it.

"Hold on," Benicio said. "Let me take your jacket off."

The boy stopped and held his arms out. Benicio slid the jacket from his shoulders, then Matthew went into the bathroom and shut the door.

Jake looked at the closed door. Every once in a while he felt as if he could communicate with Matthew. He shrugged and hung the jacket in the closet, then sat on one of the beds.

The toilet flushed, and Matthew appeared. Silently he sat on the end of the other bed.

Benicio smiled. It looked like they were playing a game, boy copying adult. But Matthew wasn't playing. Would he eventually lie down? Or drop in exhaustion, as he had in the car.

He didn't lie down.

And then Benicio remembered something the boy had said. "Matthew?"

No response.

"Matthew, can you tell me more about the Nephilim?"

No response.

"Who told you about the Nephilim?"

Nothing.

Benicio frowned. An ancient book written in a language no one understood until an autistic child came along, a child who claimed he was a member of a long-gone, probably mythical race of beings. Without the Vatican's obvious interest, Benicio would have dismissed the whole story as a psychotic fantasy. But there was no doubt that the Vatican, and more specifically Cardinal Espinosa, was interested. And his extreme measures meant he was scared.

"I really need to know what's in that book," Benicio said loudly.

Matthew didn't even blink.

"Matthew, can you tell me what you read in that funny book?

You know, the one you saw back at the big library?"

Nothing.

"It's the book you said was written in the language of the forsaken. Can you remember that book? I need to know what the book is about."

Nothing.

Benicio decided to forget about it for now. He was so tired. He hoped he could get some sleep.

A few hours, maybe less.

The Nephilim, he thought. *Why would the boy say that?*

***

Benicio had fallen asleep.

He couldn't have slept more than a few hours since this whole mess had begun. It was starting to wear him down.

He slept and he dreamed.

Images swept around, swirling as though caught up in a tornado. Men from ancient times, men with unkempt beards. He saw shimmering angels, heard women screaming, saw the hand of God reaching out.

The scene shifted.

He saw a crowd of men standing before a stone temple carved into the side of a hill. One man confronted the crowd, his face a mask of anger. He was wrapped in a rough sheet and wore sandals on his blackened feet. It was a scene from ancient times. It was a scene from men's earliest days in their newfound relationship with God.

Benicio could hear no words, but the man's outrage was evident. The crowd cowered in shame. They were being scolded.

Down the road a group of women were huddled. Their piercing eyes shone through shawls that covered their heads and most of their faces. Many of them had babies swaddled in their arms. The women were crying — pleading — for something. Benicio could not hear their words.

And then everyone stopped. Everyone. Even the outraged man at the head of the temple.

Benicio shifted his gaze and found the source of the disruption. Someone new was coming. A man was walking across the pathway to the temple. Only it wasn't a man — not a normal man.

He was clean-shaven with short hair. His robe was a pristine white without a hint of stain or dirt. He too wore sandals but his feet were not dirty. The man strode evenly, confidently to the group.

But there was something else.

The man's skin glowed. It was something you might miss at a glance but as you watched it was striking. The man's slight yellow-orange tint seemed to have a life of its own. It virtually pulsed as the man continued to walk.

And the man was tall — at least a foot and a half taller than the largest man in the assembly before the temple. As he neared them the size difference became more obvious and the crowd began shuffling to clear a pathway.

Benicio glanced at the outraged man. He no longer seemed overcome with anger but was quickly sinking into fear. He had slowly moved closer to the temple doorway.

The new man continued forward. Then something else happened. There must have been a loud noise or something because everyone, including the new man, jumped as though startled. And before anyone could regain their composure an object came hurtling down from above and slammed into the ground at the feet of the new man.

The crowd suddenly drew back, climbing over one another to put distance between themselves and the fallen object.

The new man crouched down and put a hand on it.

The thing lying in the dirt was bright but virtually transparent. Benicio was sure he could see right through it to the rocks beneath.

The glowing man put two hands against it and rolled the

thing over. It flopped awkwardly and spread out. Legs uncurled and extended from beneath it while a large wing flapped against the dirt, causing a swirl of dust.

An angel.

Benicio was looking at an angel spread out in the dirt.

An angel that had just been discarded from heaven like garbage.

The glowing man bent over and kissed it lightly on the head.

Then it grew dark. Clouds rolled through so quickly that it was as if the lights had been turned out. Benicio squinted. The angel and the man continued to provide some slight amount of illumination from the glow of their skin.

Black clouds rolled through the daytime sky, crashing against one another and diving down towards the ground as though they were alive.

Then a voice. Only this time Benicio could hear it.

Abomination no more.

Pandemonium. Everyone began running — the men in the crowd, the angry man at the front of the temple, and the group of women with their children clutched in their arms.

Everyone ran except for the glowing man and the angel.

The glowing man stood, dropped his arms to his sides, and lifted his face to the black sky.

As Benicio watched, the air around the man took life. It swirled around him, darting up and down his body. The man looked to be in severe agony, as though his life were being sucked away. He arched his back in spasm and jerked as the air continued to move.

But a face darted into Benicio's line of sight. Without warning he was suddenly staring into the eyes of one of the women, a baby still clutched to her chest. She whispered to Benicio, "The children are the key to the secrets. They belong to everyone."

Benicio wanted to answer her but couldn't. He wanted to ask what was going on.

She spoke again. "Go now. Find Dr. Tunnel. Maury and Jeremy are not the real enemies. Seventy generations has come to an end. Beware the fathers."

He blinked and opened his eyes. *Seventy generations!* He'd heard that phrase before. But where? He suddenly became aware that someone was watching him. Matthew stood next to the bed, his face only inches from the priest's. Benicio let out a little yelp.

"What are you doing?" he barked before he could stop himself. He couldn't yet tell if he was awake or asleep, but the furnishings of the room were starting to look familiar. He was in the hotel room.

Matthew didn't react, didn't say anything.

Benicio's eyes searched the room. He felt an enormous sense of urgency. He looked out the window. It was morning. He'd slept through the night.

"Put your shoes on," he said to Matthew, then got up and went to the door. He looked through the peephole, then opened the door slowly and glanced up and down the hall. No one.

He closed the door. "Let's get ready," he said. "We have to go meet someone. He's really nice. I'm sure you'll like him."

XLVIII

Jake absentmindedly watched the school bus pull away. Normally he would see Emily on the bus and then rush back to his station wagon so he could stay in front of the bus. He hated driving behind it and having to wait at every stop it made. Today he couldn't concentrate. The bus was turning the corner at the end of the street before he even started to the car.

He got in behind the wheel, his thoughts all over the map. He was worried about Wyatt. He was surprised and confused by Benicio's call on Saturday. On the one hand it would be good to see Benicio, but he just didn't have the strength to take on more problems. Not right now.

He knew his first patient was at eight-thirty. If he could just get through the morning and wrap up some business then he could be at the hospital all afternoon. He dropped into the driver's seat and put the car in gear.

***

Mrs. Tanya Meeling. Quiet, older lady. Nice. Normal. Religious. A little plump and very grandmotherly, which was appropriate given her seven grandchildren.

She perched glumly on the couch. Tears streaked her face and drew some dark mascara down her cheeks. She was one of those older women who carefully did her makeup every morning, but it only gave her wrinkled face a strange, artificial quality. Jake sat patiently. Sometimes he let the silence sit in the room for a full ten minutes, waiting for Mrs. Meeling to compose herself.

They were on minute six.

She took a deep breath. "He's such a bastard. Why does he need to do that? Doesn't he know what he's done to me?"

"I won't make excuses for his behavior. He has an illness, but that isn't an excuse," Jake replied.

Her tears surged again. "But my life is over. It's over. He's wrecked everything."

Jake opened his mouth to answer but before he could speak there was a loud bang from the waiting room. Then there were voices, then urgent whispering. He frowned.

"Just one second," he said to Mrs. Meeling, and held up a finger. He moved to the door and opened it a crack. He saw magazines on the floor and a man picking them up. He saw that everything had been knocked off the bookshelf. Then he saw a small boy.

Jake cleared his throat, and the man stood. It was Benicio Valori.

"Hey," Jake said warmly. "Ben."

"Jake!" Benicio moved toward him, hand out. "I'm really sorry to just show up here. I need to talk to you."

They shook hands. "I'm in a session right now."

"We don't mean to bother you. We'll wait."

Jake frowned, looked at the boy, then Benicio. "Okay. Twenty minutes." He returned to the office, closed the door.

"Sorry about that, Mrs. Meeling. Where were we?"

***

The rest of Mrs. Meeling's session slid past quickly. Jake forced himself to pay attention, but it was difficult.

When they finally reached their time Jake stood. "Things seem really out of control now, but you'll get through this, Mrs. Meeling. You have your children and your grandchildren to think of. They need you. You need to do what's right for yourself."

She struggled to stand, wiggling herself to the edge of the couch. "I know," she grunted, "but it's just been so long. I don't know what I'd do without him."

"I'll see you again next week," Jake said. "Don't worry about it until then. We'll work it out together."

She smiled. "Thank you, Dr. Tunnel. I don't know what I would have done without you. You're the only person I can talk to — the only person who could possibly understand what I'm going through."

He nodded, then opened the inner office door, and she stepped out. As most patients do, she reflexively looked away from the other faces in the waiting room. There seemed to be an unwritten rule not to make eye contact with other patients in a psychologist's waiting room. It would break the illusion that your visit was anonymous. She hurried to the hallway and was gone.

Jake looked at the boy and then to Benicio. "What's going on? And who is this little fella?"

Benicio shook his head. "I don't even know how to begin, buddy."

XLIX

Matthew sat in the waiting room on a futon couch, apparently unaware of anything around him. Jake was in his leather chair; Benicio was on the client couch. They were watching Matthew.

"So, who is he?" Jake asked.

Benicio hesitated. "His name is Matthew. He's autistic. I'm trying to help him."

"Help him what?"

"It's complicated," Benicio said. "I don't even know where to begin."

"On the phone you said you were in trouble with the church."

"I think I am. They want the boy."

"But you work for the church, don't you? Last I heard, you were a priest."

Benicio smiled. "I still am." Pause. "I think." He sighed, then told Jake everything. For twenty minutes both men forgot about the boy in the waiting room. When the priest stopped, there was a long silence.

"So why does the Vatican think Matthew can read the book?" Jake asked, scratching his head. He was watching Matthew again. He was pretty sure the boy hadn't moved.

"I think it might have something to do with speaking in tongues. The church has been waiting for years, decades, for the right person to come along, someone who could read the book. Maybe this child is the right person. That's what I'm supposed to be investigating."

"And?" Jake prompted.

"He might be able to read it. Unfortunately, the Voynich manuscript was stolen before I got to New Haven, so I couldn't test that theory. But there's definitely something odd going on."

"The book was stolen? From the Yale library?"

"Yep."

"Wouldn't that be pretty tough to do?"

"I think so," said Benicio.

Jake waited for more explanation but saw he wouldn't get any. "So, if the book's gone, now what?"

"I don't know. Apparently, there are copies of the whole book available online as well as other info on the Voynich. I haven't had a chance to check."

"Okay, but what about this kid? How could he read a book nobody else can?"

"Well, as I said, he's autistic. That's why I thought of you. I took the college classes, but I don't remember much about autism. I was hoping you kept up to date on your child psych."

"Nope. I've only worked with a few kids." He and Benicio watched Matthew. The boy never moved a muscle.

Benicio sighed, then said, "I suspect the church is afraid of what's in the manuscript. I think they don't want anyone to read it, ever. I think they'll do anything to keep that from happening."

"Anything?" Jake asked in a stagy, ominous voice.

Benicio nodded.

Jake was suddenly serious. "They want to kill the boy?"

"I can't be sure."

"And so you just took him? That's why you're in trouble with the church — you kidnapped the kid?"

"I felt I didn't have a choice. His foster parents were going to sell him for ten thousand dollars — then the Vatican sent those goons to get him, and the goons probably killed Father McCallum. I liked the old guy, Jake. He's spent his whole life working for the Vatican, watching the book, and the church tries to kill him. None of this is right. I needed help. And there's no one I trust more than you."

Both men looked at Matthew. He hadn't moved.

When Jake spoke, his voice was calm and measured. "Tell me again how this boy could read an unknown language."

"I've been thinking about that. Do you remember we learned about speech development in our child courses? I think he can see patterns in the book that no one else can see." Benicio waited for an acknowledgment, but when there was none he continued. "Do you remember anything about speech development from our child courses?"

"Vaguely."

"Well, I remembered reading about how complicated speech development is for young children, yet they pick it up so easily. Learning the rules of a language and being able to apply them by the age of two or three — it's nothing short of a miracle."

"I hadn't thought of it that way," Jake said slowly, "but you're right."

"Psychology tells us that humans are born with two unusual gifts: speech and written language. Humans are pre-wired to speak and read."

Jake nodded.

"Well, why should our brains be pre-wired for only one language? Maybe some people's minds are built to understand other languages, but because those languages are obscure or not used anymore, those people don't even know about their special gift."

"So there might be things we could read automatically, without any training? Our brains are ready to interpret languages we've never even seen?"

"Yes," Benicio said excitedly. "That's exactly what I mean! Language is an automatic process. Our minds read and understand things, and we don't have to do any work." He leaned over and took a piece of paper and a pen from the desk, wrote a few lines then handed the paper to Jake. "What does this say?"

U wn't hve any prblm rdng ths.
Rdng is a fnny thng nd we do it automtclly.

Jake read it out loud and smiled. "I see what you're saying. Our minds automatically try to make sense out of the world around us, fill in gaps and put meaning where there isn't any. And we do that even with language."

"And that isn't a learned ability," Benicio said. "Neither is speaking in tongues — it's a phenomenon that borrows from the way our brains are wired to interpret meaning in things around us. Looking at it in that way, the phenomenon of recognizing a language we don't understand isn't so bizarre. It's really a matter of using natural mechanisms that are already programmed."

"Okay," Jake said, "but why is the book so important?"

"Because it's about that Old Testament stuff, about angels having sex with women and the women giving birth to human angels. The church thinks Matthew is half angel and half man."

"No wonder you wanted to get the kid away from them."

Benicio nodded.

"So what can I do?" Jake asked.

"I wish I knew, my friend. I needed to get Matthew away. I knew the church was coming for him, and to be quite honest I've felt a little over my head with an autistic child. I thought you'd be better equipped to advise me."

"Because I have children of my own, or because I work as a clinical psychologist?"

"Both."

"You know I'd do anything for you. If you guys want to stay at the house or borrow my car or whatever — name it. The one thing I don't have much of right now is time. Wyatt's in the hospital and going for surgery tomorrow."

"I understand." Benicio stood. "I know everything will work out with Wyatt. I'm sure of it. You should focus your energy there."

"No. I'll help you any way I can. I'm just saying —"

"That's fine," Benicio interrupted. "I've got a few things to check on. Then I'll call you."

"You know what, I've got just a couple more patients to deal with and then I could spare a little time. Why don't the three of us go look up this Voynich on the Internet. I can meet you at Dalhousie University and we can use my computer account there."

Benicio didn't look convinced.

"I really am interested," Jake continued. "We can check this thing out online and then you and the boy will come stay at my place."

Relief washed over Benicio. "Thank you very much, Jake. I knew I could count on you."

"Now get out of here so I can finish up. I'll meet you in front of the Dal library in two hours."

Benicio looked like he was going to say something more, but stopped. He turned and moved to the waiting room. Matthew fell into step with Benicio and they left.

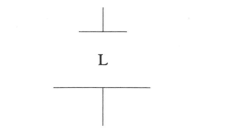

L

Jake wanted to cancel the rest of his appointments. He doubted he could concentrate after his meeting with Ben. He also felt a twinge of guilt that he wasn't going straight to the hospital, but he wasn't going to leave Benicio hanging. He looked at his watch. *Screw it, I'm going to get out of here.* He called his only remaining patient of the day, rescheduled, then grabbed his jacket. He'd stop by the hospital before meeting Benicio at Dal. The hospital was on the way to Dal anyway.

He went down the stairs and pushed into the stone lobby of the building. There wasn't usually much foot traffic, but he noticed a couple of rough, unkempt-looking guys heading across the lobby toward him. The larger man was pale and sickly looking, with a ragged eye patch. The slightly smaller, thinner man had a lopsided grin over dry lips.

"Hey," the larger one said. "You know where Jake Tunnel's office is?"

He was tempted to tell them it was upstairs and keep going. Having these guys banging on his door didn't excite him. "I'm Dr. Tunnel."

"Oh, good. We need a few minutes of your time."

"Who are you?" Jake asked.

The bigger man ignored the question. "Let's go to your office where we can talk in private."

"We can talk here. How can I help you?"

"We represent the Vatican and need to ask you a few questions about a fugitive you may have had contact with — Benicio Valori."

"Who'd you say you were?" Jake asked.

"I'm Maury and this is Jeremy."

"And what's your relationship to the Vatican?"

"I think we should ask the questions. Have you been contacted by Benicio Valori?"

"I doubt that's any of your business."

"Come on now," Jeremy urged. "Just be straight with us and we'll be out of your hair. Benicio is confused and we're here to help get things straightened out. We wanna help Benicio, even if he doesn't realize it."

"Yeah, I can see that. You two look like the helping types."

"Don't be a smart-assed prick," Jeremy said, sneering.

"Language," Jake said, faking offense. "What would the Vatican say?"

Maury looked at his brother and motioned for him to back off. "We'd really appreciate your assistance, Dr. Tunnel."

"I've got nothing to say. My son is in the hospital and that's where I'm headed," Jake announced and moved toward the door. The men shifted to physically block his way.

Maury leaned in close. He whispered, "Don't fuck with us," and slapped a card against Jake's chest. "If you hear from Valori or find out anything about where he's at — call us. If we find out you knew something and didn't tell us we'll come back. You don't want us to come back."

Jake took the card and backed away. Maury stared at him for another second, then a glimmer of a smirk crossed his lips. He and Jeremy turned and left.

Jake looked at the card for a moment and then ripped it in half. There was a garbage container nearby, and he dropped the ripped paper in it. *Ben, what have you gotten yourself into?* Things had changed. He wanted — no, needed — to know more about this Voynich book. He'd go straight to Dal and get started.

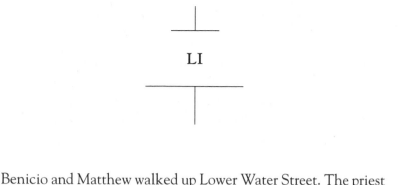

LI

Benicio and Matthew walked up Lower Water Street. The priest was glad he was meeting Jake later. Things were still on the verge of being out of control, but it helped having Jake involved. He felt guilty, though. Jake had more than enough to deal with. The guy's son was really sick. He hated to put a greater burden on him. *I guess it never rains, it pours.* He smiled weakly and glanced at his companion. *I'm on the run with an autistic child, and Jake's son is going in for major surgery.* It was certainly pouring now.

He kept walking up the steep sidewalk then noticed that Matthew had stopped. He turned to find him looking at a menu posted outside a glass doorway. He stood next to the boy. "You hungry?" He knew it was a silly question, since they hadn't really eaten yet that day. "We have some time before we meet Jake. Let's go check it out."

It was a hotel, and they went into the lobby. Benicio spied the entrance to the restaurant off in the corner. They made their way over and were soon seated in a booth near a window looking out over Salter Street.

A smart-looking young server in a white shirt and black vest and pants came over to their table. "Coffee?" she asked.

"Sure," Benicio said.

The server looked at Matthew, who was staring blankly into space. "Does your son want anything to drink?"

"Matt, do you want a drink?"

No answer.

"Apple juice? Milk?"

Still no answer. Before Benicio could offer the boy more choices, the server picked up a menu and opened it to pictures of breakfast dishes. "Do you want milk?" she asked, and pointed to a glass of milk. "Or apple juice?" She pointed again.

Matthew put his finger on the picture of the milk.

"There we go," she announced, and went to get the drinks.

"Wow," Benicio said. "Good job, Matthew."

No response.

The server was back with the drinks in no time. "What can I get you two?"

"That was a pretty good trick with the milk," Benicio said.

She shrugged. "I have a nephew who's hearing impaired. I guess you just adapt."

"Well, it's still a good trick. Think it would work again? I'll have bacon and eggs, and let's see what Matthew wants."

Benicio slid the menu under Matthew's nose and pointed to a hamburger. No reaction. Mischievously, he pointed to a plate of spaghetti. Matthew immediately put his finger on a picture of pancakes.

"Okay," the server said, smiling. "Anything else?"

Benicio looked at Matthew, who stared blankly at the wall. "No thanks."

She went to get their breakfasts.

Benicio looked across the table at Matthew. He wondered if he was doing the right thing. He thought, somehow, that if he saw Jake they'd be able to figure out an answer. He realized that was a long shot. But he knew God would lead them to an answer.

Somehow.

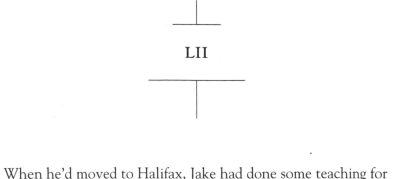

LII

When he'd moved to Halifax, Jake had done some teaching for
the Psychology Department at Dalhousie University. Teaching
a course here and there had brought in some money while he
was establishing his private practice. He'd continued his affiliation with Dalhousie, supervising practicum students from the
doctoral program and helping with research projects. It was a
good way to keep his skills honed.

His affiliation with the psych department gave him unlim-
ited access to the library and the university's massive
computerized holdings. At the moment, he wanted to learn
whatever he could about the ancient manuscript. He figured
there would be a few references on the Internet. With luck he
might find some books or journal articles.

He came to the corner of Spring Garden Road and
University Avenue and looked at the soaring column and classic architecture of the majestic Saint Andrew's United Church
— an interesting contrast to the trendy shopping district beside
it. *Old world meets new*, Jake thought, then stopped suddenly.

Harold Grower was standing in front of the church, watching Jake and waving furiously. Jake nodded once then looked
away and walked quickly past the church. As he turned onto
University he heard the slap of footsteps behind him.

"Dr. Tunnel!" Harold said as he caught up with Jake. "What
a surprise to see you around here."

Jake walked faster. "Yep."

"What brings you over here?"

"Just going to do a few things at the university," Jake said.

"That's my church," Harold announced, and pointed at
Saint Andrew's.

"That's great." Jake maintained his furious pace.

"Well, it's not actually *my* church, but God wants me to be there," Harold said. "I don't know why yet but I feel a tremendous sense of comfort when I'm there. I know it's what God wants."

"Well, don't let me keep you. You don't want to piss God off."

Harold laughed. "You pretend your heart is cold but I know better, Dr. Tunnel. God doesn't get pissed off. You know that. Or you would know that if you'd open your heart and listen. You need to open up before it's too late. God is speaking to you all the time. Like me being at the church. I don't know why God wants me there, but I go there and I wander around, just kind of exploring. That old church is full of secrets, rooms hidden in obscure corners, and hideaways in the attics. Take the basement, for example — it's a labyrinth of tunnels."

Jake stopped walking and turned to the older man. "Harold, we have an appointment next week. I really need to just get a few things done right now, okay? I don't mean to be rude but I've got a lot on my mind."

Harold smiled. "I won't keep you, Dr. Tunnel. You get going. I'm heading back to the church."

Jake kept walking. Once he was in the Killam Memorial Library, he moved quickly through the main room to a door in the back. There was an information desk just outside the door; Jake smiled at the librarian and swiped his faculty ID card over the electronic lock pad. There was a click, and he pulled the door open into a computer lab reserved for faculty. There were ten terminals, all of them empty.

He chose a computer, slung his jacket on the back of the chair and logged in. A message flashed on that he had 234 new emails. He laughed, clicked on the icon for the Internet browser, and went to Google. He typed in *Voynich*.

What flashed onto the screen surprised him.

Google reported that there were more than four hundred

thousand hits. And he'd been thinking he'd have to dig to find even one reference.

Nope.

Not only did he not have to dig but there were entire websites devoted to the Voynich. It was a massive topic.

Jake knew that quantity of information did not indicate credibility or depth of research. But still.

At the top of the listings he saw a few newspaper articles. He scanned the headlines Google provided but didn't go to the sites. The headlines told him the Voynich had been stolen four days ago and the police had no leads.

A few things became obvious from a quick scan of the Google listings. The words "mystery," "baffle," and "riddle" showed up over and over; the book was a genuine puzzle. And Jake kept seeing another word: "hoax."

The Beinecke Library was mentioned frequently, and Jake typed "Beinecke" into Google, found the Beinecke's search engine, and keyed in "Voynich." The book was stored as manuscript number 408, and the website described it:

Cipher Manuscript

Central Europe [?], s. xv^^ex-xvi[?]

Scientific or magical text in an unidentified language, in cipher, apparently based on Roman minuscule characters; the text is believed by some scholars to be the work of Roger Bacon since the themes of the illustrations seem to represent topics known to have interested Bacon (see also Provenance below). A history of the numerous attempts to decipher the manuscript can be found in a volume edited by R.S. Brumbaugh, *The Most Mysterious Manuscript: The Voynich "Roger Bacon" Cipher Manuscript* (Carbondale, Southern Illinois University Press, 1978). Although several scholars have claimed decipherments of the manuscript, for the most part the text remains an unsolved puzzle. R.S. Brumbaugh has, however, suggested a decipherment that establishes readings for the star names and plant labels; see his "Botany and the Voynich 'Roger Bacon' Manuscript Once More," *Speculum* 49 (1974) pp. 546–48; "The Solution of the Voynich 'Roger Bacon' Cipher," *Gazette* 49 (1975) pp. 347–55; and "The Voynich 'Roger Bacon' Cipher Manuscript: Deciphered Maps of Stars," *Journal of the Warburg and Courtauld Institutes* 39 (1976) pp. 139–50. Almost every page contains botanical and scientific drawings, many full-page, of a provincial but lively character, in ink with washes in various shades of green, brown, yellow, blue, and red. Based on the subject matter of the drawings, the contents of the manuscript fall into six sections: Part I: Botanical sections containing drawings of 113 unidentified plant species. Special care is taken in the representation of the flowers, leaves, and the root systems of the individual plants. Drawings accompanied by text. Part II: Astronomical or astrological section containing 25 astral diagrams in the form of circles, concentric or with radiating segments, some with the sun or the moon in the center; the segments filled with stars and inscriptions, some with the signs of the zodiac and concentric circles of nude females, some free-standing, others emerging from objects similar to cans or tubes. Little continuous text. Part III: Biological section containing drawings of small-scale female nudes, most with bulging abdomens and exaggerated hips, immersed in or emerging from fluids, or interconnecting tubes and capsules. These drawings are the most enigmatic in the manuscript and it has been suggested that they symbolically represent the process of human reproduction and the procedure by which the soul becomes united with the body. Part IV: This sextuple-folio folding leaf contains an elaborate array of nine medallions, filled with stars and cell-like shapes, with fibrous structures linking the circles. Some medallions with petal-like arrangements of rays filled with stars, some with structures resembling bundles of pipes. Part v: Pharmaceutical section containing drawings of over 100 different species of medicinal herbs and roots, all with identifying inscriptions. On almost every page drawings of pharmaceutical jars, resembling vases, in red, green and yellow, or blue and green. Accompanied by some continuous text. Part vi: Continuous text, with stars in inner margin on recto and outer margins of verso.

Written in Central Europe [?] at the end of the 15th or during the 16th [?] century; the origin and date of the manuscript are still being debated as vigorously as are its puzzling drawings and undeciphered text. The identification of several of the plants as New World specimens brought back to Europe by Columbus indicates that the manuscript could not have been written before 1493. The codex belonged to Emperor Rudolph II of Germany (Holy Roman Emperor, 1576–1612), who purchased it for 600 gold ducats and believed that it was the work of Roger Bacon. It is very likely that Emperor Rudolph acquired the manuscript from the English astrologer John Dee (1527–1608) whose foliation remains in the upper right corner of each leaf (we thank A.G. Watson for confirming this identification through a comparison of the Arabic numerals in the Voynich manuscript with those of John Dee in Oxford, Bodleian Library Ashmole 1790, f. 9v, and Ashmole 487). Dee apparently owned the manuscript along with a number of other Roger Bacon manuscripts; he was in Prague 1582–86 and was in contact with Emperor Rudolph during this period. In addition, Dee stated that he had 630 ducats in October 1586, and his son Arthur (cited by Sir T. Browne, Works, G. Keynes, ed. [1931] v. 6, p. 325) noted that Dee, while in Bohemia, owned "a booke . . . containing nothing butt Hieroglyphicks, which booke his father bestowed much time upon: but I could not heare that hee could make it out." Emperor Rudolph seems to have given the manuscript to Jacobus Horcicky de Tepenecz (d. 1622); inscription on f. 1r "Jacobi de Tepenecz" (erased but visible under ultraviolet light). Johannes Marcus Marci of Cronland presented the book to Athanasius Kircher, S.J. (1601–80) in 1666. Acquired by Wilfred M. Voynich in 1912 from the Jesuit College at Frascati near Rome. Given to the Beinecke Library in 1969 by H.P. Kraus (Cat. 100, pp. 42–44, no. 20) who had purchased it from the estate of Ethel Voynich.

Jake stretched and yawned. He couldn't imagine why the church would be interested in this particular old book. Despite what Ben had told him, it sounded as if the book wasn't even religious.

He left the Beinecke website, returned to Google, and noticed a site that offered photographs of each and every page of the book. He took a quick peek at some of the pages. The library's description had been accurate: the manuscript was littered with odd drawings of plants, obscure star systems, chubby women, and veins and arteries.

He went back to Google and typed "Voynich mystery." A list of sites popped up, and in one listing Jake noticed the word "Necronomicon." That sounded familiar.

He clicked on the listing and a site about witchcraft and magic appeared on the computer screen. Jake remembered where he'd heard about the Necronomicon. About five years ago he'd had a teenage client, Ryan, who was interested in demon worship; he dressed in black, dyed his hair black, and walked around moody and dark all the time. He'd been sinking deeper and deeper into the underground occult scene — Satan worship and black witchcraft. His parents were afraid he was getting himself into something unhealthy, and sent him to Jake. He only saw Ryan two or three times, but he remembered the teenager talking about the Necronomicon and how it was supposed to have been written by Satan — or was it about Satan?

Jake skimmed the website and found the reference to the Voynich:

Many scholars suspect that the Voynich is the only authentic Necronomicon left in circulation. There is no doubt that one of the original owners of the manuscript, Emperor Rudolph II of Germany, was incredibly superstitious and searched the world for unusual and bizarre finds. His official court was full of dwarfs, giants, and sorcerers of every description. Additionally, there is evidence that the Emperor sent numerous envoys to the Middle East in search of the Necronomicon (the original version of the book having been allegedly written in AD 700).

In order to maintain the integrity and safety of the Necronomicon, the Voynich version was written in a language that could only be interpreted with the correct cipher. The power of the Necronomicon meant that it could never be allowed into general circulation, and every version, other than the Voynich, was destroyed.

It is unclear whether the drawings represent important aspects of the Necronomicon content or perhaps a distraction for the uninitiated. Additionally, references to Sir Roger Bacon in the construction of the Necronomicon are not entirely without merit in this interpretation. Sir Roger was intimately involved in the translation of many religious documents and is widely credited with the introduction of the English version of the Bible (the exact details of which are not without their own mystery and controversy). In any event, one thing that has not been conclusively determined is whether the Necronomicon is a Satanic book of spells (as many naïve occult groups vocally espouse) or some darker version of the Bible. If the latter were the case it would certainly be plausible that Sir Roger would take care in crafting a version of the Necronomicon that could be concealed from the general public.

Jake whistled. It was beginning to look as if there really was a mystery. He clicked back to Google, typed "Necronomicon," and hit *Enter*. No results. He hit *Enter* again.

Still nothing.

He moved the mouse in a little circle. The cursor didn't move. "Damn," he muttered.

He tapped a few keys. No response. "Hell." He pressed *Control + Alt + Delete.*

Nothing.

He wondered if he could log onto another computer while he was still logged into this one. Or maybe he could find a reset button. There was a little red circle next to the power button. He pressed it.

"Excuse me, sir."

Jake turned his head. A man in a red windbreaker and khaki pants stood in the doorway, nervously shifting his weight from foot to foot.

"Yes?"

"We're having some technical difficulties with the system and I need to ask you to leave."

Jake frowned. *That's oddly worded.* "You have to ask me to leave? Why?"

The man shifted again. "It's going to take a while and, um, we need to have access to —"

Jake said, "You don't need every computer. What's going on here?" He was slightly surprised by his abrasive manner but he realized that the stress of all the recent events, including Wyatt, had left him feeling fairly raw.

The man was obviously nervous, as though he'd anticipated resistance. "I really can't get into it. You'd have to talk to my supervisor. I don't know what's going on between you and the university."

Jake stood abruptly. "What are you talking about?" *Me and the university!*

The IT guy took a step back even though Jake was still nowhere near him. He held up his hands in acquiescence. "I was told to monitor the Internet for certain search topics, and you went to some of them."

"What topics? You mean like Voynich?"

"Yes."

"What else?"

"Well, um, that necro thing. Necrophiliac, um, and —"

"Forget that. What topics were you watching for that I *didn't* get to?"

The guy looked genuinely confused. "What?"

"You were watching for specific search terms. What's on the list that I didn't look for?"

"I don't think —"

In a few strides Jake was right in front of the IT guy. "Just tell me, and then I'll go."

The IT man was sweating. He wiped his forehead with his sleeve. "I don't know. I think we were also scanning for book of the dead and nephi-something. It all sounds like gobbledygook to me."

Jake figured the technician had told him as much as he could. He pulled his jacket off the back of the chair.

"Okay," he said, and stormed out of the library.

LIII

Jeremy parked in a lot just off Spring Garden Road. Maury held the satellite phone in his lap.

"What are we going to tell him?" Jeremy finally asked.

"About what?"

"Those dudes," Jeremy said. "Are we going to say something about the bullet?"

Maury put a hand on his abdomen but didn't say anything.

"Do you think Benicio's right?" Jeremy said. "Maybe we aren't Nephilim. Maybe the cardinal has been lying to us."

"So we're just a couple of lepers?"

"I don't know." Jeremy was quiet for a moment. "I mean those guys — the ones that healed you. They said they wanted the boy. They said he was the last of the Nephilim."

"Those guys were fuckin' wacko."

"But they healed you," Jeremy said. "The dude put his hand on your gut, and you were better."

Maury couldn't argue with that. "I'm going to call," he said finally, and started pushing buttons on the phone.

"What're you going to say?"

"I don't know." He finished dialing and held the phone to his ear.

The familiar ring tone sounded twice before a voice answered. "What news?"

It was Cardinal Espinosa.

"We're in Halifax. Benicio is here with the boy."

"How long?" the cardinal asked sharply.

"Soon, I hope."

"I want the boy here. Do whatever you have to do, but get him here."

"There's another thing," Maury said tentatively.

"What?"

"There's other people interested in the boy."

"Other people?"

Maury hesitated then said, "There were two other guys. Strange guys."

"How were they strange?"

"Um, they sort of gave the impression they were, uh . . ."

"Be articulate!" the cardinal barked.

"They said they were angels and they needed to get rid of the boy. They said he's the last Nephilim."

There was a very long pause.

"Did they say anything else?" There was a definite change of tone in Espinosa's voice.

"No."

"Are you sure?"

"I'm sure."

"Don't trust them," the cardinal ordered. "Don't talk to them. They are not of God. They are banished from the Kingdom. They will deceive you."

"Whoa," Maury said, surprised at the hatred and fear in the cardinal's voice. "Why? What's going on?"

"Don't question me," Cardinal Espinosa commanded. "Find the boy. Bring him to me. Do not let the angels near him."

The line went dead.

Jeremy grinned at him. "How's the old shit doing? Does he send his love?"

Maury turned the phone off and dropped it on the floor behind the front seat. "Let's go."

"To where?"

"I'm thirsty. I'm going into that drugstore and getting something to drink and buying a map of Halifax."

Jeremy shrugged, and they got out of the car.

***

Cardinal Espinosa was shaking. He hadn't slept in a few days; he'd been sitting at his desk, waiting for news, waiting for the phone to ring.

He'd never expected to hear that the angels were back. *Seventy generations have passed. I won't let those cursed angels cause any more damage. The Voynich will be mine, as will the boy who can read it. The church will never need to worry about this again. I'll make sure of it.*

LIV

Matthew ate all the pancakes, and Benicio felt better once both of them had food in them. He also felt better with coffee in him. And he felt better because he'd made a decision. He was going to find the police station. He refused to be a fugitive any longer.

The server came to see if they wanted anything else.

"That was great, thank you," Benicio said. "I wonder if I can ask a question, though?"

She paused with the plates in her arms. "Sure."

"I think I know, but can you point us in the direction of Dalhousie University? We're meeting my friend at the library there."

She nodded enthusiastically. "I go to school there. I'm taking pre-law. Dal is just down Spring Garden. Basically, go right up to the top of the street, get on Spring Garden, and go down to the end . . ."

"That's great. Is it too far to walk, though?" He glanced at Matthew.

She shook her head.

"Thanks again," he said, and left cash and a generous tip on the table, then he and Matthew left the restaurant. They headed out through the lobby, the way they'd arrived, and ended up on Salter Street. Benicio started walking in the direction the server had suggested, and Matthew followed along.

After only a short walk, Benicio saw the sign for Spring Garden Road. He turned onto the street and kept moving, Matthew two steps behind him.

"Father Valori?"

Benicio saw two men approaching, one athletic-looking, the other heavy-set and bearded. The younger man had a large black leather portfolio under his arm. Benicio was about to lead Matthew around them to continue down the street when the younger man held his hand up.

"Father Valori?" the man said again.

"No, I'm sorry," Benicio said quickly, and tried to walk around them. Were they from the FBI? The Vatican? Either way he didn't want to talk to them.

"Please wait," the younger man said, and stood right in front of Benicio.

"You're blocking our way. Please move," Benicio said firmly.

"We won't hurt you," the bearded man said gently. "The boy is forsaken. It is the boy we want."

Forsaken? "What are you talking about?"

"Do you know who we are?" the younger man asked.

Benicio looked at the men carefully. "More goons from the Vatican?"

The bearded man laughed.

"Look again," the younger man said.

Benicio stared at him. Something was not right about the young man. The priest turned to look at the older man's face. It took a moment, but — there! A faint outline. An aura.

A slight glow surrounded each man's face.

The younger man waved his hand in front of Benicio's face. As it moved, the hand left a slight trace of gold in the air. Benicio blinked.

"Father Valori," the younger man said quietly. "You should not be involved in this. You can't possibly understand what is happening."

"Who are you?"

"I am Shemhazai. This is Azazel."

Benicio knew that was ridiculous. A zillion years ago, Shemhazai and Azazel led the rogue angels who had impregnated women. The two angels were given the harshest of punishments: banishment on Earth. Seventy generations of suffering.

Seventy generations! He remembered something from his

dream. One of the women in his dream had said, *Maury and Jeremy are not the real enemies. Seventy generations has come to an end*, and then there was something about the fathers. *Beware the fathers. The fathers of the forsaken.*

"You know who we are, don't you?" Azazel said, reading the recognition on the priest's face. "That's good."

"How is this possible?" Benicio asked. "*Non capisco.*"

"You don't need to understand," Shemhazai said in perfect Italian. "We are here to claim the boy — our descendant. He is the last of our line."

Benicio had almost forgotten about Matthew. He turned to look behind him but didn't get that far — the boy was right beside him, and he looked terrified. Seeing his fear snapped Benicio out of his stupor. "You can't have him."

"Don't try to stop us," Azazel said quietly. "Walk away now."

Benicio looked up and down the busy sidewalk and noticed two police officers across the road.

He turned to the angels. "No," he shouted. "No! I don't want to buy drugs from you! Leave me and my son alone!"

Shemhazai glared at Benicio, then saw the cops.

"Get away from me," Benicio yelled. "I'm not going to buy any drugs from you!"

"You idiot," Azazel whispered.

The policemen were halfway across the street, heading right for them.

"You haven't changed anything," Shemhazai said quietly.

"What's going on?" one of the officers asked, and stopped next to Benicio.

"Officers, I need your help. This boy has been kidnapped and these men are trying to hurt him. Take the boy and me to the police station. I can explain there."

"Maybe we better see some IDs," the second cop said.

Azazel sighed. "I think we can clear this up." He moved, his arm, a blur of muscle and speed, and he touched the forehead of the officer closest to him. The officer winced in pain, then froze.

The second officer reached for his gun, but Shemhazai pushed him into the road, right into the path of a fast-moving city bus.

Benicio stared in disbelief as the bus swept the policeman off his feet and tossed him high into the air. It was like a special effect in a movie. A few seconds later the cop slammed into a street sign then collapsed onto the road. Benicio turned back and saw the first cop on the sidewalk; his skin was an unhealthy pale gray. Benicio looked at Matthew. The boy's mouth was wide open, and he looked like he was screaming. Yet the sound seemed muffled. Everything felt dull and slow, as if the whole world was folding in on itself and crushing the sound out of everything.

He felt a tug and saw that Matthew had grabbed his arm. Fuzzily, he thought how great it was that Matthew was finally reaching out, trying to connect. Then the world suddenly unfolded again. Sound came spilling over him. People were screaming and running — towards the officer who'd been hit by the bus, towards Benicio and Matthew. He couldn't see Azazel and Shemhazai anywhere.

Benicio knew he needed to get away. He stumbled a step or two, then started moving quickly. Matthew stayed glued to his side.

After a block, Benicio turned to look for the angels. There were crowds of people, lines of cars. People crying and running around. Horns blaring. Sirens. The flash of a fire truck trying to get through the masses of people. It looked like a very small war zone. But he saw no angels.

Azazel and Shemhazai. Could it really be them?

He kept moving. He knew they were heading away from the courthouse and the police station, but he just needed to escape.

He glanced back again. He wanted to be sure the angels weren't following them.

And froze.

Maury and Jeremy were right across the street.

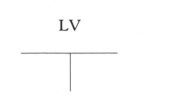

LV

Jake quickly walked away from the Killam Library, ducked down a side street, and headed toward Saint Andrew's United.

His jacket pocket rattled, and it took him a moment to realize his cell phone was ringing. He reached into his pocket.

"Damn," he said. He had found not his phone, but the big key Harold Grower had insisted he take at their last appointment. He put the key in another pocket, found the phone and flipped it open. "Dr. Tunnel."

"Jake?" Abby said. She sounded frantic. "You need to get here — I don't know — they won't give me an answer but it's happening too fast and we're not ready." She sounded out of breath, and Jake was sure she was crying.

"Whoa, hold on. I don't understand."

"Wyatt!" she said, sobbing. "You need to get here! Now!"

"What happened?" Jake asked but the bottom had already dropped out of his stomach.

"The surgery! They took him in early. They took him down to surgery. We've been trying to call you for an hour. Get over here!"

And she was gone.

Jake held the phone to his ear and stared straight ahead, his mind racing. Maybe there had been a dead zone in the Dalhousie computer room, or maybe he hadn't noticed the damn thing vibrating in his jacket. Abby must have been calling while he was searching the Internet. He'd been wasting time while his son was being operated on.

He realized he was still holding the cell phone to his ear. He folded it up and returned it to his pocket. *The hospital,* he thought. *I need to get there.*

He was only a few blocks away. He took a couple steps then saw someone waving at him.

Benicio and Matthew. Running. Behind them Jake saw Saint Andrew's United Church. And down the road he heard several sets of heavy footsteps. Also running.

"Jake!" he heard a voice scream. *Benicio's?*

Jake couldn't look away. He couldn't figure out how to make his legs work or how to turn his head. Two large, rough-looking men were pounding down the street, pushing people out of their way. He recognized them. It was the two from earlier at his office, Maury and Jeremy, and they were chasing Matthew and Benicio.

Benicio reached Jake's side, looked over his shoulder then hurried Matthew and Jake off the sidewalk and across the church lawn. He kept pushing until they were around the corner of the building, out of sight of the road. On this side of the church, a fence provided some separation from the University buildings next door. It probably helped prevent student travel across the church grounds. Unfortunately, it meant that this little alcove was a dead end. Then Jake saw a shallow flight of stairs that led down to a heavy wooden door.

"Where's your car?" Benicio asked him. "We need to get out of here."

"Over there." Jake pointed down Robie Street. "Ben, who are those thugs chasing you? What's going on?"

"Damn." Benicio swore and looked around. He knew Maury and Jeremy would be on them in less than a minute. "I don't have time to explain right now — we have to make a run for it. You take Matthew and start moving. I'll try to keep those guys here so you can get away."

Jake took his hand out of his pocket to wipe the cold sweat from his forehead and felt something hard and cold scrape along his brow. It was the heavy copper key. He looked at it as though seeing it for the first time.

"Jake," Benicio pleaded, "snap out of it!"

And he did.

He looked at the key, then at the old wooden door, and remembered Harold's words: *You need to have this. It will be your exit when you're trapped. Look to the church.*

He ran down the stone stairs, jammed the old key into the weathered brass plate on the door, and turned it. The big metal key moved easily, and the door opened. "Come on," he called to Benicio and Matthew.

***

Maury and Jeremy ran to the church.

"What the hell?" Jeremy said. He scanned the small area with the barrel of his gun. "Where'd they go?"

"Put the gun away," Maury snapped as he tucked his pistol into the waistband of his pants. "They either kept going down the street or they're in there." He pointed to the wooden door. He dropped down the few steps, pulled his gun again, grabbed the latch, and leaned hard on the door. It didn't move. He jiggled the door handle and pushed again. "Locked," he announced.

"Ah, they didn't fuckin' use that door anyway," Jeremy said.

"Let's go," Maury grumbled. "They have to be around here somewhere."

And they took off.

LVI

Saint Andrew's United Church was built just before World War I, and its foundation was a labyrinth of passages and corridors. There was another labyrinth under the city itself, a secret network of tunnels and underground trails that connected the harbor to the city's first line of defense, the old fort on Citadel Hill, and then spread out under much of downtown Halifax.

Right after the war, the military wanted to keep civilians out of the tunnels, so they sealed off and padlocked some of the entrances, but people just made new ones. Eventually, the haphazard construction and unauthorized access rendered many of the passageways unsafe. By the 1950s most of the tunnels had been sealed permanently.

The tunnels under Saint Andrew's United led in two directions: one east to the harbor and the other northwest to Citadel Hill. After the Second World War, the church had used the passages for storage. Then, during the Cold War, they considered using one of the tunnels as a bomb shelter, but the tunnel was unsafe — creaky, unstable joists, shifting dirt floors, and families of rats. The church sealed all but two of the entrances to its subterranean secrets.

One entrance, padlocked, was at the back of the rector's office. The other entrance had just been opened with the key Harold Grower had given Jake Tunnel.

Jake, Benicio, and Matthew stood in the dark. Jake had locked the wooden door as soon as they were all inside, and not a moment too soon. They could hear muffled voices from outside. Then someone banged on the door and rattled the latch. Jake and Benicio froze. Jake fought the impulse to put his hand over Matthew's mouth, to keep the boy from screaming. He squinted in the dim light drifting down from the floorboards above and saw that Matthew was standing like a statue. He seemed to be oblivious to his surroundings.

They waited a few moments.

"They're gone," Benicio whispered.

"Did one of them have a gun?" Jake asked.

Benicio nodded.

"What the hell is going on? This is crazy."

Benicio stared at Jake with a strange expression.

"What?" Jake finally asked.

"Where'd that key come from?"

Jake looked at his hand. He was still holding the oversized relic. "I don't know. I mean, I know where I got it — a patient gave it to me. But I don't know where he got it."

"When?"

Jake looked confused.

"When did he give it to you?" Benicio asked.

"Couple of days ago."

"A patient gave you the key to the back door of this church just a couple of days ago? That seems kind of unbelievable, doesn't it?"

"I don't know." He slipped the key into his pocket, trying to appear nonchalant. He wasn't. He was freaked out that the key had worked. *How could Harold have known I would need it?* "Never mind about the key — who are those goons? And what the hell is going on?"

"I don't know what to tell you. But I'm beginning to think the church would do anything to get Matthew. I think you and I are expendable."

"Expendable? Do you think you're in a James Bond movie? Never mind — don't answer that. I don't want to hear it. I need to go now. My son is in surgery. I should be at the hospital."

"Wyatt," a small voice said.

In the dark, Jake couldn't tell if Matthew had said it or not.

It hadn't been a question but more of a statement. "What did you say?" Jake asked Matthew.

Matthew stared at the wall of the tunnel.

Jake looked at Benicio. "What's the deal with this kid?"

"Jake, I just don't know — that's what we have to find out. And we have to do it before the church gets him — or anyone else."

"Anyone else? Like who?"

Even in the dark Jake could tell Benicio was hesitating. Then, finally, the priest spoke. "Something just happened. There were two guys. They assaulted a couple of cops."

"They assaulted the police?"

"Si. It was awful. So awful, I think they might not have been men at all."

"What?"

"I think I just spoke with the Grigori."

"Gregory?"

"No — the Grigori. I told you about them when we were in your office. The angels sent to Earth to help humans."

Jake remembered. "You still think this kid is half man, half angel?"

"He is. I'm sure of it now."

"Ben, come on," Jake pleaded. "I can't do this fantasy Bible crap."

"It's not crap. It's why Matthew can read the Voynich. That ability is genetically programmed in him. It's his language. The tongue of the forsaken — the Nephilim. Their story is a crucial part of the Bible. I should have realized it before. It was a part of Noah's ark."

"Noah's ark?" Jake was surprised.

"Yes. Why was God so mad at the world? Why did He want to flood it and kill everyone?"

"I don't know. Something about people being sinners or worshipping other gods or something."

"Yeah, or something," Benicio said. "Angels came down from

Heaven, had sex, and the women bore children — the Nephilim. God hated those children."

"Why, Benicio? Why would God hate those children?"

"They were an insult to Him. Earth and humankind were His creation. The angels tampered with it. The Nephilim were a bastard race, a blasphemy, an affront to nature. It's in the New Testament: second Peter, chapter two, verse three. 'For God did not spare angels when they sinned, but sent them to hell, putting them into gloomy dungeons to be held for judgment' — and so on. When he tried to kill them off, he destroyed the world. Only he didn't get everyone. A few humans survived, and a few Nephilim survived."

Jake nodded, the hint of a smile on his face. "And this boy is one of that long-ago race, the Nephilim?"

"I know how it sounds," Benicio said. "That's why I wasn't going to tell you."

"I'm going now," Jake announced. He was tired of all the nonsense. "You can have your Nephilim and your Necronomicon. I'm going to the hospital." He put his hand on the doorknob.

"Wait! Did you say Necronomicon? How do you know about the Necronomicon?"

"I looked up your Voynich book on the Internet. I came across links to the Necronomicon."

"The Necronomicon," Benicio repeated slowly. "The book of the dead."

"Yes, the book of the dead, the book of witchcraft and demonology."

"No," Benicio said slowly. "Not witchcraft. That was a story to scare people away."

"Away from what?"

Benicio looked at Jake, his eyes intense. "Only Nephilim can read the Voynich. The Voynich is their Bible — the Voynich *is* the Book of the Dead. It's so obvious — why didn't I see it before? The Voynich is the Bible of the Nephilim, the dead ones. The Book of the Dead. That's why the church wants this boy. They want to control the book. We need to protect Matthew until we find the Voynich. Until he has a chance to read it for all the world to hear."

"You do realize that you are a lunatic?" Jake said flatly.

"I know how it sounds, but we really need to get Matthew to read the Voynich."

"He can read it off the Internet. I just saw all the pages — they're all archived there."

Benicio shook his head. "I'm not sure that would work. The father told me that copies are useless — only the original manuscript can be read."

"Listen, we'll have to figure this out later. I really do need to get to the hospital. Wyatt went into surgery already."

"Oh, my God. I'm sorry. I should never have dragged you into this."

"No," Jake said firmly. "I want to help. I just need to be with my wife and son right now."

There was a thump from somewhere in the church above. Benicio held up a hand to silence Jake.

"Hey, Father Valori!" Jeremy's voice sang out. "Are you in here praying?"

"Shut up," Maury barked.

Benicio leaned close to Jake. "They're in the church. You should go, now!"

"But I want you to come with me. We can all go, and then I can take you guys back to the house after."

"But Maury and Jeremy might come after us there," Benicio whispered. "I wouldn't want to risk them following us to the hospital."

Jake said nothing. He knew Benicio was right.

"Unless," Benicio said slowly, "you take Matthew with you and I'll lead Maury and Jeremy away. I'll distract them. Matthew would be safe with you at the hospital."

"What about you?" Jake argued. "Will you be safe?"

Benicio smiled. "I have God on my side. Now go."

Jake turned to the door and opened it a crack. He couldn't see anyone.

Benicio knelt and spoke to Matthew. "Go with this man. He's going to take you somewhere safe and then I'll come see you a little later. Everything's going to be fine."

No response.

"It looks okay out there," Jake reported. "Is he ready?"

Benicio stood and nodded. "Go ahead, Matthew."

Jake started out the door, and Matthew fell into step behind him.

LVII

"Dio mi assista!" May God help me, Benicio whispered after Jake and Matthew were gone. "Now what?"

He looked into the tunnel. The entrance was framed with old planks, but the wood looked rotten and damp. He stuck his head in and saw three passages, each about six feet high and four feet wide. He barely had room to move.

Benicio hoped one of the passages would go under the church to the front entrance, so he could get out and lead Maury and Jeremy away.

He would have to move quickly. If they found him down here he'd be trapped.

He chose the right-hand passage.

The floor was hard-packed dirt, and the walls were buttressed with rough timber, which to Benicio's eye looked a bit chewed — probably rats. He *hated* rats. The plank floor of the church was just over his head, and occasional gaps let in a dim light.

He had only gone a few dozen yards when he came to a much narrower side passage. He could fit, but only just. He stuck his head in. There was almost no light. He heard a rustling sound, and before he could move something dropped from the wall to the dirt floor and scuttled between his feet, brushing against him. Then it darted into the main tunnel.

A rat.

"Che!" He jumped back. There was no way he was going down that dark, rat-infested passage. He looked into the main tunnel but could only see a foot or two; then it curved sharply to the right. He took three steps, rounded the curve — and came face to face with Maury.

Benicio took a step back and bumped into something soft. The something put a hand on his shoulder. It was Jeremy.

"Can we have a quick word with you, Father?" Jeremy asked.

Then Benicio felt something crash into the side of his head. He slumped to his knees and saw flashes of light cascading all around him. Jeremy hit him again, and Benicio fell to the ground.

Then everything went black.

LVIII

Jake walked warily up the steps from the church basement, Matthew right on his heels. Jake looked right and saw a swirling circus of people farther down Spring Garden Road. He scanned Robie Street and saw that the coast was clear. He headed down the street toward University Avenue.

Once at the intersection of Robie and University, they had to wait — the light was red. Jake kept looking all around, hoping they hadn't been followed. So far, so good.

The light changed, and he and Matthew walked the few blocks to the children's hospital. As they neared the building, Jake sped up. Concern for his son suddenly blocked his anxiety about being followed. He crossed in front of the new parkade and was about to turn into the hospital when he stopped and looked back. Matthew had fallen behind.

"C'mon, buddy," he called in what he hoped was a friendly tone. "We're almost there. Just a little further."

Matthew didn't respond or change his pace. He trotted up to Jake and slowed. Jake looked down at the boy and shook his head. He couldn't believe the enormous controversy being stirred up over this child. *How could any of it be true?*

He headed up the pathway to the entrance of the hospital. Matthew followed behind.

They went in and Jake led Matthew quickly through the lobby to the elevators. There was one standing open, so Jake stepped in, Matthew right on his heels. Jake pressed three. When the doors opened, he saw a sign: Pathology and Laboratory Medicine / Day Surgery.

He followed the purple trains to the nursing station. As he

and Matthew approached, a nurse looked up, then came down the hall to meet them.

Jake immediately recognized her. "Jenna?" he asked, surprised.

"Hi, Jake," she said quietly.

"I didn't know you were working here."

"Yeah." She noticed Matthew. "Who's this?"

"You'd never believe me. A mutual friend asked me to look after him for a while."

"A mutual friend?"

"Listen, I'll tell you later. Right now I need to know about Wyatt. What's going on?"

"I'm sorry," Jenna said quickly. "Of course. Follow me." She headed down the corridor, Jake beside her and Matthew right behind him. "There've been some complications," Jenna continued. "Your wife's in the waiting area and could use your support." She stopped at the waiting room door and motioned Jake and Matthew in. "I'll be at the nursing station if you need anything," she said to Jake. "The doctor will be with you in a couple of minutes."

Jake thanked her and went to his wife. "Abby?" he said gently. The room contained uncomfortable-looking vinyl chairs, a few tables, and a small play area in one corner.

Abby was pacing. She paused and turned to him, her face red from crying.

"Wyatt's in trouble."

"What kind of trouble?" He put a hand on her shoulder.

"Oh, Jake," she said, tears welling. "They haven't told me. He went into surgery early, and they said there were complications. They haven't told me anything else." She collapsed against him.

He wrapped his arms around her. "It'll be okay. Wyatt's a strong guy."

"Wyatt," a voice said softly.

Abby leaned a few inches away from Jake. She looked around

the waiting room. Except for Matthew, they were alone. "Who's this?" she asked through her tears.

Jake hesitated. He couldn't even think of a short version to tell her. He took a deep breath. "It's —"

"Mr. and Mrs. Tunnel." Dr. Merrot, the pediatric neurologist, stood in the doorway. He was wearing his surgical scrubs, mask pulled down, cap in his hands.

"Oh no," Abby cried after one look at the doctor's solemn face. She held onto Jake. "Tell me he's okay. Please tell me he's okay!"

The doctor's expression didn't change, which was more answer than they wanted. "I'm going to ask you to come see your son. Wyatt's resting right now. We've done all we can."

"All you can? What does that mean?" Jake asked.

"There was a bleed. That, combined with the actual location of the tumor — there wasn't any way we could —"

"What are you saying?" Jake demanded.

"I wish I could tell you something different, but Wyatt's awake right now, and I think you should see him."

"You want us to say goodbye to him!" Abby started to sob. "He's too young. This isn't right."

"Goddamn it," Jake said. "There must be something you can do! Should we get another doctor?"

"Please," Dr. Merrot said. "It would be good if you could be strong for Wyatt. He needs to see you right away."

Jake held his wife close as she sobbed. They had to keep it together. It wouldn't help Wyatt to see them like this. "Come on," he urged. "We need to go."

Abby took in deep breaths, holding them, as she walked toward their son's room. Jake knew she could compose herself in the short trip down the hall — and she did. He handed her his handkerchief, then wiped the tears from his face, before the doctor led them into the room.

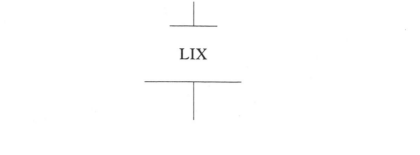

LIX

Benicio was lying on something hard. He opened his eyes and looked around. He was on a bench of some kind, and there were books lined up in front of him on the back of another bench.

Not a bench. A pew. Most of the light came through the stained-glass windows that circled the vast room.

He touched the back of his head and felt a wet, tender spot where Jeremy had hit him. His fingers felt sticky. His head throbbed.

He could hear someone talking, but the voice was dull and hollow, and he couldn't make out any of the words.

He lifted his head and took another look around. He was in a church, a very large church that could hold five or six hundred people easily. Benicio guessed he was in Saint Andrew's United. Maury and Jeremy must have dragged him up from the basement after they conked him on the head.

He stayed still and listened. Yes, he could hear the voices better, and the first one was definitely Jeremy:

"The boy wasn't with him." Jeremy sounded impatient.

"Don't be ridiculous." Benicio had no idea who the voice was — not Maury, he was sure. The next voice confirmed it:

"Listen," Maury said. "You guys claim you're angels hunting down the last bastard angel child. The cardinal has told us we share that bloodline and that's why we're sick all the time. Good old Father Benicio says everything the cardinal says is crap. You touch me once and heal a bullet wound. Who are we supposed to believe?"

"You are not Nephilim." A second voice spoke with confidence. "If you were, you'd be dead already."

"How the hell could you know that?" Jeremy challenged.

"I know," Second Voice said resolutely.

There was a moment of silence, then Maury spoke again. "We're not going to just hand the child over to you. I know what you're going to do."

"That's not your concern," First Voice insisted. "If you aren't providing assistance you are an impediment."

"Whoa, whoa!" Jeremy shouted. "We're not saying we won't help."

"The boy will die no matter what you do. There is no alternative. His life was forsaken at birth. If you do not help us, the boy will die anyway. If you help us, we will free you from your mortal illness."

Silence again. Then Jeremy spoke. "You can cure us?"

No answer.

Benicio strained to hear. He must be a few rows away from the men. Four men — at least. He'd heard four voices. Maury and Jeremy for sure, and the other two were probably the men — or angels — he'd seen on the street.

Suddenly he felt a hand on his leg and only barely managed not to scream. A man with a kind-looking face crouched next to him.

"Shh," the man cautioned with a finger to his lips. "I'm Harold Grower, a friend of Dr. Tunnel's."

Benicio looked at him, surprised.

"Just try to stay down. Whatever you do, don't get near the angels — especially if they try to change forms."

"What?" *Change forms? Who the heck is this nut?*

Harold held his finger to his lips again, then smiled warmly, stood and walked away. Benicio was too tired to lift his head to see where the guy went. He listened again.

"We should ask him, then."

"Want me to get him?" Jeremy.

"Yes." First Voice.

"What if he won't talk?" Maury asked.

"He'll tell us where the boy is." Voice Two.

My God — they're talking about me! Benicio got ready to panic. He heard footsteps as someone approached. He sat up, which made his head swim, then looked around the sanctuary for an exit. He had to do something, and running away seemed like a really good idea. He saw an exit across the aisle.

Too late. Maury and Jeremy were alarmingly close.

"Hey, Father, don't worry. We're just going to talk to you," said Jeremy.

Benicio's head was really pounding. He tried to get to his feet, but stumbled.

"Whoa," Jeremy said gently. "You're going to hurt yourself — you should let us do that for you." His laughter echoed through the church.

Benicio started to climb over his pew to the pew behind. He wanted to put distance between himself and Maury and Jeremy.

The men were moving now, cutting him off. Maury was at one end of the pew and was coming toward him. He turned and saw Jeremy blocking the other end of the pew.

Benicio realized he couldn't outrun them. "Don't do this," he pleaded. "You work for the church. You know this isn't right."

They closed in on him. Benicio put his arms up to shove Jeremy away, and Maury took advantage of his unprotected front and punched the priest in the stomach. Benicio doubled over, and the two men grabbed his arms, dragged him to the front of the church, and dropped him.

Benicio looked up and saw the men he'd encountered in the street. The men who had assaulted the cops.

"We meet again," said the younger one. Benicio saw that he held the large black portfolio under one arm.

The larger one grabbed Benicio's hair and lifted his head. "Where is the boy?"

Benicio didn't answer.

"I will only ask one more time."

"Hey, wait," Jeremy objected.

"Stop interfering." The younger man turned, reached out

and grabbed Jeremy's jacket.

Maury grabbed the younger man's arm. "Hey!" he said. "That's not part of the deal."

The young man let the portfolio fall to the floor with a thud and reached for Maury.

The older man dropped Benicio. "You should have stayed out of this," he said to the brothers.

"I just don't think we need to start smashing the priest up," Jeremy argued, struggling against the man's grip. "Let's give him another chance."

The older man looked at Benicio. Benicio hoped Jake was already at the children's hospital with Matthew.

"Where is the boy?" the older man demanded.

Benicio said nothing.

"Hey," Maury said. "Benny has this psychologist friend in town here. Some guy named Jake. We saw him and he mentioned something about having a sick kid at the hospital."

"Yeah, yeah," Jeremy chimed in. "Maybe Matthew is with him at the children's hospital."

The man released Maury and Jeremy, then shoved them both.

"Where is the children's hospital?" the older man asked.

"I don't know," Jeremy said.

Maury shrugged.

"Then you are no longer of use to us," the younger man said.

Suddenly there was a gun in Maury's hand, and it was pointed straight at the younger man. He opened his mouth to speak but was interrupted.

"I think there's been more than enough excitement." Harold stepped out from a side chapel.

"Who the hell are you?" Jeremy asked.

"Hello, Azazel," Harold said to the older man, then turned to the younger. "Hello, Shemhazai."

"Hello, coward," Azazel said harshly. "Let us finish our work. You do not need to interfere. It is our destiny."

"Destiny doesn't play a role in such matters," Harold said. "It is about your path, and you've been terribly misguided."

"You call us misguided only because your judgment is clouded by personal regrets. Don't preach to us," Shemhazai retorted. "You didn't spend generation after generation suffering. All the Nephilim must die. All of them — your adopted child had to die, and now the boy we seek."

His adopted child? Benicio thought. *What's going on?*

Jeremy looked from the two men to Harold. "What are you guys talking about?"

"Be quiet," Shemhazai said, then lifted Jeremy and threw him into the altar with an otherworldly force.

And then Benicio heard a gunshot.

Maury continued to point the gun at Shemhazai. Smoke curled from the barrel.

Benicio looked at Shemhazai. A section of his face was missing. The bullet had shattered the bone around his right eye and carved a large entry wound. Yet there was only a tiny trickle of blood.

"This isn't your battle," Shemhazai said. "You should have left."

"And this isn't the deal we made," Maury said. "Maybe you guys should fuck off."

Shemhazai flung his arms out, stretched, and a golden figure leapt from the body even as the host fell to the floor. In an instant, the golden figure wrapped itself around Maury.

Jeremy shouted.

Harold took a step forward.

Benicio prayed. But to no avail. The golden figure sank into Maury's body and disappeared. Maury stepped backwards and fell.

The body of Maury lay motionless for seven seconds, then stood up and spoke. "Hey guys, did I miss anything?"

Azazel laughed.

Harold smiled at the body of Maury. "You are now at your most vulnerable."

"What?" Azazel asked.

"You must inhabit a new host for at least twenty-four hours. If you do not, you lose your hold on the Earth and risk banishment or annihilation."

Azazel looked worried. The body of Maury frowned.

"Get out of my brother," Jeremy commanded. He had picked up his brother's gun, and was pointing it at Maury.

"Don't do it." The body of Maury held up its hands. "You'll kill me. I'm still your brother."

"He's not," Harold said. "Your brother is gone."

"Shut up!" the body of Maury shouted.

"Get out of him!" Jeremy screamed. Tears filled his eyes.

Benicio saw Azazel slowly inching toward Jeremy. Jeremy noticed the other man at almost the same time, but kept his eyes fixed on the body of his brother. "Get away from me!" he shouted at Azazel. "What have you done with my brother?" he asked the body.

"I am your brother," the body of Maury said.

"No, you're not. Don't lie to me!"

"Don't shoot. Please," the body said, and began moving toward Jeremy. "I can prove I'm still Maury. Let me show you something."

"Don't take another step," Jeremy cautioned.

The body of Maury kept moving.

Azazel started moving, too.

Jeremy fired once, and Benicio watched as the body of Maury deflated right next to him. Then Harold moved with surprising speed and tackled Azazel in front of the altar, knocking him to the floor. Azazel managed to get to his hands and knees, but stayed at the altar. As Benicio watched, a golden figure emerged from the body of Maury, then immediately writhed in agony. The golden skin began to turn red, then blistered. Shemhazai could no longer be on Earth.

Azazel pushed himself from his knees, stood unsteadily, then limped toward the back of the church.

Harold walked slowly to Jeremy, and Benicio joined them. "I need to follow Azazel," Harold said. "But first, are you going to be okay? Because there's something I'd like you to do." Harold went to the pulpit and picked up the black portfolio. Benicio held his breath.

"Jeremy," Harold said, "you've suffered a terrible loss today. I understand that, but this story is far from over. You can help make sure your brother didn't die for nothing."

Jeremy looked at Harold.

"Would you help me?" Harold asked, and put a hand on Jeremy's shoulder.

Slowly, ever so slowly, Jeremy nodded.

LX

Jake and Abby stood in the doorway of the surgical recovery room. A white curtain strung across part of the room obviously blocked the view of various machines and other equipment. There was a single bed in the room, surrounded by many small machines on carts. Wires led out of the machines, beepers beeped, and lights flashed.

They didn't see any of that.

They only saw the little boy on the bed.

Their little boy.

Wyatt lay in the middle of the bed, a blanket pulled to his shoulders, his arms outside the blanket. Wires and tubes from the small machines were taped to his arms. The top of his head was wrapped in pristine white bandages.

Wyatt looked so peaceful.

Jake and Abby stepped into the room. For the first time he noticed a nurse off to one side monitoring all the various machines and equipment. She avoided eye contact with them and kept to the side of the room.

Dr. Merrot came in behind them. Matthew was behind the doctor but slipped past him and stood near Wyatt.

Abby and Jake approached Wyatt's bed, and the boy's eyelids fluttered. He turned his head slowly and looked at them.

"Mom." He sounded like he was just waking up. He'd never been good with mornings — he needed to wake slowly or he'd be grouchy all day. Jake was stabbed by the thought.

"I'm right here," Abby said. She sat on the bed and held his hand in both of hers. "I'm right here, you hold on."

"Hey, guy," Jake said, sitting next to his wife.

"Hi, Dad."

"I love you," Abby said. "I love you with all my heart."

Wyatt smiled. "I love you too, Mom."

Jake looked at his son then pointed to his eyes, then his heart, then at Wyatt.

"I love you too, Dad," the boy said. "When can we go home? I don't like it here."

They didn't know how to answer.

Dr. Merrot spoke. "You're not ready just yet, young man. Your parents wanted to see you — they were bugging me so I had to bring them in." He smiled warmly.

Wyatt nodded. It wasn't clear how much he understood of what was going on.

"Is there anything you need?" Abby asked.

Wyatt didn't answer.

"Wyatt?" Abby said, a pitch of urgency to her voice.

"Mom." Wyatt's voice was weak. His lips barely moved.

"Wyatt, honey," Abby said very gently. Her eyes filled with tears.

Dr. Merrot came to stand at the foot of the bed.

"Wyatt?" Jake called, his eyes filling with tears.

"Wyatt, don't," Abby cried. "Not now. Don't." She was squeezing and wringing his hand in hers. "You mean everything. Everything."

Jake leaned over the bed. He bent and kissed his son on the cheek. "I love you."

Wyatt didn't respond.

"Wyatt?" Abby asked softly.

Wyatt didn't move.

"No," Abby whispered. "Please God."

Jake felt cold and numb.

"Wyatt," Abby said sadly.

Wyatt didn't answer. He couldn't. Wyatt was gone.

LXI

Benicio was rushing down University Avenue beside the man he had met in the pew of Saint Andrew's United Church. "Where are we going?" he asked. "Who are you?"

"I'm Harold Grower," he said. "I'm a worker bee."

"You said you know Jake."

"That's right."

Benicio tried to focus on making his feet work. He only had vague memories of Harold helping him up and dragging him this far. "Where are we going?"

"It's only a little farther."

"Wait," Benicio begged. "What's going on? Who are you? Where are you taking me?"

"My apologies, Father Valori. I know this must all seem unusual, but you need to trust me right now."

"But who *are* you?"

"I told you — my name is Harold Grower. I'm a friend of the church." He watched Benicio for a minute, then added, "and we are on our way to see Dr. Tunnel. It is quite urgent."

"What church do you work for?"

"I don't work for a church — I'm a friend of all churches."

Benicio tried to run things through his mind. It felt like he was putting together a jigsaw puzzle but was missing half the pieces. "What about Matthew? Is he safe?"

Harold frowned. "That's what we need to find out. We're going to see him. We really must hurry."

Benicio felt his legs go weak again. Harold quickly put a hand around his waist to steady him.

Benicio shrugged loose. "I'll be okay."

A few minutes later they reached the hospital.

"Jake's son is here," Benicio announced as though he were just remembering this detail.

"That's right."

The men hurried past the information desk to the elevators. Harold looked at a large directory posted on the wall. "Surgery," he announced. "Third floor."

There were crowds of people at the elevators. Harold looked down a corridor. "There," he said, and pointed at a sign for the stairs.

***

Jake couldn't see. Couldn't focus. Couldn't think.

Wyatt was dead. Little Wyatt.

He could have been at the hospital, earlier. He could have done something. Wyatt shouldn't be dead.

He looked at Abby. She was holding Wyatt. A nurse was trying to comfort her, but Abby was deafened by grief.

Somehow, Jake stood and staggered away from the bed. He needed to move. He wanted to be away from Abby and the comforting nurse. He leaned heavily against the wall. He knew he should sit. He knew his legs wouldn't support him for much longer, but he didn't know how to move to a chair. Jake wanted to scream for help. He wanted to tell everyone that this wasn't right. Someone had to fix this. Someone had to set things right.

The world couldn't keep going. Not without Wyatt.

Jake saw Dr. Merrot. Then he saw Matthew. The boy was moving closer to the bed.

Dr. Merrot put his hand on Jake's shoulder. Jake ignored him. He watched Matthew.

The nurse led Abby, still sobbing, toward the door.

Matthew walked right up to the bed. Then he climbed on the bed and straddled Wyatt's body.

Jake pushed Dr. Merrot aside. *What is Matthew doing?* He took a step toward the bed then stopped.

Matthew leaned forward and kissed Jake's dead son on the mouth.

At that moment, Abby turned to see Wyatt once last time. Her face flashed with distress and confusion. Her mouth opened as if she would scream, but no sound came.

The nurse turned to see the strange scene on the bed, but Abby, recovering from the shock, moved toward the bed. Jake stepped in and stopped her, folding her into his arms.

"What's going on?" Dr. Merrot barked.

"Don't," Jake whispered to his wife. Gently he began to coax her away from the bed again.

Dr. Merrot returned to the foot of the bed. Hands on hips, he shouted, "Young man, get off the bed this instant."

Then everyone froze.

A shadow had fallen across the room.

A large bearded man stood in the doorway.

"Now what?" Dr. Merrot said, clearly annoyed. "Who are you? You aren't allowed in this area."

The nurse who'd been helping Abby came to the visitor and tried to keep him from entering. He allowed her to put her hands on his chest, then he stopped. His eyes never left Wyatt's bed.

"Sir," the nurse said sternly.

The man slowly swiveled his eyes, to meet hers. "Okay," he said without inflection.

What happened next was impossible.

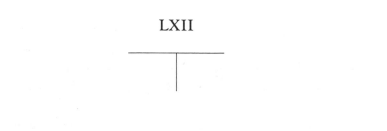

LXII

Harold and Benicio stood at the nursing station on the third floor. "Where is everyone?" Benicio asked. He and Harold were still out of breath from running up the stairs, and Benicio didn't want to waste time after all that rushing.

Harold looked worried. "I don't know — there's always supposed to be someone here."

"Hello," said a pleasant voice. "What's going on?"

Benicio turned, then stared in disbelief. The pleasant-sounding nurse standing in front of him was Jenna.

"Benicio?" Her eyes were wide. "What are you doing here?"

"Do you know if Jake Tunnel and his son are here?"

"Well, yes, they are, but —"

"Take us," Harold pleaded. "Take us there now."

Jenna looked at Harold, then at Benicio.

"Please," Benicio added.

Jenna nodded. "Come with me."

***

The bearded man lifted his arms to the ceiling in a slow, sweeping arc. The nurse instinctively stepped back, fearing a blow was coming.

What was coming was much worse.

Azazel allowed the costume of his former host to drop to the floor. The body was useless to him anyway. He stood in Wyatt's hospital room in his natural form, a massive, glowing golden figure. An angel.

Jake didn't move. He didn't dare. No one even breathed.

Azazel stretched, knowing his time was short. Already, his

skin was starting to burn. He focused on the nurse who had been watching the machines. He could almost feel her terror. He placed his strong hands on her arms and pulled her towards him, then slipped his golden self inside her skin, replacing her life with his.

Jake continued to hold his wife and tried to back away.

The body of the nurse looked at the people in the room. Then the body turned to the bed.

"Hey," Jake said softly, suddenly aware that something might happen to his son. "Hey."

The body of the nurse strode toward Matthew, who finally turned his head. When his eyes met those of the body, he looked terrified.

"Yes," the body of the nurse said. "The mistake ends here. It ends now. You are the last in the line of Nephilim."

A tear dropped from one of Matthew's eyes.

Jake let go of Abby. He couldn't allow whatever was going to happen. It was crazy.

The body put its hands on Matthew's head and lifted the boy off the bed. Off Wyatt.

Matthew screamed.

LXIII

Jake took a step but someone yelled.

"Wait! Don't go near him, Dr. Tunnel."

Jake recognized the voice immediately — it was Harold Grower

The body of the nurse, still holding Matthew by the head, turned to Harold. "You! This doesn't concern you."

"Put the boy down," Harold ordered.

"This is no boy — it's a monster."

"Put him down."

The body of the nurse dropped Matthew on the foot of the bed. "It's over anyway. The Nephilim are dead. The secrets of the Necronomicon will never be revealed. The curse is lifted."

Harold rushed to Matthew, put his fingers gently around the boy's wrist, and felt for a pulse. Matthew was dead.

"You won't see me again." The body of the nurse headed toward the door.

Harold grabbed her arm. The body flinched, then arched its back. "No," she whispered. "You can't."

Tears filled Harold's eyes. "The Nephilim were innocent. They were *innocent*."

Harold let go of the body, and it crashed onto a large machine on a metal cart, then rolled off the cart and hit the floor.

Jake watched as a faint glow surrounded the body. Azazel lay on the floor for a moment, his golden skin disappearing.

And then he was gone.

Dr. Merrot was the first to react. He rushed to the fallen nurse, crouched, and checked her vital signs.

Harold leaned heavily on the bed. Jake and Abby huddled against the wall.

"There's a pulse," Dr. Merrot announced. "I've got a pulse." He jumped to his feet. "I need to get a team in here." He ran from the room.

Harold looked at the nurse, then at Jake and Abby. Then they all looked at the door as a man entered the room.

It was Benicio.

With his head down and a somber expression, Benicio stepped into the room.

Abby put her arms around Jake and leaned in as her sobs started again. Jake wasn't sure he could support the extra weight. He just wanted to collapse.

Benicio looked at the bed, then at Jake. "May I?" He motioned to Wyatt.

Jake nodded. Benicio was a dear family friend. Of course he would want to say goodbye to Wyatt.

Benicio sat on the edge of the bed and laid a hand on the dead boy's chest. Tears blurred his vision.

And then Wyatt twitched. Benicio studied the boy's face. *A death spasm?*

Wyatt's lips parted. It was slight — ever so slight — but obviously deliberate. Wyatt was trying to say something.

"*Dio sia lodato!*" Praise God, Benicio whispered. He turned to Abby and Jake. "Hey guys," he said, his voice trembling.

Jake looked at his friend.

Abby looked up at her husband. "What?"

"Abby," Benicio said more loudly.

She turned to the hospital bed. "What?" She managed that one word through a wash of emotion, her voice barely audible.

Benicio stood and swept his hand over Wyatt, then motioned for them to come closer.

They did.

Slowly.

From near the doorway, Harold watched. Watched and smiled.

Abby and Jake sat on the bed, and Abby leaned over her son.

"Wyatt?" she said softly. There was no motion. No sign of life.

"Wyatt?" Jake said gently. "Buddy?"

The room waited, unsure.

Then there was a sound. A small whisper.

"Mom?"

Wyatt's eyes fluttered open.

LXIV

Jeremy looked at the house and shook his head.

What am I doing? he wondered. *I should just check myself into a hospital.*

He knew his entire life had been a lie, and the life of his brother. They were lepers. The cardinal had used them. Instead of giving them medical treatment, instead of giving them normal lives, he had used them.

And now Maury was gone.

Because of a book.

Jeremy looked at the black portfolio under his arm.

I'm going to do this one thing. One more thing, so the church doesn't win. So those bastards Azazel and Shemhazai don't win. This is for Maury.

He glanced nervously up and down the street. He was pleased that the homes were so private in this area. Finally, he started up the steps to the front door.

LXV

"Yes, you may be excused, too," Jake told Wyatt. Emily had already skittered away from the dining room table, and Wyatt was bouncing around.

"Thanks Dad," he said, and ran off.

"You have really great kids," Jenna said, smiling.

Jenna, Benicio, Jake and Abby sat at the table. They were just finishing dinner. From where they sat in the dining room they could hear Wyatt's feet pounding all the way down the length of the house.

"Yeah," Abby said. "Hard to believe that less than a week ago he was in the hospital." She reached under the table and gave Jake's knee a squeeze.

"So what did the hospital say when they discharged him?" Benicio asked.

"Well," Jake said, "they didn't know what to say. It was a bit of a circus." He turned to Jenna. "Any word from the inside?"

She nodded. "It's still a circus. People can't stop talking about the miracle boy. No one can explain Wyatt's unbelievable recovery. The tests they ran showed no trace of a tumor, and not only that — there's also no evidence of the original surgery."

Abby added, "They couldn't even find the stitches from the operation. His scalp was completely healed, as if nothing had ever happened." Abby could barely conceal her joy over having Wyatt back.

Benicio was tempted to say something about God working in mysterious ways, but didn't.

"You're looking a lot better, too, Ben," Jake said. "You had quite an experience."

"Just a mild concussion," Jenna answered and leaned over to

put an arm around him. "Good thing he got hit in the head —
he can be pretty hardheaded."

Benicio shrugged.

"You know what?" Abby said. "I don't even like to talk about
it. I just thank God that we all got through the — got through
whatever it was that happened." She stood abruptly. "I'm going
to start cleaning some of this up and get a pot of coffee going."
She began collecting plates.

"Coffee would be great," Benicio said.

Jenna stood and picked up a handful of dishes. "I'll help."

"No, no," Abby said.

"Too late." Jenna started for the kitchen with a stack of
plates. Abby followed.

Jake turned to Benicio. "Jenna's great."

"I think so."

"Any plans?" Jake asked.

"I love her," Benicio said matter-of-factly. "I've always loved
her."

Jake laughed. "But you're a priest!"

"For now," Benicio said. "I need to report to the Vatican in
a day or so. I'm not sure what I'm going to tell them."

That surprised Jake. He thought about pursuing it but felt it
wasn't any of his business. Benicio obviously had some difficult
decisions ahead of him. Jake decided to ask a different question.
"I still don't know what to think about anything that happened.
Can you explain it?"

Ben glanced toward the kitchen. "We should talk — but not
here. Why don't you show me the deck?"

Jake understood. They got up from the table and walked to
the side door. "We're just going out on the deck," Jake called to
Abby.

The Tunnel residence had a large deck that wrapped around
two sides of the house. It was a little brisk but not uncomfortable outside. The two men stood side by side leaning over the
railing. The nights were coming earlier, and light from the

house cast patterns across the lawn.

"What have you told Abby?" Benicio asked.

"Not much. Even if I wanted to tell her something, I couldn't — I have no idea what happened."

"Right."

"Are you going to tell me what happened?" Jake asked after a long pause. "Who was that kid? What happened to Maury and Jeremy? What happened to the book?"

"That's a lot of questions," Benicio said softly.

"Pick any one of them."

Benicio paused then finally asked, "Where do you stand now on your belief in angels?"

Jake laughed. "I'd say I'm a lot more open to the idea."

"Well, I guess that makes two of us."

"But you're a priest. You were always supposed to believe in angels."

"I believed in angels as energy, as part of the mystery of something greater. I never thought of angels as individuals. I never thought the Bible stories were literal."

Jake nodded. "Bible stories like the Nephilim."

"Exactly. Yesterday I spoke to a few scholars at the Vatican. I think I was right about the Voynich."

Jake arched his eyebrows. "And?"

"A long time ago, God sent angels to Earth to watch over people. Those angels lay with women and fathered the Nephilim. Then God sent a flood to wipe out everyone — humans, Nephilim, and angels. But the angels had already told people the secrets of heaven, secrets humans were never supposed to know. I think they shared the secrets by recording the information in a book — the Nephilim bible, the Necronomicon. We've been calling it the Voynich manuscript. Those two angels, Azazel and Shemhazai, had been sentenced to seventy generations of exile because they had revealed the secrets, and to avoid further punishment, they needed to destroy the book and eliminate every last Nephilim. We could only know God's secrets if we put the book in the hands of a Nephilim."

"Now we won't ever know," Jake said. "Matthew was the last of the line, the last person who could read the book."

"And no one has found the Voynich manuscript, either. It's probably lost forever, as well."

"Wow." Jake scratched his head. "I wonder what was in that book."

"Dad!"

Jake turned. Wyatt was standing at the screen door.

"Dad, do you wanna play Lego with me?"

Jake laughed. "Do I ever!" He looked at Benicio. "We'll talk more later. Why don't you go on in and get a coffee? I'll be right there."

"Jake." Abby was at the screen door behind Wyatt. "There's someone at the door. He says he's here to see Father Valori."

"Oh my gosh!" Benicio's face lit up. "He made it!" He turned to Jake. "I hope you don't mind, but I invited someone to join us tonight."

Jake and Ben stepped into the house as Wyatt ran off to find the Lego.

"Who?" Jake asked.

The men looked up to see the smiling face of Father Ronald McCallum.

LXVI

Cardinal Sebastián Herrero y Espinosa sat behind his ornately carved oak desk. The massive top held only a small brass lamp and a single file folder.

The cardinal's office was tucked into a corner of an administrative area no tourists ever saw. At regular intervals, Vatican security swept the office and telephone of the Cardinal Prefect of the Congregation for the Doctrine of the Faith, looking for listening devices. Cardinal Espinosa distrusted those who might wish the Catholic Church harm. His job was to ensure complete protection of the church.

Sometimes that protection required unusual tactics.

Over the years, Cardinal Espinosa had made many decisions that would shock the lesser members of the faith — members who didn't understand what it took to protect the church.

Sometimes the cardinal issued orders that made the church very proud. Sometimes he had aligned himself with people who had been openly rebuked by the Vatican.

Nova Scotia had been a disaster. He knew that. Maury was dead. Jeremy had disappeared. The Voynich was still missing. At least the boy was gone.

But that wasn't enough. Not nearly.

The cardinal had promised God that the secrets of that book would never be told. He couldn't keep his promise. There was a chance Jeremy would resurface. He would need the medication the cardinal provided, the elaborate lotions and pills that slowed the disintegration of the flesh.

But the cardinal knew that didn't matter.

Nothing mattered anymore.

He was a failure.

There would be an investigation. There were rumblings in the Vatican. Soon, there would be strangers in his office. Strangers asking questions that shouldn't be answered. Questions that couldn't be answered.

Questions about Father McCallum.

Questions about Maury and Jeremy.

Questions about how the cardinal had used the vast powers the church had provided him.

Everything was ruined.

"I'm so sorry," he said as he stared at the ceiling. "I'm not worthy to hold this position. I've failed You. I've failed the church. And I've failed myself."

He opened his desk drawer, pulled out the familiar black case, and set it on his desk.

The light on his phone blinked. That would be the receptionist. Perhaps there were people here already. People with questions.

He took the knife out of the box. He wouldn't answer this call.

He would never answer another call.

LXVII

Jake sat in his office, doodling. *Back to normal*, he thought, and smiled. He wondered if things could ever be normal again. It was good to be at the office, to listen to the problems of his patients. Listening helped restore his balance.

Although he would much rather be at home.

A week ago, Wyatt had been in the hospital. A week ago, there had been a miracle.

He felt truly blessed.

By God?

He still didn't know. But he had a good idea who might know: his next appointment. His next client was a very special one.

Jake stood and went to the window, gazing idly at the harbor. He had a lot of questions for his client. Questions about what happened in the church, what happened to Benicio — and what happened to the angels.

The client was Harold Grower.

He glanced at his watch and frowned. It was five minutes past the hour. He went and looked in the waiting room. Empty.

That's odd — Harold is never late.

He left the waiting-room door open and went to his desk. He'd clear up paperwork until Harold arrived.

He picked up the stack of correspondence he needed to answer and saw, right at the top of the pile, the papers from Blue Cross declining to pay for Harold's therapy. First was the paper with the CLAIM DENIED stamp, and beside the stamp the rubric 28a P/D, which was supposed to tell him the reason for denying coverage. He couldn't remember all the codes — why couldn't they just use English? — but he was pretty sure he'd never seen this one before. He searched through a drawer full of Blue Cross papers for the sheet that explained the codes, then realized there was a second sheet stapled to the letter about Harold. *Aha, the code for the codes!* He went down the column until he found the one he wanted.

28a P/D: Patient deceased.

***

Wyatt was playing a video game, his mother on the sofa beside him, when he felt her shift and stand. "Honey," she said. He *hated* it when she called him honey. It was kind of girly. "I need to do some laundry. Could you go play in your room for a bit?"

"Can I play with Emily?"

"I think she still needs to finish her homework. You can play with her in a little while. But for now, can you play in your room, please?"

"Okay," Wyatt said, and started toward the stairs.

"Wait," Abby said abruptly.

Wyatt jumped.

"Come back here for a second," she said sternly.

He frowned but obeyed. She scooped up him and gave him a big hug.

"Mom," he yelped. Hugs were even worse than being called honey. Sheesh! She'd hardly left him alone since he'd come home. His dad too. He hoped they would get over it soon. Emily was the only one who didn't make a big fuss all the time. He liked playing with his sister.

"Okay," Abby said, then set him down and kissed the top of his head. "Away you go. You can play more video games tonight."

Wyatt pounded up the stairs and along the hall to his room. He liked his room okay, but the best part was the closet — it was huge. He had a secret playroom in there. His mom knew he kept his toys in there, but she didn't know about *everything* he had in there. He went right to his secret playroom and reached for his

Hulk action figure. Wyatt sat cross-legged and made the Hulk leap through the air, defying gravity, then soar to the top of a closet ledge. He had barely touched down when Spider-Man landed beside him.

"Oh yeah," Wyatt said in his deepest voice. "Let's see you do *this* jump!" The Hulk was airborne again.

***

Deceased? That's a new one.

He looked in the waiting room. Still empty. He looked at the letter from Blue Cross. *Deceased.* The insurance company had cancelled Harold's coverage six months ago. And six months ago was when Harold had had his accident on the helicopter.

Jake stood. He looked in the waiting room again. Harold was almost fifteen minutes late. Jake shut the waiting-room door then sat at his desk again, Harold's file in front of him. He drummed his fingers and thought about calling Harold's wife.

How many times had Jake asked Harold for permission to call her? And every time, Harold had said no.

He opened the folder and found the basic information sheet they'd completed at their first session. The home phone number was right there. He checked Harold's wife's name. Linda.

He dialed. Part of him almost hoped no one answered. He wasn't entirely sure what he was going to say.

And then he heard a woman's voice say, "Hello?"

"Uh, hello. This is Dr. Jake Tunnel. I'm a psychologist in Halifax and I wondered if I could talk to Linda Grower."

"This is Linda."

"Linda, hi. Is this a bad time to talk?"

"No," she said, but Jake thought she sounded uncertain.

"I'm sorry to bother you but I had some questions about Harold."

"Harold?" she said, surprised.

"Uh, yes — I had an appointment with him today and he

hasn't shown up."

She laughed. "You must have booked that appointment quite some time ago."

"Why do you say that?" Even as he waited for an answer, he felt sure he knew what it would be.

"Was it booked in relation to our son?"

"Your son?" He hadn't expected that question.

"Yes, Lucas. Harold was a mess after Lucas left us. I thought maybe the military had booked the appointment back then."

"No, actually, I was seeing him about the helicopter accident."

Silence.

"Mrs. Grower?"

"What do you mean, seeing him about the helicopter accident? That's not the slightest bit amusing."

Jake could tell she was crying. "I'm sorry. I didn't mean to upset you."

"Harold passed away that night. It was one of the worst nights of my life. We lost our son, and then I lost Harold so soon after."

Jake was speechless.

"Is that all?"

"I'm sorry for your loss, Mrs. Grower. But could I ask one last question? I'm just going to close my file."

"Ask it if you must."

"What happened to your son?"

"Why do you want to know about that? It's none of your business."

"I'm sorry. I don't mean to pry. I'm just trying to finish up your husband's file." There was long silence, and he could hear Linda Grower crying.

Then she spoke. It was obviously a story she'd told before. "Lucas was a special boy. We knew that when we adopted him. A lot of people told us we wouldn't be able to handle an autistic child but Harold and I knew better. We'd never had children of our own, but we had a lot to offer.

"Lucas was seven when he came to live with us. He went to regular school — we helped pay for a full-time aide, and it was worth it. Lucas seemed to really enjoy going to school and coming home again. I don't know if he realized what school was, but he went off with his aide every morning without fuss. Then one day, I don't know, everything went wrong. The aide took Lucas to school but then she got sick and — and our Lucas disappeared. At first we kept hoping he would try to come home on his own."

There was another pause, and Jake heard more crying. She took a moment to compose herself.

"Anyway, they found Lucas the next morning, in the woods behind the school. The medical report said he died of exposure. Harold never believed that. Some kids at the school said they'd seen a couple of strange men talking to Lucas. Harold thought there was something else going on, but Lucas hadn't been hurt in any physical way — the police checked that very carefully. There was no sign of other people in the woods where Lucas was. But Harold just never believed it."

"What *did* Harold believe?"

"I don't know," she said, and started sobbing. "I really need to go."

Jake sighed. He had a thousand more questions. "Of course," he said. "Thanks so much for your time. And I apologize again for bothering you."

"Good day," Linda Grower said, and hung up.

Jake set the phone in the cradle.

There was a thought in his head, and he didn't want it there. He waited, but it didn't go away.

Lucas was Nephilim.

Harold had stayed on the Earth to protect the last of the Nephilim. To make sure the world would not lose the secrets of the Voynich manuscript forever. Harold wanted to do right for his son.

Only Harold wasn't exactly Harold anymore. Back at the hospital, Azazel seemed to recognize Harold, as though Harold were of some divine origin. Jake wondered if Harold was on a mission direct from God. A mission to stop Azazel and Shemhazai from destroying the last of the Nephilim and taking away humanity's chance to know the secrets of the Voynich manuscript.

A mission that had failed.

Matthew was dead, the Voynich lost.

Jake slowly closed Harold's file.

The Nephilim's secrets were lost forever.

***

The Hulk smashed into a neat stack of books on the closet shelf. Mom always made him keep the bedtime books in the closet so his room didn't get *cluttered* — one of her favorite words. Most of the time the books were in heaps on the floor, or scattered under piles of action figures. Wyatt wondered who had put them in such an orderly stack, then decided it didn't matter, as long as he didn't have to do it.

Spider-Man followed the Hulk and hit the books hard enough to knock one to the floor. The others shifted and started to fall off the shelf.

Wap, wap, wap. They hit the floor one after another.

Wyatt stepped back. He didn't want any books to land on his foot — probably one of his toes would die if it got hit. He waited. After the books stopped crashing down he looked around nervously, waiting for his mom to yell about the noise. Then he remembered she was in the laundry room. *Good,* he thought. *The machines are a lot louder than a bunch of books.*

He'd better pick the books up, though. He stacked a couple of them and stood, reaching high to set them on the shelf. He bent to pick up a couple more.

Uh-oh. One of the floorboards was loose. The books must

have broken the floor. *I'm going to be in big trouble.*

He knelt beside the board and tried to push it down so it wouldn't wobble.

It wobbled even more.

He pushed on the other end of the board, and it seemed to jump into the air. *Oh man, oh man.* He grabbed it and pulled the whole thing out of the floor so he could see why it wouldn't stay where it belonged. There was a big hole under the board, and one of his bedtime books was in there. He pulled it out and tossed it aside, then tried to push the board down again. Then he stopped. There was something else in the hole. He threw the board behind him and looked down. There was another book in the hole — a big book.

He reached in to get it, but it was really big and pretty heavy. He got up and walked around the hole and knelt on the other side, then tried pulling the book out from there. When he finally got it out he dropped it on the floor. It weighed a ton!

And it was really dirty.

It looked pretty old, and it smelled kind of funny.

He frowned. *How'd that get in here?*

He opened his mouth to call his mother, then closed it. She would ask him how the floor got wrecked. She probably wouldn't even care about the book. And what would he tell her? Spider-Man did it? She'd never believe him.

I guess I'd better see what the stupid book is, he thought, and looked at it. The cover was kind of torn up, so he pulled the book open near the middle and saw silly pictures of fat, naked ladies. He laughed, then turned the page. The book had weird letters. He knew his alphabet already, but he didn't recognize any of the letters or words in the old book. But as he stared at the page, the letters started to dance and spin. It made him feel dizzy.

And then the letters stopped.

He blinked once, twice.

He looked at the page again.

That's better, he thought. *At least now I can read it.*